NOT JUST FOR CHRISTMAS

BY
STEFAN JAKUBOWSKI

Published in 2013 by Zygmunt Stanley.

ISBN 978-0-9574625-0-2

© 2013 Stefan Jakubowski.
www.stefanjakubowski.co.uk

The author's rights have been asserted in accordance
with the Copyright, Designs and Patents Act 1988.

In this work of fiction the characters, places and events are either the
product of the author's imagination or they are used entirely fictitiously.

All rights reserved. No part of this publication may be reproduced,
stored in or introduced into a retrieval system, or transmitted, in
any form, or by any means (electronic, mechanical, photocopying,
recording or otherwise) without the written permission of the author.

Cover illustration and design by Neil James.
www.neiljamesartwork.co.uk

Pages designed and typeset by Rachel Jones.

Printed by Gomer Press, Wales.

THE AUTHOR

Originally from Reading, Stefan moved to Wales in the latter part of the last century. (He wishes to point out that he is not as old as that makes him sound.) (Nia, his wife, wishes to point out: 'Oh yes he is!') He lives with Nia and Peaches the cat somewhere in Pembrokeshire.

For
the child in all of us.

Special thanks to
Rachel Jones
and
Neil James
and special thanks also to
Millie and Marley
for letting me use their names!

Tom Tyme
in
The Missing Christmas Sock
or
'Where's me batteries?'

Chapter 1

Tom Tyme, the time travelling pensioner, always stayed with his daughter Lucy over Christmas. It was *cost effective*. And, although his favourite word at this festive time of year was humbug, he always looked forward, secretly, and with a huge amount of child-like glee, to the big day. Especially to the morning of the big day when, with that child-like glee tempered with child-like enthusiasm, he would awaken to search for that "surprise" sock of goodies, which duly appeared at the foot of his bed. This morning though, Tom was to be disappointed.

Tom woke with a start, which was his wont on Christmas morning, and instantly wiggled his feet beneath the duvet, hoping to make contact with the sock Santa had spirited there at the midnight hour, as was Santa's wont.

Nothing to the left. Nothing to the right. Tom tutted. It must have rolled off the bed during the night. *Horrors*, he thought, *I hope there isn't anything breakable in it.* He quickly sat up, and switched the bedside lamp on.

The bed was surveyed. There were no tell-tale signs of festivity. No tinsel. No misplaced pressie, cast erringly from the sock. The duvet was thrown back. Tom leaned to the right and surveyed the floor. He frowned. Nothing but carpet. He leaned to his left.

'Blast,' said Tom, furiously rubbing at his forehead. He had forgotten the lay of the land in this bedroom was different from his own. Wall to the left. Still rubbing, but less furiously – there would be a bruise – Tom eased his sorry carcase from beneath the duvet and headed, on all fours, to the last place the sock could be, on the floor, at the foot of the bed. No wall there.

Tom reached the end of the bed and, with a rising feeling of apprehension, though he knew not why, peered over the edge. His heart skipped a beat. Nothing. The floor was empty of a Christmas sock. What was going on? He had a sudden fearful thought, *blimey, I've missed it? I've slept through Christmas?* Then he had a more rational one. *Perhaps it's too early. Perhaps I've been too excited to sleep properly, and woken too early.* He observed through a chink in the curtains it was still very dark outside. *That's it then*, he thought, *I've woken much too early, panic over.* But, just to be sure, he reached for the alarm clock. Disaster, it read seven of the clock on Christmas morning. It wasn't too early. A child-like panic started to rise in Tom's gut. Had Santa forgotten him?

Deciding, due to the emergency of the situation at hand, to get up, Tom got up. He then had another thought, *what if the sock had rolled under the bed?* He decided, without a thought as to how such a thing could happen, a rolling sock, to look. Back on all fours again, he did just that. He peered. He was to be disappointed once more that morning.

'Blast,' said Tom, who now remembered that his daughter preferred those bed bases that left barely an inch space to the floor. No room for a pot. He stared at the space, it stared back. It was then that Tom heard a tap-tap-tapping noise.

Tom looked up. The noise seemed to be coming from the direction of the window. *What now?* he thought, grumpily. But as grumpy and disappointed as he was, he decided to investigate.

Free from the carpet, Tom, dressed in his best yuletide jammies – they had reindeer printed on them – went to the window and pulled a curtain aside. He was eager to see what new misery sought to add to his sockless torment.

It was Cat. She was Tom's familiar. An Egyptian Mau. She was training him in the art of time travel, and all that that entailed. She would be his companion once the process was complete. Which she didn't see happening anytime soon. She was sat on the window sill, licking a paw. Tom scowled. He was on holiday. Cat knew he was on holiday. They had agreed. Still, he couldn't leave her there, sitting in the cold. Tom took the key that hung on the wall beside the window and put it to the window's lock. He opened the window, as far as it would, which wasn't far. Tom shivered as the cold from outside reached in and embraced him.

'What do you want?' said Tom, in the grumpy tones of one who has been missed by Santa.

'We need to talk,' said Cat.

'I'm on holiday,' said Tom. He blinked as a sudden draft of cold air tickled his face. 'Drat,' he said, turning to find Cat now sitting on his bed. 'I didn't think you could come in until you were invited,' he said, closing the window.

'That's vampires,' said Cat. 'Nice jammies by the way.'

'Vampires?' said Tom, eyebrows rising. 'Are there vampires?'

'How should I know,' said Cat, sure that they had had this conversation before.

'But you said…'

'I take it you're aware of the situation?' said Cat, eager to dodge from the topic of mythical fanged ones.

'What situation?' said Tom, closing the curtain.

Cat cocked her head to one side, not sure if Tom was being deliberately obtuse this morning or his normal self, which wasn't much better. It might save some time if she came straight to the point. 'The Santa's been kidnapped situation,' she said.

'Santa's... What did you just say?'

'All knowledge of the jolly fat fellow has been erased,' said Cat.

Well that explains that, thought Tom. But the knowledge that the knowledge was no longer knowledgeable, did squat diddly to ease the disappointment he was feeling. 'Does that mean Christmas is cancelled?' he asked, fearing the worst.

'There's more to Christmas than a jolly fat man dressed in red,' said Cat.

'Don't tell Sandy that,' said Tom, referring to his mate who was the resident Santa in the local department store, and had been for as many years as Tom could remember. 'He lives for that jolly fat man as you call him.'

'I won't,' said Cat. 'Now, time to get dressed I think. We have to get to the bottom of this before it gets any worse.'

But Tom was way ahead of her and was already struggling with a sock that wasn't of the festive type. A struggle that saw him slide off the side of the bed.

Chapter 2

It should be explained, before the adventure progresses, why Tom was not affected by the erasing of Santa from memory, and so had been still expecting a sock full of goodies. It is because Tom is a time traveller, existing in his own time. Imagine a bubble with him in it, a time bubble if you like, protecting him, leaving him unaffected by any time ripple that should arise, sent from the past to change the present. Tom remains at all times the old, stuck in his ways, irritable self, that he is. Some would say it is a shame. Cat has thought it on numerous occasions.

Socks on, shirt on, jacket on, trousers put on, taken off, put back on the right way round, second time lucky. Cap of the Universal Translator kind placed firmly on head. Tom was ready.

'Shoes?' queried Cat.

Shoes on. Tom was ready. But first he had to have a little sit down on the bed for a moment. The blood had rushed to his head. Tom sucked on a finger.

'Didn't your mother ever tell you not to put your shoes on without first undoing the laces?' said Cat, stifling a smile.

Tom had caught a finger between his heel and the back of his shoe. But at last the blood was beginning to return to where it should be. His head was clearing. He looked at Cat. 'Kidnapped you say?' He was back on track.

'So it would appear,' said Cat. 'We should go.'

Tom went to the bedroom door but stopped short of it, he had had a thought. 'They'll hear the car start,' he said, fearing an explanation would be needed. He wasn't very good at explanations. Not the ones that involved a lie.

'You came by taxi,' said Cat.

'Ah,' said Tom. That complicated things. It was a bit of a jaunt from his daughter's to his cottage, where his time machine stood. It could take a little while, unless... 'Cat?'

'Way ahead of you,' said Cat. 'I've brought a hitchhiker with me.' A hitchhiker was a small device that, when squeezed, could track and then latch on to the time stream of any passing time machine, handy in an emergency. But handy as it was, it sometimes meant travelling the scenic route. And sometimes you just didn't have the time. Thankfully, Cat had tinkered with hers, and re-modulated it to attach itself to the time space surrounding the nearest time machine, which in this case was Tom's.

Cat clenched her tiny buttocks – cats are sadly lacking in the thumb and pocket department – and squeezed the hitchhiker. An instant later they were standing in Tom's time machine. Tom's time machine was a portable toilet, or portal-loo, that stood in his garden. And no, it wasn't bigger on the inside. Who ever heard of such a thing?

Tom thought about his destination, connecting with the loo through his mind – that's how it worked if he wanted to get somewhere – which in this case was home, and an instant later he and Cat were in his bathroom. The portable toilet could take Tom to any toilet in the world – a massive saving on bus fares – and from there he was able to travel back in time to the exact spot he wanted. Of course, on this occasion, he could have just stepped from the loo, crossed the garden, and entered his cottage the more traditional way. But as it was cold outside and Tom wasn't wearing a coat, and as yet hadn't had any breakfast, he had the time machine take him to his bathroom.

'Cuppa?' Tom enquired, as he left the bathroom and stepped into the hall.

'Milk will be fine, thank you,' said Cat, following him out.

They walked along the hall to the kitchen.

'So,' said Tom, filling the kettle, 'What do we know?'

'That Saint Nicholas has disappeared,' said Cat.

'Saint Nicholas?'

'One moment he was on his way to do his famous good deed, and the next whammo, he was gone, taking his bags of gold with him.'

''ere, I thought you said Santa had been kidnapped,' said Tom, flicking a switch.

Cat gave Tom a long hard look. 'The story of Santa,' she said, 'Or at least the catalyst of the story.'

Tom did some of his famous frowning. 'What?'

'Suffice it to say,' said Cat, 'if we don't put Saint Nicholas back where he belongs, no more Crimbo presents.'

Enough said as far as Tom was concerned, as a look of horror spread across his face. He needed that cuppa and as it was the festive season, perhaps a drop of the hard stuff. Then a thought struck.

'Did you say he disappeared with bags of gold?' said Tom, the cuppa forgotten for a moment.

'I did,' said Cat, wondering where this line of enquiry was going.

'Then that's it,' said Tom. 'He's done a runner with the money.'

'For goodness sake Tom, the man's a saint,' said Cat, suitably disturbed. 'Besides, it was his money.'

'Oh,' said Tom, 'robbery then?'

'Maybe,' Cat conceded, 'but he's still gone.'

The kettle beeped. The water had boiled. Tom poured that water into a mug holding a spoon of coffee, tea wasn't going to do it for him, he needed a stronger hit. He added milk, and then some of the hard stuff. Not too much, he would need his wits about him. Maple syrup sometimes made him hyper.

'You want some?' said Tom, offering the syrup to Cat.

'Just a little,' said Cat.

Tom dropped a couple of drops into her milk and stirred it. Cat lapped it up.

Nothing like the hard stuff, thought Tom, putting the syrup back in the cupboard. He was proud to tell anyone that asked, that his syrup was the real McCoy, not that sickly rubbish some shops tried to pass off as the real thing. He returned to his cup and took a sip. It was lovely.

'So,' said Tom, between sips, 'what do we do now?'

'We find him,' said Cat, licking milk from her whiskers.

'How?' said Tom, who hadn't even heard of the saint chappie until a minute ago. Or had he? In one ear, out the other was the usual with Tom.

Cat stopped her whisker cleaning and her little face took on the look of the serious. 'I shouldn't,' she said, 'but I suppose it won't hurt.'

Tom didn't like the sound of this. He didn't like any sentence that had the word hurt in it. 'What won't?' he asked, carefully.

'Giving you your Christmas present now.'

Tom's eyes lit up. Now that was a sentence he could live with. Then they dimmed. Cat hadn't said anything about exchanging pressies. This wasn't fair, he hadn't got her one. What did he do? Think on his feet, that's what. 'Are you sure?' he said. 'Only yours is back at Lucy's and, you know.'

Cat didn't. 'I can wait,' she said, not believing a word the old fool was saying.

Putting his mug on the kitchen table, Tom tried not to look too excited. Perhaps Cat's pressie would make up for the lack of Christmas sock? No, silly talk, but still, one never knew. He decided he needed to sit down. No, he needed the toilet. *Flipping excitement,* he thought. 'I won't be a moment,' he said, excusing himself.

When Tom got back, there was a rectangular shape, wrapped in Christmas paper, waiting for him on the kitchen table.

'Hope you like it,' said Cat.

So do I, thought Tom, eyeing it eagerly. 'I will,' he said. He sat at the table. 'May I?'

'You won't know what's in it if you don't,' said Cat, wisely.

Tom duly attacked the wrapping paper.

'You're getting blood on the table,' said Cat.

Tut-tutting, because of the forced delay in unwrapping time, Tom went to the first aid box, got out a plaster, and carefully placed it on the paper cut he had just given himself. He returned to the table and, with a bit more care this time, finished tearing the wrapping from his gift.

'Well?' said Cat, when Tom had finally beaten the wrapping paper into submission. 'What do you think?'

'What is it?' said Tom, eyeing the box he had unearthed with suspicion.

'It's a laptop,' said Cat. 'You said you wanted to give one a try. It'll save us having to run to Marc for information.'

Marc was Lucy's son, Tom's grandson. Marc cost Tom a small fortune in bribes. Tom liked the idea of saving time. He liked the sound of saving money even better. Trouble was, Tom didn't know what the heck it was he was looking at. He didn't remember wanting to try one, whatever this lap thing was. Should he ask for a little more information? No, open the box first. Play along. Perhaps it was one of those thingy's you ate your dinner off when watching television. Though he couldn't remember wanting one of those either. And how would that help him with information? He didn't know. Tom opened the box.

'It's shiny,' observed Tom. It was a good start; Tom had a penchant for all things shiny. His grandmother had often wondered if he was half magpie.

'It's ready to go,' said Cat. 'I've already charged it.'

Charged it, thought Tom. Now he really was at a loss. This thing had given Cat money? Why? Good grief, was it something magical? From Cat Land? Perhaps the shiny housed something living?

'Turn it on,' said Cat.

'Turn it on?' said Tom, horrified. Now Cat was going too far. They hadn't even been introduced. Tom gave Cat a glare. What was in this thing?

'You still don't know what it is, do you?' said Cat.

'Of course I do,' said Tom, giving Cat the look of the indignant. 'It's a...'

'Computer,' said Cat.

'Is it?' Tom looked mystified. 'In there? That tiny little thing?'

Sometimes, thought Cat, *sometimes.* 'It's a laptop computer. Look, take it out of its box, and lift the lid.'

Not without a little apprehension, Tom was expecting something to pop out at any moment, he did as Cat asked, and was surprised to find that the lid, when at the perpendicular, displayed what appeared to be a small television screen, one of those flat jobbies. Problem was, it appeared to be broken; it was blank. 'It's broken,' said Tom.

'Press the button.'

'Which one?' There were so many.

'The one at the back, beneath the screen.'

The button was pressed. The screen came to life, with a tuneful bing-bong, and then went off again. Now it was broken. Typical. Nothing worked properly these days. Tom blamed the yuppies.

No, something was happening. There was sound again. A ditty. And there was...

'What are those?' asked Tom, pointing to the screen.

'Icons,' said Cat. Then, noticing Tom's confused expression. 'I'll explain later. First we have to get the info we need. Click on there.' Cat pointed to a button with her paw. 'It will take us to the internet.' She gave Tom a guilty look. 'I... er, took the liberty of having you connected. But if you want a different service provider, we can sort that out later too.'

Tom pressed the button, but wasn't sure about being connected. Connected to what? Or what service was going to be provided. He would make a point of asking later. Something was happening on the little television screen.

'The world wide net at your service,' said Cat. 'Now, type in Saint Nicholas in that box at the top, and press search.'

Tom did.

'Now get rid of press search from the box, and click on that little magnifying glass beside the box. That's the one.'

Tom did that, and then couldn't believe his eyes as lines of information, pertaining to know about Saint Nicholas, appeared on the screen. Well he nevered. But it was typical of this day and age. Nothing was sacred anymore. All those people working on Christmas Day. 'Shouldn't be allowed,' he said, as Cat directed him to a likely source.

It took a while, Tom kept oohing and aahing at things, but finally enough information was gleaned to be going on with.

'Well, that's apt,' said Tom, closing the lid on his shiny thing, when they had finished.

'What is?'

'Him living in Turkey like that.'

'So?'

'Christmas – Turkey,' said Tom. 'Who'd have guessed?'

'Come on,' said Cat, intent on more ignoring of the old buffoon.

Chapter 3

Stepping into Tom's bathroom, Cat gave him the once over. He had pulled a woolly hat over his cap, donned a heavy ancient donkey jacket over his jacket, and wrapped a thick scarf around his neck. And to set the ensemble off, he had balanced a pair of sunglasses on the bridge of his nose.

'Your jacket will be fine you know,' said Cat.

'It's winter,' said Tom.

'It's Turkey,' said Cat, 'mid-teens.'

'Sunglasses,' said Tom, 'middle-aged.'

'What?' said Cat.

'It was you that started with the ageism,' said Tom.

'I don't understand.'

'There you are then.'

Cat shook her head. 'I meant the temperature. It won't be hot, but it shouldn't be too cold.'

'Mid-teens *is* cold as far as I'm concerned,' said Tom, taking a pair of gloves from a pocket and donning them.

'You look a right Charlie,' said Cat.

'A warm one,' said Tom.

Feeling the battle was long lost, Cat decided it was time they moved on. 'Ready to go then are we?' she asked.

'About to think,' said Tom, eyes closed, his face contorting with the effort. "Demre" popped into his mind, the modern name for Myra, the destination they would eventually be heading for. Tom's eyes opened. 'We there?' he said.

Cat had opened the door as soon as Tom had stopped gurning. They appeared to be in a rather posh restroom. A hotel she guessed. But she would have to check further afield to see if they had reached their intended destination. Time travel wasn't an exact science, especially with Tom at the helm. 'Hang about, I'll go look.' Cat scooted out the door.

A couple of minutes later Cat was back, choosing a cubicle. The portable toilet didn't travel you see, just the inside of it. The portable loo itself was still in Tom's garden. So when Cat pushed open the right cubicle door, she stepped back into the inside of the portable toilet.

'Well?' said Tom, who had made himself as comfortable as one could in the confines of said portable loo.

'Demre it is,' said Cat, with just the hint of lingering surprise that came with Tom getting things right.

'Myra it is then.'

'You remember the date?'

'Of course,' said Tom, looking hurt. 'I still have most of my marbles left you know.'

This of course depends on how many you had in the first place, thought Cat, not unkindly. 'Just checking,' she said.

Cat had, in this instance, given Tom a precise date to aim for, which was just as well considering the vague offerings the internet had conjured up. Tom had smelt insider information at play. Cat had called it an educated hunch. But Tom wasn't going to argue, a magical creature was just that after all.

'Thinking it,' said Tom, which was the equivalent of "fasten your seat belts".

'Concentrate,' said Cat.

He did, and when that concentration was spent, Cat again did the honours. It was dark outside.

'Coo!' said Tom, peering from the confines of the portable loo, 'it's a bit dark.' He sometimes forgot that the world of the past didn't exist in the near constant light of the present. 'Pitch black,' he said, holding out a hand in front of him. 'I can't even see me hand.' He also sometimes forgot he was wearing sunglasses.

'It's night,' said Cat, 'and you're still wearing your sunglasses.'

'I'll get the torch,' said Tom, deftly removing the offending blinkers.

'No need,' said Cat, 'I'll be your eyes, better we don't give ourselves away, just stay close.' Cat could conjure a *glamour* around Tom and herself, to hide them from any prying eyes. Something that always worked exceedingly well, that is unless someone – no names mentioned – pokes a finger out through the edge of the glamour field, causing consternation and fainting amongst any innocent onlookers, faced with a floating dismembered digit. 'And keep your hands in your pockets.'

'I can hardly see you,' said Tom, clawing blindly ahead of him.

Checking that Tom *had* removed his sunglasses, which he had, Cat relented, and told him to fetch his torch. 'But keep it pointed to the ground.' She hoped she wouldn't regret it.

Tom went back and got the torch. He flicked it on.

'Batteries?' said Cat, when the torch failed to work.

'Just needs a little TLC, that's all.' Tom then proceeded to bang the torch on the ground. After a moment, when the torch could take no more, it succumbed and flickered into life. 'There,' said Tom, pleased with himself.

'You happy now?'

'Yes siree,' said Tom, waving the torch about. 'Let's get those doggies mo... oops. Sorry.'

'No offence taken,' said Cat, 'and keep that torch down.'

'Which way?'

'Just follow me.'

They travelled here, there, but not everywhere. And after a while of this, Tom soon realised that Cat was right, it wasn't cold. He wanted to go back. He was cooking beneath his layers. 'Aren't we there yet?' he grumbled, as they headed down yet another dark back street, the only light drifting from a window here and there. He took his woolly hat off and stuffed it in a pocket.

'Nearly,' said Cat.

'You said that ten minutes ago,' moaned Tom.

'And I'll say it again if you ask me before we get there,' said Cat.

Three *nearlys* later, they arrived at their intended destination. But where was that, Tom wanted to know.

'The house where everything started,' said Cat.

'With the bags of gold and the daughters?' said Tom, who had swotted.

'Exactly,' said Cat.

'I'm going to see Santa,' said Tom excitedly, the street trudging forgot about, as his child-within came embarrassingly to the surface.

'How old are you?' said Cat. 'And before you get too carried away, no you're not.'

'I'm not?'

'No,' said Cat. 'That's the point.'

'Is it?'

'Yes, it's clues we're here for.'

'Ah,' said Tom, 'clues.' He sounded just a little deflated.

'Clues,' Cat confirmed.

'So what is it we're looking for?' said Tom, playing the *hardly worth the effort* beam from his torch across the ground.

'Anything that will throw a little more light than that torch of yours, on the how's and why's of Saint Nicholas's disappearance.'

Tom gave the torch a shake. It helped a little, but it would soon need new batteries. Batteries that he was sure would have been in his surprise sock. You couldn't have enough batteries. He played the torch beam on the ground again, where it cast a yellowish circle of light the size of a basketball. This searching lark was going to take a while.

Chapter 4

'Oh-oh-oh, woe is me,' wailed the chappie, observing the yellowish basketball sized beam, apparently appearing and waving about from nowhere. The observer knew a torch light when he saw one, and he also knew that they didn't exist here in the fourth century.

The observer was a natural worrier. He had worried when he had kidnapped Saint Nicholas. He had worried after the dirty deed had been done. He had worried when he found out he had inadvertently left behind some evidence of his identity, during the struggle; Saint Nicholas had put up more of a fight than had been expected. Now he was worried that he was to be found out. But what had he expected, hadn't he been worried that might happen? Oh, woe was he. Woe, woe, woe!

The worried observer chewed nervously on his knuckles. Any moment now they would find it. Or would they? He hadn't been able to find it, and he knew what he was looking for. Perhaps he was worrying about nothing? Perhaps he hadn't left it here. Maybe it had been lost somewhere else. But where?

Turning away from the intermittently appearing torch beam, the worried observer made tracks to his time machine. Why oh why had he done it? Because of what he had read, that's why. Why did he ever buy that darned computer? Why had he looked? Why wouldn't he? That's what the flipping things are there for, to be looked at, to be surfed. Was that the right word? Never mind. It was done. But what did he do now? Think, that was it, go back and think. Think where he might have lost it. Think of ways to cover his tracks.

The worried observer climbed aboard his time machine, said the words that needed to be said, and was gone.

Chapter 5

'What was that?' said Tom, ears pricking.

'What was what?' said Cat, busy investigating.

'That noise,' said Tom.

'What noise?' said Cat, un-busying.

'I thought I heard someone shout,' said Tom.

'I never heard anything.'

'Haven't you got super hearing or something?'

'What can I say, I was busy,' said Cat. 'Perhaps if you had been busy instead of waving that poor excuse for a torch about, you wouldn't have been hearing things either.'

'I wasn't hearing things,' Tom protested.

'I thought you said you had,' said Cat.

Sometimes Cat could be as infuriating as Tom was. This was one of those times. Tom wanted to tut, stamp his feet, and get generally huffy. He had heard a shout. He was sure. It was a man's voice, shouting something, no, commanding something. 'I did hear something,' said Tom, the beginnings of a pout forming on his lips.

'Go on then,' said Cat, preparing to humour. 'What was it you thought you heard?'

'I… It…' And in that moment, as Tom struggled with his words, he suddenly realised just why that might be. *I couldn't have,* he thought, as what he thought he heard hit him. He looked at Cat, who was giving him the curious eye.

'Well?' said Cat.

'I…' He couldn't. He would sound silly. Sillier than usual. He must have made a mistake, surely. Perhaps he hadn't really heard anything. Perhaps he was hearing things. He didn't want to sound silly. 'Nothing,' he said.

'Nothing?' said Cat, still giving Tom the curious look.

'Must have been the wind.'

'Must have been,' said Cat. There was no wind.

Tom played his torch on the ground and picked up from where he had left off, aimlessly shining it at nothing in particular.

'Tom?'

'Yeah?'

'Nothing.' Cat discarded her curious look with a worried one. Tom was worrying her. But then again, when wasn't he? She watched as the torch beam disappeared beyond the glamour.

'Tom?'

'Yes?'

'You are keeping the beam within the glamour, aren't you?'

Wrinkled brow. 'Er... Yes.'

'Good, we don't want a repeat of what happened before.'

'Good grief, no,' said Tom, slyly moving the beam back into the confines of the glamour. It was a good thing he had been searching the opposite way to Cat. No harm done.

'Let's move on.'

'But we've already been here for hours,' Tom protested, feeling increasingly uncomfortable under his donkey jacket.

'Fifteen minutes,' said Cat.

'Feels like hours.'

'Hot are you?'

And bothered. 'No,' lied Tom, his red face telling a different story.

'Just a little while longer, but we do have to be thorough.'

Tom did some huffing, but they continued with their search, scouring the area Cat believed to be the scene of the kidnap, until it was completely covered. It drew a blank. No incriminating evidence. But there was something. And it meant there was one more place she needed investigate, and if she was proved right, it would be outside the window of the house where the story of Santa began, the window of the house where the man and his three daughters lived. The place where Saint Nicholas was to have performed his act of generosity. Cat set off. Tom followed behind, grumbling under his breath.

When they arrived, a pale light shone from the window, initiating caution, but they had to get close. Something might be waiting to be found.

'Quiet now,' said Cat, as she got closer. Something had caught her eye. She hoped it was the something she was looking for.

'As a mouse,' whispered Tom.

Cat cut him a look, but Tom was oblivious to it as he concentrated on the task at hand.

They neared the window. Someone was moving about inside. They would have to be careful. A noise out of place could start a whole new story echoing into the future.

'Why are we here?' whispered Tom.

'Evidence,' said Cat, in hushed tones.

'But why would there be any here?' said Tom.

'Footprints,' said Cat.

'Footprints?' said Tom.

'Leading from the scuffle to here,' said Cat.

Tom hadn't noticed any footprints. He played the torch on the ground and along the way they had come, and sure enough Cat was right, there were footprints. But footprints were footprints. 'Could be anyone's,' said Tom, who had a valid point.

'Sssch,' hushed Cat.

'Sorry,' whispered Tom, 'but they could be.'

'Not with that tread print,' said Cat, 'modern boot.'

Tom took a closer look. By jingo, Cat was right; he had a pair of boots with the exact same tread.

'I've...' But Cat had already made her way beneath the window. Tom scurried after her.

'What do you see?' she asked when Tom arrived.

'What do you mean, what do I see?' said Tom, not liking the sound of the question.

'Inside.'

'I'm not looking inside,' said Tom, 'someone might see me.'

'You're *glamoured*.'

Tom had forgotten about that. But nevertheless, he proceeded with caution as he peeped over the sill.

'Well?'

'A man,' said Tom.

'What's he doing?'

'Pacing back and forth.'

'Is he looking this way?'

'Why?' said Tom, not liking the sound of this either.

'Because, I want you to reach up and grab that piece of white fluff.'

'White fluff?' Tom looked up, and sure enough, caught on one of the jambs, was a piece of white fluff. Tom immediately went to grab it.

'Wait,' said Cat. 'Carefully.'

'He can't see me,' said Tom.

'But he can see the fluff if he's looking this way. We don't want to frighten the man with sudden disappearing fluff.'

Tom once more peeped over the sill. The man was pacing away from him; he took his chance and grabbed the fluff. He inspected it. 'What do you think it is?' he asked.

'Evidence I hope,' said Cat.

Tom smiled. 'Does that mean we can go home? I could do with a cuppa.'

'No time, I'm afraid,' said Cat.

'But I'm thirsty, all that detective work.'

Cat could see how playing a torch's beam aimlessly on the ground for forty odd minutes could make you thirsty; if you were Tom. 'We've still got detective work to do.'

'More?'

'We have to find out if that white fluff is what I think it is.'

'And what's that?' said Tom, studying it in his hand.

'Synthetic.'

Tom furrowed his brow.

Cat didn't have the time to explain. 'You want your sock back, don't you?'

'Yes,' said Tom.

'To Smokowski's then,' said Cat.

Tom immediately brightened. Smokowski could always be relied on to provide a cuppa for a pal in need, even perhaps a dodger, of the jammy kind. Tom's mouth began to water.

Chapter 6

The worried observer wasn't so worried anymore; he had found what he had thought he'd lost. But that didn't mean he could stop worrying altogether, he wasn't safe yet. That mysterious beam of torch light he had seen was still serious food for thought, so much so, it was giving him indigestion.

Also a concern was the worried observer's conscience. He hadn't thought it would worry him so, but that poor man, pacing with worry, going to go without, and those poor daughters of his. The worried observer shivered. And it was all his doing. What had he done?

But it had to be done. But what did he do now? Maybe he hadn't thought things through properly. He definitely hadn't given a thought as to what to do with Saint Nicholas, now that he had him. The worried observer glanced at the man, all dressed up in his bishop's garb, tied to a chair, gagged. He looked younger than he thought he would. He looked downright miserable. Perhaps a cuppa would cheer him up.

Chapter 7

'Tra-la-la-la-la-la! Tra-la-la-la-la-la!'

'Sounds like someone's having fun,' observed Tom, as he and Cat stepped from the loo in Smokowski's storeroom. Smokowski owned the local mini-mart cum post office. He knew about Tom and Cat, and the time travelling. A bit of a mystery, rivers ran deep where Mister Smokowski was concerned. He was also trained in unarmed combat. He was also one of Tom's best mates.

Cat had decided it best to arrive at Smokowski's just after closing time on Christmas Eve; yesterday. That way there was less chance of bumping into any of Smokowski's customers. But she hadn't banked on arriving in the middle of a sing-song.

'I know that voice,' said Tom, after a moment.

Sadly, so did Cat, to her consternation.

Gently pushing on the storeroom door that led to the shop, Tom opened it just enough for he and Cat to see what was going on behind it. What was going on behind it was Darren, Smokowski's hapless shop assistant, Cat's constant worry, Lucy's loving husband, and therefore Tom's pain in the butt son-in-law. He appeared to be doing the conga all by himself. Smokowski was standing behind the counter looking on, his face a mask of despair, and one of desperate concern for his stock. Darren was also something of a myth, but we won't go there. Suffice to say, he found the present somewhat more difficult than the past.

'Smokowski,' hissed Tom, as he opened the door wider. If possible, it would be better if they could conduct business without attracting the attention of Darren.

'Thank goodness,' said Smokowski, on seeing Tom. 'But I thought Lucy was picking him up?'

Cat's attention was immediately turned to the door of the shop. They would have to be quick. Lucy seeing them there, when she had just left Tom at home sat in front of the fire warming his tootsies would be hard to explain. Lucy wasn't privy to Tom's time travelling exploits. One had to draw the line somewhere. Besides, it was in the rules.

'Sorry mate,' said Tom, 'not here to collect, got a small problem.'

'So have I.' Smokowski nodded towards Darren. 'He's been like this since we closed. Says he can't wait for New Year.' Smokowski grimaced, Darren was conga-ing along the wine and beer aisle. He hadn't noticed there were visitors.

'Leave him for the moment,' said Cat, 'Lucy will sort him out when she arrives. In the meantime, we need your help.'

In the privacy of the storeroom, with Auld Lang Syne ringing in their ears, Tom quickly filled Smokowski in on what was afoot. He showed him what they had found.

'Fur,' said Smokowski, without hesitation, 'without a doubt, fur.'

'Fur?' said Tom, providing some of that missing doubt. 'But Cat said…'

'Synthetic fur.'

'Ah,' said Tom.

'Fur?' echoed Cat, but more questioning than doubtful.

'Some sort of blend,' said Smokowski, studying it. 'Superior stuff though, very realistic, wouldn't be cheap.' Even though Smokowski was in the grocery business, he liked to keep tabs on all sorts in the world of trade and commerce. It was called having your fingers in as many pies as you could. 'Doubt you would be able to buy something like this retail. Do you want me to have a dig around? I've a few contacts.'

'On Christmas Eve?' said Tom.

'Not everyone celebrates it you know.'

'So I've been told,' said Tom.

'Would you?' said Cat.

'A pleasure,' said Smokowski. The shop doorbell rang. 'That must be Lucy. Look, I'll give you a call when I know something.' Smokowski doffed an imaginary hat, and returned to the shop.

'So,' said Tom, 'what do we do now?' He hoped the answer would have the word cuppa somewhere in it.

Chapter 8

Saint Nicholas had not wanted a cup of tea. What he wanted was to go home – Tom wasn't the only one with a Universal Translator – but that wasn't possible.

The worried observer paced a little. He then paced some more. He then paced even more. He then stopped, the phone was ringing. Who could that be? he wondered, phoning him on Christmas Eve? Didn't they know it was the busiest time of the year? Still, it was the time for goodwill to all men, and women, so the worried observer went to it and picked it up.

'Yes?' said the worried observer. It was one of his suppliers; an amiable enough chap called Honest John. Honest John yattered.

The worried observer put the phone down after wishing John a merry one. It was worrying news, which made him worry even more. He went to his coat and checked it. It was as he feared. And now someone was onto him, or would be if he didn't act quickly.

Honest John had done what any man would have done in the same situation. Someone had been nosing around, asking questions about fur and wondering where he might get some? Ordinarily, Honest John would have only been too happy to help, but as the enquirer lived within the same area as another customer – the worried observer – he had thought it only good manners to inform interested parties as to the interest.

The worried observer had no time to waste.

Chapter 9

There was a sharp rapping on the mini-mart door.

'We're closed!' shouted Mister Smokowski, who had just finished totting up the day's takings. He was sat in the storeroom cum office, with the door to the shop slightly ajar. But the rapping became all the more insistent.

Mister Smokowski tutted, but got to his feet. He was in no two minds as to who it was knocking at this time of the night. He wondered what Darren had forgotten this time.

In the shop proper, Smokowski peered through the insufficient light the freezer units gave off, narrowing his eyes as he did. Outside was dark, inside not much better. He couldn't see who was at the door, but it wasn't Darren; Darren would have had his face pressed against the glass, as was his habit. Tutting again, he decided it must be some old dear who had forgotten her stuffing. He went to the door and peered outside.

To Smokowski's surprise, it wasn't an old dear at his door, but an old boy. He stared harder and realised it was someone he knew, old Mister Corrs. *I wonder what he wants*, thought Smokowski, stuffing no doubt.

Smokowski unlocked the door and opened it a little way, no point in letting the heat out. 'Hello,' he said. 'What can I do for you?'

'I'm sorry to trouble you on this most special of evenings, but I have something to show you.' The old boy had spoken in almost a whisper.

'Sorry?' said Smokowski.

'I have something to show you.'

Sighing inwardly, Smokowski opened the door so that Mister Corrs could come in; it was the season of goodwill after all. 'Please come in,' said Smokowski, who didn't think the old boy looked too well.

'Thank you,' said the old boy, stepping inside.

'Now, what is it you want to show me?' said Smokowski, raising a quizzical eyebrow.

'Just this,' said Mister Corrs, producing something from a pocket at a speed that belied his apparent age. 'I call it my forty winks spray.'

Smokowski never stood a chance. Mister Corrs had been very quick on the draw. Mister Smokowski fell against the door and slid down it onto the welcome mat. There he sprawled unconscious.

Chapter 10

'But I can't understand why we can't just turn up before this Nicholas bloke was kidnapped and stop it from happening,' said Tom, putting forward, what he believed to be, a perfectly good argument. He brushed his hands together. 'Job done!'

'Because it isn't how things are done,' said Cat.

'But it makes sense,' said Tom.

'Then answer me this,' said Cat. 'If we go back and stop whoever it is from doing what they did, how would we know that anything had taken place for us to go back and stop?'

'But we'd know,' said Tom. 'We're in that time bubble you talk about, aren't we?' He was starting to get one of those headaches. The ones he got from trying to think.

'Would we?' said Cat.

And as Tom's headache had arrived, and as Cat had spoken with that degree of finality that meant, *enough on the subject already,* Tom decided to call time on the questioning; for the moment. Until the time came for the need for another, which just happened to be right that very second.

'Where are we?' said Tom, momentarily disorientated, as the world as seen through the loo door suddenly changed. How did Cat do that? One minute Smokowski's storeroom, and the next, a billionaire's junk room. Tom was sure he hadn't thought Egypt at any time. Egypt, because he now knew exactly where it was he was.

'Home sweet home,' said Cat, stepping from the loo. 'I need to look something up.' She wandered off, leaving Tom to stare in bewildered awe, as he always did, when he visited Cat's abode.

Cat lived in a secret chamber, a large secret chamber, a very large secret chamber, beneath one of the ancient pyramids of Egypt. Which one, and in which timeline, no one but she knew.

Awe staring over for this visit, Tom headed for the kettle. At least a cuppa was at last in the offering.

Freshly brewed cuppa in hand, Tom decided to do some wandering while he waited for Cat to finish what it was she had come here to do.

Tom liked to nose, and who wouldn't, the place was amazing, jam packed as it was, with antiquities and curios of all kinds, enough to fill a museum ten times over. But Tom had to tread very carefully, most objects he was allowed to touch, some he wasn't. And some of those he wasn't came with a threat that something nasty might happen to him if he did. Cat had even mentioned something about, *on the pain of death to do so,* or something. Tom had laughed. Cat had not. Thankfully, these had been pointed out to him. But just to be on the safe side, Tom tended to err on the side of caution at all times. Tom's version of caution that is.

Blowing on his cuppa, then taking a careful sip, Tom stopped beside a huge chariot. The like that that Ben chappie rode on in that film with the name Tom could never remember. He climbed aboard carefully, so as not to spill his cuppa – he was good like that – and then, with his free hand, took up an imaginary whip which he swished at the imaginary horses in front. So far so good, Tom was observing the rules. Do touch – don't touch.

Finished with cracking his whip, Tom clambered from the chariot to see what else he could find. He idled from one object to another, avoiding the do not touch, and investigating the ones he could, sipping on his drink as he went, until… 'And what do we have here?' said Tom, to himself.

On the floor, lying between a Chippendale what-not, and an unknown painting by some famous artist or other, was a huge sword, the double handed type, the sort the knights of old may well have wielded in some adventure or another. Tom balanced his still hot mug on the top of the Chippendale what-not – he was bad like that – and, fancying himself as being a bit of one of those knights in shining armour, he bent to pick it up. It was on the okay list as far as he could remember. It wouldn't just be lying there if it wasn't, would it?

Three unsuccessful attempts later, to even lift the thing a millimetre from the floor, a huffing puffing Tom, gave up. He looked, but couldn't for the life of him see where it was fixed down. And why in the world Cat would want to do such a thing, unless it was valuable, but still a silly place to put something, on a wall yes, but the floor? Tom groaned as he straightened up. *Flipping silly thing,* he thought, his lumber area giving him gyp. He took a kick at the sword out of frustration and saw it spin like a child's top, so well balanced was it.

'Well I…' exclaimed Tom, who then glanced furtively behind him. No Cat to be seen. Tom, embarrassed but thankful no one had been privy to his pathetic failure, quickly reclaimed his mug, gave a tut when he saw the ring it had been covering – how can people be so inconsiderate – and moved swiftly on. Or as swiftly as someone could whose back was intent on telling the world how old one was.

Five minutes later, his back a little better, and the thought in mind that another cuppa might be a good idea, Tom came across something else; something very, very, interesting.

Tom couldn't remember ever seeing the object before; not that he had seen everything. He hadn't seen the sword before. But if he hadn't seen it before, then it hadn't been shown to him as being something to be avoided, which meant, it had to be safe, didn't it? He took a step towards it. What was it?

'Tom!' shouted Cat, who had at last found what she had been looking for, an ancient scroll with scrawled co-ordinates on it, 'I've found what I was looking for!' But she got no answer. She tried again. 'Tom!'

That's funny, she thought, when still no answer was forthcoming. She then rethought her thinking. No it isn't, it's worrying. It was Tom. 'Tom?' Cat went into search mode.

But all was well. A couple of turns later in her maze of amazement, Cat came upon him sitting quietly on the floor. Relieved that nothing untoward had happened to him, she immediately set about freeing his head.

Chapter 11

Mister Corrs, the worried observer, was accumulating problems. He had kidnapped Saint Nicholas, he hadn't wanted to. He had also kidnapped Mister Smokowski, the proprietor of the local mini-mart. He hadn't wanted to do that either. But what choice had he had? None, that's what. He had guessed right, the shopkeeper had had a very incriminating piece of evidence on him. How he had got hold of it though was worrying. It had to do with that dratted torch beam, but he just wasn't able to join the dots.

But there were other, more immediate problems facing Mister Corrs, the lack of chairs for one thing. There had originally been four of them, a set, but wear and tear meant that there were only three left, and two of them was occupied. He didn't know what he would do if he had to kidnap someone else. Perhaps he could borrow one from that nice old lady, Missus Wigguns, from next door.

Mister Corrs slumped wearily into the unoccupied chair, took off his hat and, as he placed it on the table, sighed heavily. Oh woe was he. If only he had given more thought to his plan. It had seemed so simple when he had first thought of it. He started to ponder on the last few hours. He began to fidget. No, silent cogitation wasn't the answer. But what was? Sit and rue? Oh woe was he. Mister Corrs gave another deep sigh and then got to his feet. Perhaps a cuppa would help.

Chapter 12

As Tom endeavoured to rid his ears of the last of the margarine, Cat worked out exactly what was needed when they got back to Smokowski's storeroom. And as the co-ordinates on the scroll needed a constant focal starting point, which Cat's home was far from being, she decided there would be no place better to start than a few feet from where Tom's time machine now stood; Mister Smokowski's shop wasn't going anywhere soon. At least she hoped not; though stranger things had happened.

It was, still there, the mini-mart. Tom and Cat stepped from the loo and back into Smokowski's storeroom, no more than a second or two after they had left it. Tom was still complaining about the object that had *accidently* fallen onto his head.

'But you didn't say it was a *don't touch*,' moaned Tom, who was sure some of the margarine had got into his brain.

'That's because it wasn't,' said Cat.

'But it was dangerous, you should have warned me.'

'I would have if you'd been younger than six,' said Cat.

'What do you…?'

'Ah, here we go.'

'We go? Wah! Where are we now?' Such was the sudden change in scenery, Tom didn't realise he still had his little finger in his ear. But that changed when he realised his feet were suddenly cold. He removed his finger and looked down. 'Snow?'

'A little surprise,' said Cat, 'but don't look round.'

And as Tom hardly did what he was told, he did. 'Wah!' he exclaimed.

'Told you not to look.'

Tom took to stammering. 'Bu-bu-but, there's nothing there,' he managed.

'That's why I told you not to look round,' said Cat.

'But how can that be?' said Tom, starring into oblivion.

'Because Tom, we are somewhere that is slowly ceasing to exist.'

Tom didn't like the sound of that. 'Why are we here then?'

'Like I said, I've a little surprise for you,' said Cat, purposely evasive.

Deciding it might be wise to try and put what was, or wasn't, behind him for the moment, Tom bravely asked if Cat thought he would like it.

'Depends,' said Cat.

'Depends?' said Tom.

'Depends on whether you like cookies and hot chocolate or not.'

Tom was now more confused than usual. And that confusion grew further, when a huge red door mysteriously appeared in front of them. 'Cat?'

'Follow me.'

As Tom fell in behind Cat, the huge red door swung silently and easily open. A soft warm light greeted them. Cat stepped over the threshold. Tom wasn't happy, but there was no going back. He had the horrible feeling, that if he didn't step through that doorway, oblivion would swallow him up, and never spit him out. He nervously glanced behind him, and then quickly followed.

Behind the door a hundred or so small faces turned to greet the, one furry, one old and befuddled looking, visitors as they entered. Small faces aglow with rosy cheeks broke into cheerful smiles. Small faces with pointy ears adorning each side of them. And on top of the heads that these small faces belonged to, sat merry green hats trimmed with red, a small bell atop them.

Now someone else greeted the visitors. A large elderly chap with cheeks that rivalled those of the small faces, and a belly huge, that wobbled like a huge bowl of...

'Who the heck is that?' whispered Tom.

'Who do you think it is?' said Cat.

A huge beard of white the large man bore, a jolly hat of red and white, trousers and jacket to match, he wore. A large black belt, buckled with silver did gleam, and to match, boots so shiny and clean.

'Nope,' said Tom. 'Is he off the telly?'

'Santa,' said Cat, 'how are you?'

'Well-well-well,' said the large chap, in a voice as cheery as his cheeks. 'Is that you Cat? Well I never. Come in, come in and sit by the fire, and if you're lucky I may just play my lyre.'

'Santa?' said Tom.

'And this fine elderly fellow with you must be Tom, and I apologise, if I've got that terribly wrong,' said Santa, offering Tom a mitten encased hand.

''ere,' said Tom, frowning, but taking hold of that mitten. Santa or no Santa, the elderly remark was a bit much, and not in the least bit true.

'Now come in Tom, Tom come in. Oh I must sit down, all this excitement, my head's all in a spin.'

Yeah, thought Tom, *I could do with a good sit myself.* But not because of his age you understand. No, it was all the excitement. *Drat!* thought Tom.

Santa sat and clicked his fingers. He then removed his mitten and tried again. A young chap dressed all in green appeared. 'Ah, Rinkel my dearest dear chap,' Santa said with a smile, 'would you be so kind as to draw Tom here a map?'

'Will do Santa,' said Rinkel, looking at Tom. 'I thought he was a myth.'

'A map?' said Tom. ''ere, what do you mean, myth?'

'Of course,' said Santa, cheeks still aglow, 'for the cookies and hot chocolate are in the kitchen I say, and I'm sure you'll be wanting to know the way.'

Tom gave a Cat a quick worried look. Cat took the map. 'This way,' she said.

Out of earshot Tom aired his worries.

'Just go with the flow,' said Cat, which wasn't very helpful.

Then suddenly they were at another door.

'Whoa!' said Tom, just stopping short of walking into it. 'Where did that door come from?'

'A shop that sells doors?' said Cat, as quick as you like. She nudged it. It opened up to reveal the beating heart of the house; the kitchen. And at its midst, amongst the steam and bubbling pots, stood a woman. A woman dressed in red and white. A woman bearing an uncanny likeness, less the whiskers, to the man Cat had called Santa.

'Well I'll be!' exclaimed the woman. 'Is that you Cat?'

'It is,' said Cat.

'Then this, forgive me for staring, must be Tom,' said the woman, removing a pair of oven mitts.

'It is,' said Cat, speaking for Tom, who was stood with open mouth.

'Well I'll be,' said the woman. 'And there's me thinking he was nothing more than a myth.

Chapter 13

'You going to tell me what is going on?' whispered Tom. They were alone, Missus Claus had had to pop out for a moment after making them their hot chocolate, but you never could tell. He was sat beside Cat at a huge table, in front of him his large mug of hot chocolate. Cat had her hot chocolate in a bowl. 'And what is it with this myth business? It's giving me the heebie-jeebies. It's as if they didn't think I existed.'

Cat paused in her lapping of her hot chocolate. It had just the faintest aroma of roast chicken about it. 'You're a star Tom,' she said. 'No one can quite believe what you've done, in such a short time, and still be in one piece.'

Up until that last bit of Cat's explanation, Tom had started to harbour a sense of smugness. 'What do you mean, *in one piece*? Is that supposed to make me feel better?' He put on a grumpy face and stared at the multitude of marshmallows that were piled high in his mug.

'Depends how you were feeling in the first place,' said Cat, getting back to her lapping.

'Not helping,' said Tom.

Ceasing in her lapping again, Cat decided to fill Tom in. She tended to keep Tom informed on a need to know only basis, if she could, he was still only a newbie, but sometimes it couldn't be helped and she had to give out more than she really wanted to. 'We're here to find out if Santa knows anything about what is going on. If anyone knows what is going on in the world of Santa, it's Santa.' Failing that, she was going to have a word with someone else that might be able to help her, Elven. Elven was a familiar like herself but an elf, a real elf, whose love of the world of Santa was so great, he had made the North Pole his home. And, like Cat, he was also assigned to a time traveller. But, unlike Cat and most of the other familiars, when Elven went on a mission with his traveller, he liked to leave an interacting hologram of himself behind so he was ever present at the North Pole, should Santa need him. Either Elven or his hologram would do to have a word with, but Cat didn't intend on worrying Elven if she could help it, he would be having his own problems somewhere no doubt. She suspected that was why she hadn't seen him or his hologram as yet.

Tom nearly choked on his mallows. 'What?' he spluttered, just missing Cat with a pink one. He started to cough.

'It's rude to choke on someone you know,' said Cat.

Coughing subsiding, Tom managed to remember how to breathe again. 'What did you just say?' he said, in that first breath.

'I said it's rude…'

'Not that, the bit about Santa?' A mallow fell from Tom's jacket lapel onto the floor; a white one.

'Which bit?'

'The bit about that big bloke out there thinking he's Santa.'

'He is Santa,' said Cat. 'And the nice lady, who provided us with our hot chocolate, is Missus Claus.'

'Claus?'

'Claus, Kris Kringle, Santa, all the same,' said Cat.

'That fat bloke out there is really Santa. That's what you're trying to tell me?'

'Yes,' said Cat, trying to get back to her lapping. The hint of roast chicken was divine.

'But I thought Santa was just a…'

'Whoa there Tom,' said Cat, stopping Tom dead in his vocal tracks. 'You don't know who might be reading this.' Cat looked from the page and gave the reader – you – a sheepish grin.

'Reading?' said Tom, his best non comprehending look on his face. 'What are you talking about? And who are you smiling at?'

'No one,' said Cat, eager to get back to the story. 'Now, drink your chocolate before it gets cold.'

Sometimes Tom had no idea what Cat was going on about. This was one of those times. He picked up his mug and took a sip, taking mind to miss the marshmallows that he was sure were out to get him, then took a furtive glance to where Cat had smiled. There was nothing there, wait… just a moment… there's something…

'There,' said Missus Claus, slapping Tom hard in the middle of his back. She had heard Tom coughing and had rushed in as quickly as she could; which wasn't that fast as she had stopped off in the stables first to feed the reindeers. But she was here now, and that's what counted.

Mind now most certainly off things that didn't concern him, Tom fought for the suddenly misplaced breath he had just been about to take. He found it and spluttered. If it wasn't the mallows trying to disrupt his breathing regime, it was the wife of Santa.

'Better out than in, eh?' said Missus Claus, proud that she had done her bit to prolong the life of the time travelling hero.

It was a good job Tom had all his own teeth. 'Much better,' said Tom, only now realising it hadn't been a runaway bull that had smacked into him. And on that point he felt it only polite not to mention her tardiness. *Now, he thought as feeling returned to his back, better check the old spine.* He wriggled his toes. All okay there. He reached for his mug. No problem there either. All seemed fine. Though it was doubtful he would ever touch another marshmallow again.

'Likes his hot chocolate, doesn't he,' said Missus Claus, winking at Cat.

'He sure does,' said Cat, winking back.

This has to be some surreal dream, thought Tom, hoping he would wake up soon if it was.

'Right,' said Missus Claus, 'if you'll excuse me I have a table to lay in the dining room. And if you're after wanting more hot chocolate, and I think I know someone who might,' she winked at Tom, 'you just help yourself. See you in a jiffy.' Missus Claus gave a little wave, and left the kitchen.

Alone again, Tom took no time in turning and glaring at Cat. He had heard what she had said, but now he wanted the truth. *Santa, my ar... aromatherapy set,* thought Tom. 'Right Cat old friend, what is really going on?'

'They're real,' said Cat, 'Santa and his wife, and the elves, all real, in the sense of the spirit of it.'

'The spirit of it?'

'Yes.'

'You going to elaborate on that?' said Tom, frowning.

'All that you see here is real, because that is how people see Santa. See mother Claus. See the elves. This is that belief personified.'

'Personified?' Tom would have to start keeping a dictionary about him, the way Cat was going on.

'Made real.'

'Santa's real?' Tom took a swig of his hot chocolate. He should have made a bigger Christmas list.

'As real as you and me,' said Cat.

'Well I'll be,' said Tom. He let the thought sink in. No different than travelling in time, he supposed. 'So we've got to ask old whiskers out there what he knows about the kidnap.'

'That was the plan,' said Cat, 'but I fear he might be beyond helping us.' This meant she would need to seek out Elven and have a word with him, see what he knew, if anything.

'You think?' said Tom, thinking about the rhyming.

'But it's not all in vain, not just yet, we've still got time.'

'Do we? For what?'

'To save the old fellow.'

'How do you figure that then?' said Tom.

'He's still here isn't he, for the moment.'

'I don't understand,' said Tom. He really didn't.

'Look,' said Cat. 'Saint Nicholas has disappeared, so has the pressies on Christmas morning.'

'Got that,' said Tom. He really did get that.

'But Santa here... You listening?'

'Of course I am, just taking it in,' said Tom, who sometimes couldn't help looking blank.

'But Santa here, the personification of yule...'

'Mule?'

'Yule, as in tide,' said Cat.

'As in high?' said Tom, complicating things.

'As in yuletide,' said Cat.

'Ah-ha,' said Tom.

'Can I continue?'

'Please do.'

'Survives on the belief of him, and as he is still here, there is still time to put things right, but not much.'

'How much?' said Tom.

'Remember the huge red door we came through?'

'Yes,' said Tom, always up for a quiz. He used to love that television programme, open the box and give me your money, or whatever it was called.

'Remember what was on the other side?'

'Us,' said Tom.

'And?'

Tom's brow furrowed.

Cat began to think perhaps the hot chocolate was having an effect on him.

Tom's face suddenly darkened. 'The nothingness,' he said.

'Well, just before I came to get you, I'd popped here to deliver Santa and Missus Claus their presents.'

'You deliver presents to Santa?' said Tom, who had never given as much as a thought to whether Santa received a present on Christmas morning. Well, now he knew.

'It's only polite,' said Cat, 'to give a gift when you're invited over to dinner.'

'You have Christmas dinner with Santa?' said Tom, impressed.

'For years now,' said Cat, 'unless there's an emergency in the offing.'

'Like today.'

'Exactly,' said Cat, 'but we're getting side-tracked. What I was going to say was, when I had visited earlier, there was less nothingness.'

'How much less?'

'Snow and ice as far as you could see less.'

'Ah,' said Tom. 'But can't you protect the place somehow? A glamour or something?'

'I put something in place when we arrived, but I don't know if it will help. It's belief we're talking about here. No belief, no existence. If they disappear I fear they will never be remembered again, whatever we do. They didn't even remember I'd already called. And as for the rhyming, I fear the place might be unravelling from the inside as well. We might be too late.'

'I'll remember,' said Tom. 'And you.'

'It won't be enough.'

'It's bad, isn't it?' said Tom, gravely. 'We had better find that Saint chappie smartish.'

'Bad, but not hopeless,' said Cat. 'I've been thinking, there's a chance we might be able to stem the flow before finding Saint Nicholas.'

Tom had a sudden bad feeling about the *we* part of Cat's thinking. 'We?' said Tom, nervously.

Cat told him what she had in mind.

'Oh,' said Tom. He had been right to be nervous.

Chapter 14

Just after Cat had explained her plan to Tom, Santa and Missus Claus came into the kitchen, they were holding hands and were looking very worried, their jolly demeanour had all but left them.

'What's wrong?' said Cat, fearing the worst. Or nearly the worst, as Santa and his missus were still with them.

'It's Elven,' said Missus Claus, 'he's missing.'

'Elven?' said Tom.

'Elven?' said Cat, who was mortified by the news. 'When?' He would never go anywhere without leaving his hologram. This was serious if it was true. And it would explain why she hadn't seen him. Bang goes that chat with him. But were Santa and Missus Claus totally compos mentis as of this time? For all Cat knew, because of what was happening, they may well have just forgotten what he looks like, or something. But the lack of his greeting her was now very worrying, in light of things.

'Roughly two bells ago,' said Santa, revealing his little known nautical side, 'as the cock doth crow.' Revealing just how addled he had become.

'This morning sometime,' said Missus Claus, who thankfully appeared to be still functioning with all her faculties, 'just after breakfast we think. He usually helps me with the dishes you see.' Disturbingly though, she didn't appear to be noticing her husband's poetic endeavours.

'Who's Elven?' asked Tom.

Cat quickly explained.

'And you've only just noticed now?' said Tom.

'I just thought he was busy with something else, but when he didn't turn up to help me lay the table as he always does, well, I got worried; he never misses that,' said Missus Claus, looking increasingly upset. 'So I sent Rinkel to find him, but he says Elven is nowhere to be found.'

'His traveller?' said Cat, sounding out a long shot. A long shot because she knew Elven's traveller was a special case. But there was always a chance, even familiars slipped up now and again. Not her of course.

'No one knows who he is,' said Missus Claus, confirming Cat's thoughts.

This wasn't a mystery, very few Travellers were known outside of the familiars, but occasionally the odd traveller was known to be known to no one but his or her own particular familiar. These Travellers were designated *deep cover* Travellers, for a number of reasons. Tom wasn't one of them, a *deep cover* traveller that is, not one of the reasons; as far as anyone knew. But Elven's was.

'Alas no one knows who he is, and that is very true, and if someone doesn't find Elven very soon, he may end up as glue,' Santa chipped in.

'Oh shut up Santa,' snapped Missus Claus, hitting him with a mitten. She turned to Cat. 'Will you look for him Cat?'

'I'll do my best,' said Cat, seizing on it as a reason for them to now leave. 'Come on Tom, there's no time to waste.' She leapt from her seat to the ground. Tom got up to follow her.

'Well I never,' said Missus Claus, suddenly blinking, 'it's you Cat. And if I'm not mistaken this must be…'

'Tom,' said Tom, passing Cat an anxious glance.

'Tom, that's right,' said Missus Claus. 'You know, I always thought you were a mug of hot chocolate.'

'Come on Tom,' urged Cat urgently.

But Tom needed no encouragement.

'Phew,' said Tom, as they arrived back in Smokowski's storeroom, 'that was getting weird. Do you think there's a connection, you know with Saint Nick and that Elven?'

'Could be,' said Cat, thoughtfully, 'but first things first, we need to put my plan into action.'

Tom knew she was going to say that. 'But where are we going to get three bags of gold from?' he said, hoping he had found a hole in her plan.

'The same place we're going to get a bishop's robe from,' she said, squashing those hopes.

Tom was aghast. 'You're not thinking of robbing a…'

'Certainly not,' said Cat, disturbed by the very thought of whatever Tom was going to say. 'We're going home.'

Tom couldn't remember having a bishop's robe in his wardrobe, but if it meant the chance of a cuppa. Come to think about it, he couldn't remember having any gold either. 'But I…'

'My home,' groaned Cat, 'not yours.'

'Ah,' said Tom. He then took on the look of the constipated. 'Why have you got a bishop's robe?'

'Never mind,' said Cat, who had just had a thought. 'But first let's go see if Smokowski's found anything that might help us.'

'Good idea,' said Tom, suddenly cheery. Especially if Smokowski had found something that would save them from having to carry out Cat's plan. But then he took a turn on the thought merry-go-round. 'But Smokowski won't have found out anything yet would he? We've only been gone a couple of minutes.'

'Unlike some people,' said Cat, 'Smokowski isn't one for hanging about. Besides, we've been gone for more than a couple of minutes.' She started for the shop.

'Have we?' Tom checked his watch, but for some reason, it had stopped, probably the battery. He went to follow Cat but then stopped himself. There was something he had meant to ask Cat. 'Is Elven really an elf?'

Chapter 15

Mister Corrs had made Smokowski a cuppa. He wasn't able to drink it, his hands were tied and he was gagged, but as always, it was the thought that counted. Mister Corrs had thought about spoon feeding Smokowski with the brew, another thoughtful thought, but because of the way Smokowski was glowering at him, he had thought better of it. So, with all his latest thoughts behind him, Mister Corrs turned once more to fretting and worrying.

The biggest worry of which, was the occasional bump and bang emanating from below his feet. And as he knew what was making that occasional bump and bang, it was good cause to fret. He should go down and sort it out really. But Mister Corrs was frightened by what he might find. So he stood and listened and worried and fretted.

Chapter 16

'That's odd,' said Tom, stopping yet again.

'What is?' said Cat, who was just about to nose her way into Smokowski's shop.

'He's left his takings out.' Tom stared at the pile of money and empty bank bags on Smokowski's desk.

Cat turned and did her own staring. Smokowski would never, ever, leave his money lying around for a moment. He was almost, but not quite, as miserly as Tom was. This wasn't good. Cat's feline sense for trouble clicked up a couple of notches, her tail grew noticeably bushier. Tom's sense for trouble did likewise, his bladder urging him to find a loo.

But there was no time for that. The atmosphere in the storeroom had heightened. Cat was gently nudging the door to the shop open. The hairs on Tom's neck were standing on end. The tension could suddenly be cut with a knife. Cat opened the door.

Beyond the door the shop had an eerie feel to it, lit only by the blue-white light from the refrigeration units; the only noise their gentle humming.

'Easy,' cautioned Cat, as Tom joined her at the door. 'See anything?' she whispered.

'You're the one with the night vision,' Tom whispered back.

'I'm down here,' whispered Cat, from her position behind the counter.

'Fair do,' whispered Tom. 'No, I should have brought my torch.'

'It's in your pocket.'

So it was. Tom reached into his pocket and took it out. He aimed. He clicked the switch. The anticipated flicker of the *not in the least bit blinding light*, never materialised. 'Drat,' said Tom, as he shook the torch to see if that would help.

'Ssssch!' hissed Cat.

It did, the torch flickered into life with a beam ten times brighter than it had ever shone before. Which to be honest wasn't that much better, but the effect was still enough to make Tom jump, causing him to lose his grip on it. The torch fell to the floor with a thump. 'Bother,' said Tom, whispering a thing of the past. He dropped on all fours. This, because of Tom and his touch of arthritis and what have you, wasn't quite as quick as it sounded.

Shaking her head in disbelief Cat, now happy the element of surprise, if they had ever had it, was long gone, leapt onto the counter, eyes wide, claws fully extended, ready for anything she might encounter. But there was nothing, no one. The place was as empty as Tom's head sometimes was. But that didn't mean all was well.

'This isn't good,' said Cat, under her breath, 'not good at all.' She didn't need her feline senses to tell her that something untoward had happened here, and not that long ago. The front door standing slightly ajar, wedged open by the welcome mat that lay rumpled half in half out, signs of what may have been a struggle, dust still settling, did that for her. Something bad had gone down in Smokowski's shop. Something she couldn't help but feel was connected in some way to the disappearances of Saint Nicholas and Elven. But there might be a chance, whoever it was who had been here, might well still be in the immediate vicinity. There could still be time to catch them, if she was quick. Cat prepared herself.

'Coo-ee!' said Tom suddenly, waving a hand towards the window. He had retrieved his torch.

'Grief,' said Cat, starring at Tom in startled, unfettered horror and disbelief. 'What the heck are you doing?' Any chance of catching anyone in the close vicinity unawares was now miles out with the washing, thanks to Tom's sudden appearance.

'Sandy,' said Tom, peering through the shop window this way and that at the street outside. He could because of the street-light outside, though to be fair street-dim might be a better word. Smokowski had complained to the council that it was too bright and was causing his window display to fade. The council decided it best just to go along with him, so they changed the bulb. It would save a couple of pence in the long run.

'Sandy?' said Cat. Surely the need to call a doctor was imminent. Had he banged his head? What was he going on about?

'Thought I saw him,' said Tom.

'Who?'

'Sandy.'

'Sandy?'

'Outside the window, on the pavement, I'm sure it was. Could be wrong, but he's usually wandering the streets late at night this time of year. Collects for charity you know.' Tom, oblivious to the way Cat was looking at him, tried his torch. It worked first time. 'Anyhoo,' he said, playing the torch through the window, 'did you see anything?'

Cat wished for something to give her strength and then, after counting to ten, told him what she had seen and what she thought it meant.

'Broken crackers!' exclaimed Tom, 'You think Smokowski's been kidnapped as well?'

'Looks that way,' said Cat, who was still rueing what she thought was a missed opportunity. If only her concentration hadn't been confined to the shop, otherwise she might have seen what Tom had seen, only clearer. It might have thrown some *light* on what was afoot. 'Smokowski would never leave the shop unattended like this. And it wasn't a robbery. It's the only explanation. And it's got to be more than coincidence that he just happens to disappear just after we give him that material.'

'Then we've got to find him,' said Tom, fearing for his old mukka.

'We will,' said Cat, 'but first we have another job to do.' And before Tom had the chance to utter a word in protest, they were somewhere else.

Chapter 17

The noise had got louder and more insistent, and that meant Mister Corrs would have to go down to the basement sooner or later. He didn't want to, so had decided on later for the moment. He had to think you see. But the noise wasn't helping.

'So-so wrong,' said Mister Corrs, as he paced, while he fretted, as he worried.

'Wot ith?' said Mister Smokowski, through his gag. He had been in hostage situations before and knew you had to try and engage with your kidnapper. At least he figured it was a hostage situation, no one had told him otherwise. Besides, he had been watching Mister Corrs for some time now, watching and waiting, for just the right moment. Perhaps this was it. Mister Corrs wasn't looking so good.

Mister Corrs stopped pacing. He looked at Smokowski. *This won't do*, he thought, *I can't be doing with more noise. It won't do at all.* He reached into his pocket and pulled something from it, out of Smokowski's line of sight. A moment later, the moment Smokowski had thought might be the right one had passed. Mister Corrs put the forty winks spray away, back into his pocket as Smokowski slumped forward onto the table.

'Ouch,' said Mister Corrs, as Smokowski's head made contact. He felt a little sorry for the shopkeeper, but all was fair, as people say, and it *was* so much quieter. Too quiet in fact he realised. The noise from the basement had stopped as well. Now that *was* worrying. He now really did have to go down and sort the problem out.

Chapter 18

Back in the pyramid the last thing on Tom's mind for once was the making of a cuppa. How could anyone think of tea at a time like this? His mate, mukka, comrade, fellow miser, was missing. Taken, no doubt, by some deluded maniacal kidnapper, with who knows what in his mind. It beggared belief. And all he could do was wait around while Cat collected her bits together. He wished she would hurry up.

Cat, who had left Tom for barely five minutes while she rounded up the gold she would need and the appropriate bishop's robe, came back to find him sipping on a cuppa.

'For my nerves,' explained Tom, slopping some of his tea over the edge of the mug as he raised it towards Cat. He had suddenly felt a pang of guilt, but a cuppa was a cuppa.

'Your robe,' said Cat, standing aside. Behind her, hovering three inches from the ground was a rather lovely red robe, hanging from a hanger. It was of a type bishops of Saint Nicholas's time might wear.

'My grief,' said Tom, managing not to spill tea down his front when he saw it, 'I can't wear that, it's a dress.'

'It's a robe.'

'It looks like a dress.'

'But it's a robe, and a fine one at that,' said Cat, who had been expecting just such protestations. 'You can wear your trousers underneath.'

'But I'm too stressed,' said Tom. 'I can't do it.'

But he would in the end, after a long game of delaying tactics of one kind of another. He knew it, and Cat knew it. But today Cat's patience was a tad thin, and time was short. She waved her tail.

'What the...' said Tom, as he suddenly found himself wearing a red dress. Amazingly, he still remained dry.

'*That* is a red dress,' said Cat, a mobile phone hovering before her. 'And if I press this button, your picture will go viral in a matter of seconds.' Cat held her paw menacingly over the camera button. 'Your choice.'

Tom didn't have the faintest idea what Cat was going on about, but that didn't matter, he was in a dress. And just that fact alone was enough. Minutes later he was in the robe, under his own volition.

'Now, hold still,' said Cat, as she steered three small bags of hovering gold into one of the robe's pockets.

'Oof!' said Tom, as he listed to one side.

'Oops, sorry,' said Cat, quickly transferring a bag to the other pocket. 'That better?'

'Suppose,' said Tom.

'You look just like Santa, but without the beard,' said Cat, trying to brighten the atmosphere. She knew Tom was worried about Smokowski; so was she, but he had to learn that there were priorities in their line of work, sometimes there were no choices.

'Only if he looks like an old guy in a dress,' said Tom.

'Grumpy.'

'Well.'

'Just remember you'll be getting a sock after all this is over with.'

'I haven't forgotten,' said Tom. He had.

'I never thought you had,' said Cat. She knew he had.

'Suppose we'd better be going then,' said Tom, with all the enthusiasm of someone with none. But being reminded of his sock had cheered him a little.

'Better,' said Cat. She gave the hitchhiker a squeeze.

Smokowski's storeroom was just as they had left it. The money still out on his desk.

'Shouldn't we put that away?' said Tom.

'Crime scene,' said Cat. She had made sure the door to the shop was shut and locked before they had left for the pyramid, it should be safe.

'I still think we should put it away,' said Tom, approaching the desk.

'And if there is some missing?' said Cat. 'Who's to say the kidnapper didn't have a small dip.'

Tom froze, he hadn't thought of that. 'Fair dos,' said Tom. No touch, no blame. It was a good philosophy.

'Ready?'

'As ready as I always am.'

'Then let's go.'

They stepped into the storeroom loo.

Chapter 19

Chewing his knuckles, Mister Corrs listened at the door to the basement. All was quiet. Was that good or bad? Did he go in or stay outside? Did he stay here or go back to the kitchen? Mister Corrs was in a right tizzy. A song sprang to mind, that described his predicament, as it does. Should he something or other, or should he something else, or words to that effect. He was useless at remembering words to songs, to all but the important ones that is.

But this wasn't helping him he decided; he changed hands and chewed on fresh knuckles. He would have to make a decision. He made one, he took knuckles from mouth, but it worried him. Had he decided too quickly? Was it the right one? He would go back in time and stop himself from doing it in the first place. That would work, wouldn't it? No, there was the rule about being in the same place at the same time. But he was a rule breaker. But it was supposed to be dangerous. He could leave himself a note. But what if someone else found it first? No, too many if's and but's. What about just taking Saint Nicholas back to where he belonged, all would be all right again then, surely. Or would it? Knuckles went back to mouth. Saint Nicholas would remember. Who could forget being kidnapped for goodness sake? He could spray him, with his special amnesia spray. But then he might forget who he was. That could be a good thing. No it wouldn't. What was he thinking? And then there was Smokowski, he'd remember. Maybe he could spray…

The banging started again.

Chapter 20

Somehow, Tom had managed to leave his cap in the portable loo. Any other time this would have posed a serious cause for concern – a universal translator being an intrinsic part of any serious minded time Travellers' kit – but as Cat thought there was little chance of Tom conversing with anyone this late at night, and if he kept himself to himself, the absence could be lived with. Besides, they really didn't have the time to go back for it; this mission was all about timing.

Tom and Cat, mostly Cat, had to time this just right. The plan was to arrive after the kidnap of Saint Nicholas, but not so long after that they lost the small window of opportunity they had to try and put things right.

'You ready to do your stuff?' Which meant it was time for the dangerous part; Cat had to drop the surrounding glamour so Tom could act the part of Saint Nicholas. It had to be done, so that any passer-by that had chanced on the deed of Saint Nicholas giving the gold would still do so.

'I still can't see why we can't just go look see who it is doing the kidnapping,' said Tom.

'Like I've said,' said Cat, 'if I'm right, he knows someone is onto him so he'll be on his guard. He'll probably come back before he's done it, just to make sure no one is snooping around.'

Tom was starting to get one of those headaches again. 'No.'

'No?'

'I'm not ready to do my stuff.'

'Good,' said Cat, dropping the glamour.

'Did you hear that?'

'Hear what?'

'A shout.'

Not again, thought Cat.

Tom frowned. He was sure he had heard something. And he was also, nearly ninety-nine per cent sure it was what he had heard the first time he was here. But that was silly; what he thought he had heard. So he decided to forget about it. He didn't want Cat to think he was going doolally.

'Tom?' said Cat, wondering if he had gone doolally. 'You okay. You look a bit odd?'

Tom snapped too. 'Right,' said Tom, 'ready.'

'Deep breath,' said Cat, shaking her head. Tom was something else.

Tom took a deep breath.

Grief, thought Cat, *did I just say that out-loud?* She realised she had. She suddenly feared that Tom might be rubbing off on her. Better get on.

'Let's go then.'

'You'll stay close?' said Tom.

'Like a tick on a cow,' said Cat.

'Sorry?'

'I'll be a curious cat, just sniffing around.'

'Good,' said Tom, who was understandably nervous. Tom also doubted he would meet anyone, but you never knew. Anyone could be wondering about doing whatever. The time his cap had gone on the blink when looking for Excalibur was enough of a trauma; no one should be carried in a net and poked with sharp sticks.

'To the window then,' said Cat.

'On my way,' said Tom. Feeling downright naked without his cap, and subconsciously looking for those nets, he took a step forward.

'Quickly now,' whispered Cat. She didn't want to be there any longer than was necessary.

Faster than a speeding snail, but only just, Tom at last made it; to halfway to where he was supposed to be.

'Faster,' encouraged Cat, from behind a water butt.

'I am going fast,' countered Tom.

'You're dithering,' said Cat, moving behind a handy crate.

'It's the dress, I keep standing on it.'

'It's a robe, and be careful I've just had it cleaned.'

Tom attempted to lift the hem, but the weight of the gold wasn't helping. The robe was heavy. The gold was heavy. Tom's heart was heavy. And three heavies equalled a plod.

'Think about your sock,' said Cat, trying to encourage.

'I was,' said Tom, hence the heavy heart. That and Smokowski of course.

'Think of it full,' said Cat.

Tom tried, but as much as he filled it, it was no match for gravity's grip.

'Nearly there,' said Cat, now behind a cart.

And then it happened. The moment Tom had been dreading, the net moment, but without the actual net.

'Good evening, Your Excellency,' said a deep, well to do, voice.

Cat, who was doing a good job of being almost invisible as she popped from one shadow to another, stopped dead at the sound of the mans' voice. Tom on the other hand, who didn't have the luxury of a shadow to hide in, did a bit of classic panic dithering.

'I said good evening, Your Excellency,' repeated the voice, with added firmness.

Is he talking to me? wondered Tom. It was a rhetorical thought, of course he was. What did he do now? Perhaps he should just ignore and quickly shuffle off. But he had to deliver the gold. Throw it through the window and run. Run in the dress? Tom didn't think so. Just ignore him then, perhaps the talker would shuffle off. But whoever it was that was talking, wasn't going anywhere. Now the owner of the voice was politely coughing.

Against his better judgement, but lost for anything else to do, Tom turned around, doing his best to keep his face hidden. He was greeted by the vision of a large man dressed in, what Tom would call, Sunday best. Cat, still hidden and wondering what to do without causing a time scene, figured the man a person of substance, a merchant perhaps. But that wasn't helping her.

'A beautiful night is it not?' said the merchant, gesturing to the sky, which was full of sparkling stars.

Cat was staring at Tom, almost willing him to do something, anything. Well, maybe not anything.

Tom was staring at the merchant, trying to will the man from existence; it wasn't working.

The merchant was staring at Tom, a puzzled expression on his face. He took a step towards Tom. There was expectancy in the air.

Tom took a step back. The merchant took another step forward, his expression slowly changing from puzzled to suspicious.

Now Tom, thought Cat, who knew that one more step forward by the merchant would spell disaster. But what could Tom do? She started to rack her brains for a way out of the situation; a safe one.

Come on Cat! thought Tom, as his identity, of not being who the bloke in his Sunday best thought he was, looked likely to be revealed. But Cat was nowhere to be seen. Maybe something had happened to her? *Oh, broken biscuits!* he thought, *I'm on my own.*

But he wasn't, and Cat was at that moment working on a plan of diversion.

But Tom didn't know that. *What am I going to do?* thought Tom, as the merchant went to take another step towards him. And then the old light bulb popped on. Tom had had an idea. He was an old codger; by most definitions, a grumpy groggins; by his grandkid's definition, and a moaner, by his own admission. And what did a grumpy, moaning, old codger do, when he was disturbed? Why grumble, that's what. So that's what he did.

Throwing his arms in the air in an irritated way, Tom started to grumble and moan. 'Grr,' grumbled Tom. 'Ahwaywityer,' he moaned. 'Wah-wah-wah,' he added, in a grumpy voice, which didn't make much sense but didn't really matter, as it was in the true tradition of the grumpy groggins, so there. And all this, whilst making shooing motions with his hands. He even threw in a few shooing noises for good luck. Tom huffed and puffed and gesticulated for all he was worth. He then surprised everyone, even himself, by hefting his robe to his knees, running to the window, and throwing the bags of gold through it. Luckily they were open to the world outside, so no damage done.

Cat, quick off the mark when a diversion was needed, and even quicker as she had just planned one, gave out her best *I've just seen another cat in my garden* wail, then charged headlong at the merchant, her eyes wild, her demeanour wilder, her tail as big as a rich man's loofah.

The merchant's eyes, which were already wide after the grumpiness he had just encountered, grew even wider as a mad cat hurtled from nowhere, towards his feet.

Cat ran between the merchant's legs.

The merchant, now off balance as he tried to dodge the mad cat, twisted, got his legs in a tangle, tripped, and fell to the ground in an untidy heap.

Tom saw his chance, and legged it. The lack of gold in his pockets having the effect of him feeling he was almost walking on air. He wasn't, and a few paces later, his knees told him so, in no uncertain terms.

Meanwhile Cat, emerging from behind the stricken merchant, saw Tom and made a dash for him.

They met, Cat glamoured, they headed as quickly as Tom's knees would allow to the loo. Safely inside, Tom concentrated for all he was worth on a certain storeroom toilet.

Chapter 21

Mister Corrs had returned to the kitchen, not to take Saint Nicholas back, or Smokowski, but to collect something he needed, something to stop that infernal banging coming from the basement.

In the corner of the kitchen, beside the old brick larder was the old brick coal bunker. Mister Corrs opened the door to it, but not to get coal. Inside stood a number of containers, not unlike divers' oxygen tanks. He selected one and lifted it onto a small wheeled hand truck. He checked it was firmly in place then wheeled the truck from the room.

Back outside the basement door Mister Corrs unclipped a rubber hose that ran from the top of the tank. He listened. The noise had stopped, but he knew it would start again. He placed the hose, equipped with a special fitting he had designed himself, against the door's keyhole, and clipped it into place. Happy all was secure, he then opened the valve on the top of the tank. There was a hissing sound. Moments later the banging started again.

But was one tank enough? Perhaps another tank would be needed, just in case? With this new worry in mind, Mister Corrs headed back to the kitchen for a reserve tank. Elves, you see, were notoriously hard to knock out.

Chapter 22

'Well, that went well,' said Tom, no irony in sight, as he emerged from the storeroom loo, the bishop's robe tucked safely over his arm.

'You think?' said Cat.

'Why not?' said Tom. 'We put the gold where it was needed. We got back in one piece. And, all being right with the world, my sock should be back as it should. Good job, I say.'

Cat didn't want to rain on Tom's parade, but nothing was proved just yet. And there were other concerns. 'But the job isn't finished yet,' she said, 'we've still got to find out who's behind all this, and rescue Saint Nicholas, Smokowski, and Elven, if indeed he has been kidnapped.' Rain clouds started to gather.

'Oh,' said Tom, one of those clouds crossing his suddenly guilty face.

'You'd forgotten, hadn't you?' said Cat, giving Tom an accusing look.

'Not actually forgotten,' said Tom, squirming just a little, 'more filed for future reference.'

Tom never failed to amaze her. But no time to dwell on Tom's shortcomings, they needed to get back to the pyramid, and more importantly, check to see if Christmas was indeed back to normal.

Bishop's robe safely returned to its hanger, but needing a trip to the dry-cleaners, Cat and Tom returned to Smokowski's storeroom. A discussion on how best to establish whether their labour had indeed borne fruit was in full swing.

Tom wanted to go back to Lucy's to see if his sock had arrived. But Cat reminded him of the dangers should two Tom's meet. Worse still, what if Lucy or the kids happened to see two Toms, how would they explain that away?

In the end Tom agreed that one Tom at any time was probably enough. Cat didn't hesitate in agreeing with him. They then went on to agree on something else. They would visit a few high street stores and engage in a quick bit of window shopping. There would hopefully be enough clues in the window displays to tell them if the giving of gifts was once more on the Christmas menu.

They decided, as it was less complicated to do so, to walk to the high street; it wasn't far. The tension built. The apprehension started to rise. They turned the corner and...

> What a sight it was that they did see
> Santa's galore, presents,
> and more than one Christmas tree
> For happiness it more than did the trick
> it was smiles all around
> but frowns at a peppermint stick!

'Not keen on those,' said Tom, face against a window.

'Those?' said Cat.

'Them peppermint sticks,' said Tom, screwing his face up.

'You tried one then?' said Cat.

'Not as such,' said Tom, 'but seen them in films. Never seen anyone eat one though.'

'Fair dos,' said Cat.

They then set off back to Smokowski's, feeling a lot happier than they had, when they had set off.

'So,' said Tom, when they got back, 'what's the order of things?'

'Find Smokowski, then the others,' said Cat.

'Where do we start?'

And sadly, there in, lay their next problem. Cat didn't have the slightest idea. And to make it worse, the only piece of evidence they had, was with Smokowski. 'I don't know,' she said.

'You don't know?' said Tom, taken aback. This was disturbing. Downright worrying. Tom had never heard Cat talk like that. If Cat didn't know what to do next, who did? Not him. Perhaps, maybe, a small trip to see the new Head Traveller? But thinking about it, he suspected Cat would have thought that and got the t-shirt. Tom looked at Cat, who appeared to be deep in thought. Tom decided to join her. He wondered if they could go back and see who had done the kidnapping. But Cat had said they couldn't. No she hadn't, she had said they couldn't go back and stop it happening. Was there a difference? It wouldn't hurt to throw the idea into the ring. 'Why don't we go back and see who did it, before it happened? Saint Nicholas I mean,' said Tom, now thinking it didn't sound a bad idea, said out-loud.

But Tom was to be disappointed. 'I already thought of that,' said Cat. 'I went before coming to see you.'

'You did?' said Tom, clearly disappointed.

'You were on holiday, remember?'

'What happened?'

'The felon was cloaked.'

Tom's eyebrows did some rising. 'It was a cat in a coat?'

'Felon,' said Cat, raising her own, 'not feline.'

'Oh,' said Tom. 'Then who was in the coat?'

'I… never mind. Suffice to say, going back is a no-no.'

Then Tom had what he would call a brainwave. 'What about Smokowski?' he said, grinning like a cheddar cat; not so yellow. 'You haven't gone back to see who kidnapped him.' He was right, seeing as she had been with him since it happened. Or had she? Yes she had. But then a doubt crept in; you never knew with Cat. 'Have you?'

'How?' said Cat, giving him a look of the incredulous. 'I've been with you since it happened.'

'Just checking.'

'Besides, I doubt the outcome would be any different. He'd be cloaked like last time.'

'How do you know it's a man, it could be a woman?' said Tom, brightly.

Cat studied Tom. 'The gender unspecific would be cloaked like last time,' she said.

'Er?' said Tom. But as the saying goes "you can't keep a good man down" or for that matter Tom. 'But what if it was a different kidnapper?'

This, Cat had to admit, she had not thought of, as doubtful as the idea was. *But, any port will do when you've run out of sherry. And as there wasn't any port available either,* she thought, *why not, couldn't hurt. And who knows, they might just get lucky.* 'Good thinking,' she said.

'Was it?' said Tom.

'Let's go.'

Chapter 23

Ear hard to the paint, Mister Corrs listened intently at the basement door. The gas canister had emptied. The noise had stopped. It had come to an abrupt end as someone slumped unconscious to the floor.

Mister Corrs, waited a moment or two then unclipped the hose from the keyhole. He produced a key, but didn't use it straight away, instead he listened again. Elves could be tricky, but then again, he had emptied a whole canister into the room; enough to take down a bull elephant. All was still quiet. He put the key in the lock. He turned it. He held his breath. He opened the door.

The basement was in darkness. The light switch was to his right. He reached for it after pocketing the key. He flicked the switch. He tensed as he did it, ready for anything. A stun gun in his left hand, taken from another pocket; he hoped it was powerful enough should it be needed.

Elven was laying on his side, on the floor, his little green hat with its little bell, still attached to his head. Mister Corrs inched forward and prodded Elven with the toe of his boot, then quickly stepped back, the stun gun at the ready. The Elf didn't move.

Mister Corrs gave Elven another tentative prod and then, happy Elven was truly out for the count, he released a huge sigh of relief and headed for the chair the elf had been sat in; different from the ones in the kitchen. Rope, an inch thick, lay snapped and in pieces on the floor beside the upended chair.

Drat, thought Mister Corrs, picking the rope up and inspecting the frayed ends where it had been snapped. He would need something stronger.

Chapter 24

From inside the confines of the portable loo, which was now in Smokowski's storeroom loo, Tom and Cat listened, as Smokowski moved about the storeroom. It was dangerous. Smokowski mustn't know they were there; mustn't know he was about to be kidnapped. But a contingency plan was in place, should Smokowski feel the need to visit the smallest room; disappear toot-sweet, come again another moment in time.

They listened. There was the clink of coins, the rustle of notes, a grumble, Smokowski's voice.

'We're closed!' shouted Mister Smokowski. A few moments of silence followed. Then there was the sound of a chair being pushed back. Smokowski tutted.

'There's someone at the shop door,' whispered Cat, relaying what was beyond Tom's hearing.

'The kidnapper,' said Tom, whispering right back at her.

'Could be,' said Cat.

They heard Smokowski open the storeroom door. The sound of the counter flap being lifted. Cat heard him tut.

'Let's move,' said Cat. She left the loo, Tom hot on her heels. They reached the storeroom door. Tom eased it open. 'Gently,' warned Cat.

Door safely navigated, they slipped into the shop. Cat leapt lightly onto the counter top. Tom peered over it. They couldn't be seen, Cat had glamoured them, but they could still be heard. Cat urged caution. They watched Smokowski approach the shop door.

'Any minute now,' whispered Tom, getting excited.

'Sssch,' said Cat.

Smokowski was now peering through the door. He opened it slightly. He said hello to someone. Asked them how he could help. But it was hard for Tom, even Cat, to see who it was Smokowski was talking to. The shop was gloomy, the street outside just as bad.

Then Tom got a tad animated. 'He's not cloaked,' he said excitedly, noticing a movement beyond Smokowski.

'No,' said Cat. 'I doubt Smokowski would have opened the door to an invisible door rapper.

'Oh, yeah,' said Tom, feeling just a little silly.

Cat pricked her ears, hoping to catch a snatch of conversation, but whoever was at the door was talking in a whisper. She wondered if Tom had caught anything, as doubtful as that was. 'Can you hear what is being said to Smokowski?' she asked, turning to him.

'Sorry?' said Tom.

'Never mind,' said Cat, turning her attention back to Smokowski, just in time to watch him slump unconscious to the floor.

Tom, on seeing his old mukka slip to the floor, instinctively moved to help him. But Cat was on the ball.

'Wait,' she said, stopping Tom in his tracks with a light restraining spell, 'look.'

Tom looked, and his jaw dropped. Smokowski was beginning to rise as if part of a magician's trick. A sack suddenly appeared. Smokowski started to disappear into it. 'What the...'

'He's cloaked himself,' said Cat, throwing caution to the wind as to Smokowski's kidnapper's gender.

Tom managed to close his mouth then open it again. 'What now?' he asked.

'We go,' said Cat.

'But what about Smokowski?' said Tom, 'We might be able to follow.'

'No time,' said Cat. 'I think we might be about to arrive.'

'We...'

But there was no time to explain. Cat clenched her cheeks. A second later the door from the storeroom inched open.

'That was close,' said Cat.

'What was?' said a bewildered Tom, puzzling at his new surroundings. 'And why are we back in here?' They were back in Smokowski's storeroom.

'Listen,' said Cat.

Tom listened. And then listened some more. 'Is that...'

'Yes,' said Cat. 'It's you.'

'But I'm...'

'Time to go.'

'Where?'

'Back to the pyramid, I've got to think.'

Chapter 25

With a still unconscious Elven again bound and secure in his chair, this time with steel cable, Mister Corrs left the basement. He hoped this time the binding would hold him, but if not, he still had a full canister of his knock out gas. With this reassuring thought just holding worries at bay, Mister Corrs closed the door and locked it behind him. He felt safer as he did it, the door was iron lined, as were the walls, ceiling and floor of the basement, precautions taken should he need a safe place and keep things out, but now coming in very handy for a different reason, to keep something in. Elves didn't like iron, or so the rumour went. Managing a weak tuneless whistle, Mister Corrs headed back to the kitchen.

Smokowski was awake when Mister Corrs returned, and as he fancied a cuppa after his successful trip to the cellar, he asked Smokowski if he would like one as well. Smokowski deigned not to answer, but that mattered not. Something strange was afoot. Something Mister Corrs was having trouble putting his finger on. Then just like that, he had it; he was feeling a little cheerier, happy almost. He then realised there was something going on with his face, something alien, something he hadn't felt in a while. He put a hand to his lips. A smile was forming, growing.

And then it stopped dead. Mister Corrs had stopped it. He had stopped it because he couldn't understand it. Couldn't understand, under the circumstances, why he would want to. Something was up.

Standing at the kitchen window, something now caught his eye; something that he was sure hadn't been there before he had gone down to the basement. He slowly put the kettle down. Something was flashing behind the drawn curtains. Glints of colour occasional peeped through the crack between the curtains. For a split second Mister Corrs had the horrible feeling the police had somehow found him. But other colours, as well as blue, were flashing. He reached for a curtain and gently pulled it aside a smidgeon. His eyes widened. The house across the street, flash Jenkin's place, was covered in a myriad of sparkling Christmas lights, colourful snowflakes, icy blue icicles. There was a red steam train puffing merrily in a window, going nowhere, its car full of presents. A huge snowman in the garden eclipsed the shrubbery. Plastic reindeer and sleigh appeared to be waiting for someone on the lawn. Mister Corrs's eyes were drawn skyward, he gasped. A plastic Santa Claus was on the roof, his cheery red cheeks glowing. But how? It shouldn't be. But why shouldn't it be? It was Christmas after all. But it had all disappeared. It had all disappeared when he had stopped Saint Nicholas from doing his deed. But now it was back. What was going on?

Mister Corrs took a staggering step backwards. Something was wrong. Worryingly so. But that was the problem, he wasn't, worrying. Instead he was filling with Christmas spirit. His face was changing again. He couldn't stop it. Something was very amiss. Mister Corrs, a huge smile spreading across his face, headed for the weapons cabinet.

Chapter 26

Cat paced. Tom paced, but with a cuppa in his hand.

'So that was us?' said Tom.

'Yes,' said Cat.

'And we're not allowed to meet?'

'That's the gist of it.'

'Weird,' said Tom, slurping at his tea.

'Weird,' said Cat, not really listening. She wanted to think, and Tom wasn't helping.

'So what next?'

'Think,' said Cat, wishing she could. 'Think about what we've just seen.' The journey to Smokowski's seemed fruitless. But she had to think, surely there had been some clue in what they had just seen that could help them.

Tom took a long noisy draw from his cup.

'Do you have to do that?' said Cat.

'What?' said Tom.

'Slurp.'

'Did I?'

'Yes.'

'Oh.' Tom stared at his cup as if it somehow was to blame. He decided it wasn't. 'Shall I go and sit somewhere?' He was tired of pacing anyway. He had only been doing it to keep Cat company.

'Might be a good idea,' said Cat.

'I can think better when I'm sitting,' said Tom.

'As can I,' said Cat.

But she wasn't sitting. 'But you... Oh.' Tom knew when he wasn't wanted. It sometimes took a while, but he usually got there in the end. He took his leave and wandered off to find somewhere to sit.

As Tom searched, his thoughts turned to other things. Like, why did biscuits go stale so quickly in a pyramid? Even in a tin? He could do with a biscuit, a dodger perhaps, or a choccy digestive. His mouth watered at the thought of a good dunk.

Many tried and rejected seats later, Tom alighted on one that looked right up his street. It was huge. It was a throne no less. Its arms wide enough to take his cup, its seat padded enough for his bony posterior. 'Begging your pardon your majesty,' said Tom, as he sat.

Tom swivelled his backside. He settled. He relaxed. He took a sip of his tea; no slurping, it was a throne for goodness sake. That was better. He thought he could get used to this. He then thought of Smokowski. He thought of Cat trying to do her best. He suddenly felt guilty. He with his tea and comfy throne, Smokowski somewhere out there all kidnapped like, Cat looking so worried. But what could he do? He was still a newbie at all this, a trainee, until Cat told him otherwise. Therefore, leave it to the professionals. Best to perhaps. Leave the worrying to those who could do something with it. He took another sip of his tea and admired his seat. He could do with one of these at home. He wondered if the front lifted to raise the old legs. It didn't appear to. Something to think about should he get his own. But never mind, it was comfy with its great gold arms, which looked solid, not your painted on leaf stuff, soft padding, plush red velvet covering. It was... wait a doggone moment.

Tom lodged his cup on an arm of the throne and stood up. Something, somewhere, in Tom's mind was doing something. He looked the throne up and down. Stared hard at it. Tom's brow creased. A thought was forming.

'Slithering Santa's!' exclaimed Tom, as the thing in his head set to clanging a bell or two. He had remembered something. No, two things. He had to find Cat, right away.

Chapter 27

Smokowski watched Mister Corrs leave the kitchen then worked at his bonds again. They were tight, expertly tied. His wrists were raw, but he had to get free of them, find Cat, and discover just what the heck was going on.

But Mister Corrs wasn't gone long. He returned a few minutes later, armed to the teeth, but not with what he had set out to get. Instead of weapons, his arms were full of festive cheer, candy canes, chocolate Santas, chocolate reindeers, Christmas crackers, a plethora of Christmas treats and goodies. He set them on the table and stared at them in wonder. He didn't know why he had just done what he had done, just that he couldn't help himself. Something was truly amiss. Oh so worryingly so. So why couldn't he? Worry.

Cat wasn't exactly at the end of her tether, there were avenues she had not yet explored, the traveller's link for one, but that would take time. Time she doubted she had. And then Tom appeared, his jacket covered in tea. He looked excited, very excited. Cat wondered what trouble he had found this time.

'Calm down,' said Cat, dodging slops from Tom's cup, as he hopped from one foot to the other. It has to be noted that Tom's cup was on the large size.

'I remember,' said Tom.

'Remember what?' said Cat.

'No-no,' said Tom, shaking his head. 'I mean I know.'

Tom wasn't making much sense, which was par for the course, but this session of senselessness seemed worse than usual. Perhaps he had hit his head this time. 'What do you know?' said Cat, not expecting a lot.

'What I heard. No, what I saw.' Tom put his cup down. 'What I mean is... What I meant was... Oh dodgers!'

'Whoa there,' said Cat. 'Take it easy. Look, sit down and take a breath.' She couldn't ever remember seeing Tom this animated. He was worse than that time she had left him overnight in that small shed.

Tom sat. He took a breath. He opened his mouth, closed it. He took another breath, deeper this time. He tried again with the mouth. This time it worked. 'The fur, I think I know where the fur came from.'

'You do?' said Cat.

'And it was what it was I heard. It sounded crazy, but I did. You know, when we went back to find clues.'

'I thought you said you hadn't heard anything?'

'No, that was the second time, when I forgot my cap, but I had, and it was the same as the first.'

'You were hearing things again?'

'Yes... No, I mean I was hearing things, but I wasn't. I heard someone shout the same thing both times.' Tom's face contorted with the effort of explaining. Of trying, but not able to, tell Cat exactly what he had heard. She would think him a silly billy.

'What was it you heard?' said Cat, making it easier for him.

'You'll think me a silly old fool,' said Tom.

'If it helps,' said Cat, 'I already do.'

It did. 'Fair dos,' said Tom, who then told her what he had heard.

Raised eyebrows from Cat.

'There, that's exactly why I didn't tell you in the first place.'

But Cat was being open-minded. 'And the fur?'

Tom needed a drink, so he reached for his cup and was surprised to find a couple of mouthfuls still surviving. He knocked them back. He was now ready to put his head back in the lion's mouth, or Cat's, as it were.

'It's what I remembered,' said Tom.

'Go on,' prompted Cat.

'When we went back, you know, to see if we could catch a glimpse of Smokowski's kidnapper.'

'And?' said Cat, squeezing, sure they would get there in the end. Others may well have cried "enough" by now and fled, but not Cat, she was made of sterner stuff. Plus the fact that she had no choice but to stay. And this was all they had so far. And...

'I thought I saw my mate, remember, I waved?' Cat remembered. 'Well,' Tom continued, 'whoever it was I saw shouldn't have been wearing it. It was before we returned the gold and made everything all right. Well, with Christmas anyway.'

'Wearing what?' said Cat, wondering if you got medals for patience.

'The Santa suit!' exclaimed Tom. 'He was wearing a Santa suit, but he shouldn't have. That part of Christmas was still on hold. It was after Saint Nicholas was kidnapped, but before we made it all right again.' Tom was fairly frothing at the mouth.

Cat was getting a Tom headache.

'And then, just now, when I was sitting on the throne, I realised something else.'

Too much information, thought Cat, but she played her part. 'What?' she said.

'That I knew the voice that had shouted. Back there in Saint Nicholas's time. And it belonged to the person I had seen. Don't you see?'

Cat was trying.

'The fur was from a Santa suit, Saint Nicholas and Smokowski were kidnapped by Santa!'

And then it dawned on him, why he had come back with sweets instead of weapons. He had returned to his old self, his old Christmas loving, Christmas living, self. He had just slipped back into it without realising it. The role he played every Christmas, and wished he could play every day. But it was different now. He couldn't, wouldn't be able to do it ever again. He had done a bad thing. Nothing would be the same. He began to fret. Worry. Mister Corrs turned from the table and stared at the plastic Santa on the roof opposite.

All Travellers had a sixth sense, some more than others, Mister Corrs had it in bucket loads. But he didn't need it to tell him things had taken a turn for the worse. The Santa opposite told him that. But what the plastic Santa couldn't tell him, but his sixth sense could, was that someone was on to him, and that someone was on their way. Mister Corrs turned from the window and headed for the hall.

It was too risky to actually arrive in the suspected kidnapper's bathroom, so Tom and Cat had returned to Smokowski's shop and foot padded it from there to the suspect's premises. It wasn't far.

There were no lights on in the front of the house when they arrived. Tom and Cat, glamoured as they were, inched forward cautiously.

'I can't believe it,' said Tom, as they approached the gate. 'And him a traveller to boot. Who'd have guessed?' He gently lifted the latch and pushed on the gate.

'Believe it,' said Cat, knowingly. 'You lot come in all shapes and sizes, and sometimes, when the pressure gets to those that can't cope, kerpow!'

'Kerpow?' said Tom, giving Cat a worried look. 'Will I go kerpow?'

'Not very likely,' said Cat, who then ushered Tom on before he could ask why.

They moved into the garden, keeping low. Tom eyed the windows with suspicion. 'Do you think he knows we're coming?'

'I doubt it,' said Cat, offering a little reassurance. 'But you never know.' Reassurance negated.

*

Mister Corrs, sixth sense blaring like a foghorn on a sugar trip, had scurried from the kitchen to the front room. There he sidled up behind a curtain and peeped outside, just in time to see the garden gate open by itself.

'So,' said Mister Corrs, slamming a fist into an open palm, 'you're here.' He didn't know exactly who it was who was here, but being able to verify someone was, was enough. He scurried, shadow to shadow, back into the hall, to the only room with a light on, the kitchen, stopping once on the way, to retrieve something from the weapons cabinet.

'Did that curtain just move?' said Cat.

'What curtain?' said Tom.

'Never mind,' said Cat, as she brought their advance to a halt.

'Why are we stopping?'

'He knows we're here.'

'He does?'

'We need a strategy.'

'We do?'

'To catch one, we need one,' said Cat, all cryptic like.

Too cryptic for Tom. 'Do we?'

'We need to split up. I'll take the obvious route, you the less obvious. With a bit of luck he might think there's only one of us.'

But none of it was obvious to Tom, less or not. 'Say again?' he said.

Cat explained, 'I'll continue towards the house and see if I can get in through a traditional avenue. You're going in from above.'

'Above what?' said Tom, looking up.

'The house.'

Tom didn't like the sound of that one iota. 'I think I've left the cooker on,' he said.

'You haven't been home for days.'

'I've left someone else's on then.'

'Don't worry, I'll levitate you, then give you a dose of Santa magic,' said Cat, having none of Tom's nonsense.

Tom still wasn't taken with Cat's idea, but the mention of receiving a dose of Santa magic had him intrigued. 'A dose of magic you say?'

'Enough to get you down the chimney. It could well be our best chance of taking him by surprise.'

Did she just say, down the chimney? 'Did you just say, down the chimney?' said Tom.

'Yes,' said Cat, gearing herself up for the expected protests.

Tom surveyed the roof. Not too much of a slope to it. But it was the roof, and roofs of houses were generally, because of their position, high up, as this one was. Tom really didn't like the idea, but the other idea, of being privy to a bit of Santa magic, well, magic has to trump roof, surely. 'I'll do it.'

'You will?' said Cat, taken aback by Tom's unexpected willingness.

'When do we start?' said Tom, taking his gaze from the chimney stack, to look Cat straight in the eyes. 'Waa!' exclaimed Tom. He quickly looked down. Had he stepped in a hole?

'We've started,' said Cat, smiling at little Tom. 'Just the levitating, and down you go.'

'But…'

But it was too late for buts, Tom was on his way. Up-up-up and away went Tom, higher and higher and higher until he was just a protesting dot in the night sky. But deciding enough was enough with the toying with him – she was a cat after all – Cat brought him lower and landed him on the chimney. Tom made a grab for a chimney pot and held on for dear life. He looked down and shook a little fist in Cat's general position; she was still glamoured so he couldn't actually see her. Cat returned his gesture with a smile.

From his eyrie up above, Tom vowed to have words with Cat when he got down; if he got down. Which he was sure he would. But whether that would be in one piece was another matter. He started to clamber up the chimney pot.

Cat watched Tom start to clamber, then with the smile still firmly in place, headed for the house.

Smokowski sensed something was afoot. Mister Corrs looked more agitated than usual, his mind on something other than his captives. He took the chance to have another go at his bonds.

Tom climbed to the top of the chimney pot and looked down into its waiting black maw. Thankfully there was no cowl attached, or smoke, unless it was smokeless fuel being used, but then he would still be able to smell fumes if a fire was going on below, wouldn't he?

He shook off such thoughts, Cat wouldn't let him go if it was dangerous, would she? Then, still shaking off those thoughts, he wondered if the gap he was looking at was in fact big enough for him to climb down. He suddenly doubted it. He needed to be smaller. And suddenly he was.

'Waa!' said Tom, just managing to stop from falling in. 'I need to be bigger. Bigger!' he yelled. To whom, he didn't know. And suddenly he was. 'Blimey,' echoed Tom's surprised voice, as if he were in a tunnel. Cat had given him the ability to change size. And once he realised that, he would be able to make himself smaller again, thus able to free his head which was stuck in the top of the chimney pot. Oh woe was Tom. Tom wondered if there was any margarine left in his ears from last time.

Mister Corrs, his sixth sense on the verge of doing itself a mischief, was no longer smiling. It was him or them. He had been a bad person and would undoubtedly deserve the punishment that would be meted out, but banishment was on the cards. Banishment to the outer edges, where the BIMBO'S – don't ask, highly classified – operated. There would be no Christmas there. Mister Corrs didn't think he could handle that. He looked down at his lap, at the weapon he had taken from the cabinet, his weapon of choice. Hopefully he wouldn't have to use it. Hopefully he could still escape. Make a break for it if he couldn't talk his way out. Better a fugitive, than banishment.

Wary of traps, Cat cautiously headed for the back of the house. A small pathway running down the side of the house, led from the front garden to the back. She took it.

A shed took centre stage in the back garden, smaller than Tom's, but large enough for any man. Cat cast a wary eye over it. A lean-to angled from it, covering something that covered something else in a large weathered tarpaulin. Cat instinctively headed for it, suspecting she knew what was hidden beneath. If she was right, she would have to disable it.

'Smaller-smaller!' yelled Tom, who hadn't yet realised the extent of what he could do with what Cat had given him, but as luck would have it.

'Waa!' yelled Tom, as he again found he was small enough to fall without touching the chimney's sides. It then came to him, as he hung to the rim of the chimney pot, the significance of what his yelling had achieved so far. Apart from it being lucky no one had heard him yet. Or had they? Therefore he tried a tentative *slightly bigger*, whispering it this time. It worked. Tom grew slightly bigger.

'Ha,' whispered Tom, realising this Santa magic needed to be treated with kid gloves. 'Slightly bigger again,' he said, in a whisper. He grew slightly bigger again.

By the fourth slightly bigger, Tom was a lot happier. He was big enough, or small enough, depending on how you looked at it, to climb down the chimney quite comfortably. 'Okay,' he said, peering into the dark, 'here I come, whether I'm ready or not.'

They were loosening, Smokowski was sure of it. He glanced at Mister Corrs. He was staring at his lap. That was fine. Just a little bit more.

Mister Corrs twitched, like a rabbit's nose sensing something. He stared straight at Smokowski, with the look of the suspicious. Smokowski returned his look, with the look of the innocent.

Mister Corrs stood up, placed his weapon of choice on the table, and took a step towards Smokowski. Something was going on, he was sure of it. He walked behind Smokowski.

'Think I'm stupid do you?' said Mister Corrs, reaching down. Smokowski cursed under his breath. 'Got to have this tight,' he said, tightening Smokowski's gag. 'Can't have you shouting a warning now, can we?' He turned to Saint Nicholas. 'That goes for you too.'

Both gags checked, Mister Corrs reclaimed his weapon of choice, and went to the kitchen light switch. He flicked it, sending the room into darkness, and went back to his seat to wait.

Across the room, Smokowski sighed a huge sigh of relief.

Down, down, deeper and further down went Tom. It was pitch black in the in the chimney, apart from the small dint of light somewhere down below. Tom just hoped it wasn't the first glimmers of a roaring fire. But still he went down, heading for that light. And then it went out.

It was no surprise to Cat that the house was suddenly in darkness, the only light she had seen so far having just gone out. She had expected it. As she had suspected they had been discovered with that twitch of the curtain. Any traveller worth their salt, who was expecting trouble, would want to make it as difficult as possible for any approaching assailant. It's what she would do. The question now was what was waiting for them inside?

Any thought Mister Corrs may have harboured regarding escape using his time machine, had just taken a knock. His gut had told him to go to the kitchen window. There he had seen the tarpaulin covering his time machine, twitch and lift, and then twitch and lift again. And he knew why. Whoever was out there had disabled it. It's what he would do; cutting it out of the equation as an escape route. He should have taken steps to make sure it couldn't happen, but his mind had been occupied with other things. He ducked back out of sight. Whoever it was out there knew what they were doing. Whoever it was that was out there was good. Only one thing for it then, sit and wait, he switched the kitchen light back on as he passed, and hoped an opportunity for a different means of escape would present itself should they make a mistake. His gut though told him they wouldn't.

It was dark. Tom was finding it hard to know up from down. The sudden disappearance of the light from below hadn't helped. Any light from above, which had been meagre to begin with, as it was dark, was no longer reaching him. He stopped. He was still going down, wasn't he? He looked to where he thought down should be. Suddenly Tom wasn't sure; reason taking a break. What if he had turned without knowing it? Then reason popped back when he realised he was still wearing his cap. Gravity would surely have seen to his losing it if he was going the wrong way. Panic over. And then, as if to throw weight to this reasonable reasoning, the light below appeared again.

Now that was a surprise. Cat hadn't expected the light to come on again. And it could only mean one thing as far as Cat was concerned; she had been invited in.

It was going to be touch and go with Mister Corrs sitting so close, but as the man seemed to have all his attention focused on the back door, it was worth taking a chance. Smokowski, so very close to ridding himself of his bonds, struggled on.

The back door, which led from back garden to the kitchen, opened.
 'Please do come in, Cat,' said Mister Corrs.
 Cat, who until that moment had been hiding behind a glamour emerged from it. 'I don't believe I've had the pleasure,' she said, scanning the room as she spoke.
 'No,' said Mister Corrs, 'but I know you. Or should I say, heard of you. Everyone has.' His heart was beating hard, as if it was about to leap from his

chest. He had never felt so anxious. But he had to try and stay calm. 'You alone?'

'Yes,' Cat lied, 'my Traveller's on holiday, it's Christmas Eve.'

Mister Corrs winced at Cat's words. He knew what day it was. He should be out working, playing his part. But he had to stay in control. 'I need your traveller's time machine. I take it you've taken care of mine?'

'I told you, he's on holiday,' said Cat, treading warily.

It could be true. Some Travellers liked to take Christmas off. But as Mister Corrs wasn't privy to whom her traveller was, or know enough about Cat to warrant believing her, he had to err on the side of caution, and her telling fibs. He would play along. 'Then you have a hitchhiker? That will do.'

'I have,' said Cat, bringing a disbelieving stare from Smokowski. 'And I'll be using it to take you to headquarters, where you no doubt will be severely dealt with for your crimes.' Smokowski now looked at Mister Corrs.

Cat's words brought a narrowing of Mister Corrs's eyes. He couldn't be taken. He wouldn't be able to stand banishment.

'You will be given a fair trial,' said Cat.

That's what Mister Corrs was worried about. He was guilty as charged. So he needed to get away, desperately so, but to do that he would have to go through Cat. An impossible task so the stories went. His heart beat harder. So be it then. There was only the one option left for him. He raised his weapon of choice.

The dint of light was getting larger all the time, and now he could hear voices, Cat's voice. She was in already. Tom started to hurry. She might need his help. He was nearly there.

Mister Corrs aimed his weapon of choice.

'Don't do it,' said Cat.

Smokowski wriggled frantically in his chair, he was almost free. Beside him, Saint Nicholas was rigid with fear at the sight of the cat that appeared to be having a conversation.

'I've no other choice,' said Mister Corrs, his finger tightening on the trigger, 'unless you let me go.'

But the cat was not for bending. 'You know I can't do that,' said Cat.

Smokowski needed just a second or two more.

Tom just needed a second more.

Saint Nicholas could take no more, and fainted.

Mister Corrs finger tightened further.

And then Tom was there, at the bottom of the chimney, staring into the kitchen from behind a glass door.

Mister Smokowski's fidgeting finally got him somewhere. His chair tipped. He with it. Together they fell to the floor.

'Don't do it,' said Cat.

'You know I have to,' said Mister Corrs. He pulled the trigger. As he did a voice screamed out. A voice muffled by the glass of the cooker stove it was trapped behind.

'No, Sandy. No!' screamed Tom.

But it was too late.

Chapter 28

Elven had tears in his eyes as he sat at Sandy Corrs's kitchen table. He dabbed at them with a green hanky. 'He wasn't a bad man, truly he wasn't,' he sniffled, burying his nose in the hanky. Elven had been Sandy's familiar for years.

'And locking you in the cellar was a good thing, was it?' said Smokowski who wasn't in such a forgiving mood, as he rubbed at his sore wrists.

'He knew I'd try and stop him, if I found out what he was planning,' said Elven, nose still buried.

Beside Elven, and looking a little shell shocked, dishevelled, sooty, and sombre, but now back to full size, sat Tom. 'I thought he was going to kill Cat,' he said.

'It was never his plan,' said Cat, who was neither shocked nor dishevelled, just her normal cool self. 'He just wanted to disappear, and when I made it clear I wouldn't allow him to, well…' Cat's voice trailed off. She had known she was in no danger, as soon as she had seen what Sandy had been holding, and the way he had been holding it.

'I don't think he was himself,' said Elven.

'You can say that again,' said Tom, still trying to get his head around old Sandy the mall Santa, being one of him, a Traveller.

'But why did he do it?' said Smokowski, shaking his head. 'Kidnapping his Saint-ship like that. He must have known he was never going to get away with it.'

'I doubt we'll ever know,' said Cat.

Elven removed his nose from his hanky. 'I do,' he said. 'Or at least I think I do.'

All eyes in the room turned and stared at Elven.

'You do?' said Cat.

Elven nodded. 'It started with that new computer he had for his birthday a couple of months ago.'

Tom exchanged a knowing look with Cat. He knew those flipping things were trouble.

'Go on,' said Cat.

Sniffing, Elven continued, 'He spent hours on it, day and night, surfing for everything and anything to do with Santa Claus.'

'I would've thought he'd have loved all that,' said Tom. 'Right up his street.'

'He wanted to better himself you see,' said Elven. 'Be a better Santa. But not all he read was good. He was particularly upset about this one article.'

Elven dabbed at his nose again. 'He started to grow moody after reading it; stopped being his usual jolly self. But never in my wildest dreams did I think it would come to this.' Elven started to sob again. 'I thought once the big day was here all would be fine, return to normal. I thought he'd forget all about it.' Elven's body was racked by a sudden almighty sob. 'It's all my fault,' he wailed.

'Good grief,' said Tom, wondering whether to pat the poor chap on the back and utter some "there-there's". He decided not to. Instead he gave his own insight on Sandy. 'I just don't understand it, Sandy lived for being Santa. I never thought anything could upset him where Santa was concerned. Mind you, having said that, say something against the old fellow and yes, he could be tetchy, even the odd round of fisticuffs.'

'Yes, thank you Tom,' said Cat, giving Tom her sternest look.

'Do you know what the article was about?' said Smokowski.

Nodding, Elven wiped away his latest tears. 'It had said that Santa was grumpy.'

'Santa grumpy?' said Smokowski.

'Saint Nicholas,' Elven explained.

'That would have done it,' said Tom. 'To Sandy, Santa was jolly; full stop, whatever his monocle.'

'I think you mean moniker,' said Cat.

'And her,' said Tom.

'But kidnapping him?' said Smokowski.

'Like I said,' said Elven, 'he wasn't himself for a long while.'

'Obviously,' said Smokowski, remembering his wrists and giving them another rub.

'So what do we do now?' said Tom.

Cat looked at Saint Nicholas who was still slumped face down on the kitchen table. He hadn't yet come round from his faint, and she had seen no reason to rouse him from it. 'Firstly, we take old sleepy head there back to where he belongs. Secondly, I'll work a little of my mojo on him to make sure he remembers nothing.' Cat sighed. 'And with a bit of luck all should then be back to normal again, give or take.' Both Tom and Smokowski raised an eyebrow.

'And Sandy?' said Tom, giving him the thumb.

'I'll take care of him,' said Elven. 'It's the least I can do. I'm sure headquarters will be able to find him some shelf room somewhere.'

And so that was that. The story was at an end. Saint Nicholas was safely returned to where he belonged. Smokowski returned to his shop, where he securely locked the front door before attending to the day's takings. And Elven to headquarters, where Sandy was found room on the largest shelf available, not only out of respect for his many good years of service but also because of his last ever choice.

You see, Sandy had in fact chosen banishment, but under his own terms. The weapon of choice Sandy Corrs had removed from the weapons cabinet, hadn't been a weapon at all. It had been a SCUP; Snowglobe Containment Unit Provider. It was so called because the containment unit, when deployed, resembled a snow globe. On this occasion, Sandy had turned the SCUP on himself. A SCUP that had been modified so that the containment unit it fired could only be closed down from the inside, configured so that its occupant would be captured within, forever frozen in a tableau of the occupant's choosing, in this case, as a smiling Santa, cheerfully carrying a sack full of toys. And if you pressed the large red button on the side, another modification, snow would instantly fall as Sandy's voice urged certain special reindeer onward and upward. Words Tom had heard Sandy shout a couple of times, way back there in time.

As for Tom and Cat, they were heading home. Tom to search for that sock, and Cat to scratch an itch of curiosity that was annoying her, regarding a certain suspicion she had. But before they did, they were going to pay a visit to a very special couple.

Chapter 29

'Well I'll be,' said Tom, as he and Cat followed a path through a wilderness of snow and ice that stretched as far as the eye could see, which hadn't been there the last time they had visited.

'Thank goodness, I say,' said Cat.

'Does this mean we've saved Santa?' said Tom.

'It sure looks like it,' said Cat, dodging the sudden arrival of a snowball. 'Missed!'

The smiling face of an elf appeared from behind a snowdrift. 'It was a warning shot,' laughed the elf. He had been waiting for Tom and Cat to arrive, which mystified Tom, who wondered aloud how anyone could possibly know they were paying a visit, especially when he had only found out himself, a few seconds ago. Cat did little to clarify the situation, by telling Tom, Santa knows all. Tom hoped not.

Led by the elf, they soon reached the familiar huge red door which, on their approach, was swung open to reveal a jolly red face, just bursting with yule-time joy.

'Come in, come in,' said Santa, his face wreathed in smiles, his eyes sparkling like diamonds. 'Dinner is on the table.'

'Dinner?' whispered Tom. 'I can't eat dinner. I haven't had my breakfast yet.'

'Don't worry,' said Cat, 'it's only the personification of a Christmas feast.'

A regular occurrence now took place; the frowning of Tom's brow. 'But I thought you said that means it's real?'

'It is,' said Cat, causing deeper brow furrowing from Tom, 'but the extent of the personification is up to you.'

'Eh?'

Cat saw that she would have to explain further. 'What you see is what you get, but what you eat doesn't have to be all it seems.'

'Eh?'

Cat now saw that Christmas would be over before Tom understood; maybe even Easter. She would have to simplify things to something he could understand; she hoped. 'Think turkey, taste turkey, swallow lettuce leaf.'

A furrow twitched. 'Er... wait a minute... oh-right.'

By Crimbo, I think he's got it, thought Cat.

'I think I've got it,' said Tom.

'Good, let's go. I for one will be thinking turkey all the way down.'

And Cat was right. And even though Tom managed to put away three Christmas dinners, and as many Christmas puddings – and we're talking family size here – he never once had to let out his belt. In fact, when it was time to go, Tom decided that as far as breakfast was concerned, a good old fashioned fry up wouldn't go far amiss.

Feast over with, Tom and Cat bade fond farewells, and headed for home; Lucy's home.

But as they left Santa's home, just as Cat prepared to squeeze the hitchhiker, Tom aired a worry that had suddenly come to him. 'Whoa there,' said Tom, 'what if Lucy's already tried to put the sock on the bed and discovered I'm not there. How am I going to explain that away?'

'But we're going back a couple of seconds after we left,' said Cat.

'But a second is a second,' said Tom, still with the worry.

'She won't have missed you, trust me,' said Cat.

'But you can't know that for sure.'

'Oh but I do.' Cat squeezed the hitchhiker.

Chapter 30

'Look,' said Cat.

Tom gasped. They were back in Lucy's spare room, just after they had left, as Cat had said they would, but with one small difference, on the bed was a Christmas sock brimming with goodies.

But it wasn't the long lost sock that lay at the foot of the bed that had caused Tom's sharp intake of breath. Indeed not, rather it was the huge lump in the bed that suggested someone was in it, that had Tom goggled eyed and wincing in horror.

'What the…' said Tom, pointing, fearing the worst. Only the worst he feared was too fearful to think about, so he was fearing something that he couldn't even imagine. In effect, he was fearing the worst, when he didn't know what that might be.

'Don't worry,' said Cat. 'Just something I did earlier.' And glad she was she had. Lucy, it appeared, was quicker than Cat had realised. It also proved that one should never second guess.

'What? When?' said Tom. He stared at the bed.

'Pull the duvet back,' said Cat.

Tom took a tentative step forward.

'Go on,' said Cat.

Gripping the duvet with a shaking hand, Tom pulled, and nearly jumped out of his skin.

'It's you,' said Cat, verifying what Tom was seeing.

'I can see that,' said a visibly shaken Tom, who wished he didn't. 'What am I doing there?' He then suddenly remembered that two of him, in close proximity, was seriously frowned upon. He jumped again.

'Don't worry,' said Cat, suddenly remembering there was something she had forgotten to tell Tom. 'It's only a hologram.' Cat waved her tail and the sleeping Tom dissolved from existence. 'I popped it there as a precaution.'

'Well you could have said something,' said Tom, as he wondered which had been the most disturbing; he seeing himself asleep, or seeing himself disappear.

Cat, noticing the return of the famous frown on Tom's face, decided to change the subject or she would never hear the end of it, and what better subject to change it to. 'Ooh,' she said, 'what a big sock you have.'

It worked, Tom's face immediately brightened at the word sock. He had forgotten all about it. And what a sock it was. With all thoughts of the other Tom rapidly draining away, Tom reached down and picked it up.

Cat smiled. She so very much preferred the happy Tom to the grumpy one. Not grumpy like Saint Nicholas had been. The other Saint Nicholas. The one the merchant had had the misfortune to bump into. The merchant who had started the rumours that led to some quarters believing Saint Nicholas a grump. Wonder what he thought about the accusation? Funny, she had thought, when her suspicion had borne fruit, how things happen. A real chicken-egg moment it had been, but that's time travel for you. She watched Tom up-end his sock onto the bed. Best he didn't know of course.

'Wow!' said Tom, as he marvelled at his hoard. 'Have you ever seen so many batteries?'

'No,' said Cat, her smile growing. 'I haven't. Merry Christmas Tom.'

'And a Merry Christmas to you too Cat,' said Tom, who then turned, squinted, and appeared to stare straight out of the page. 'And a Happy Holiday to you too, whoever you are.'

Richard Ross (and relatives) in A Christmas ~~Carol~~ Richard

The first thing you should know about Richard is that he is dead. Dead as a Dodo. Brown bread. He is dead.

The second thing you should know about Richard is that he still gets excited when Christmas comes around.

Our story started a while ago, when Richard was alive, when he was visited by his past lives; four of them. Lives he hadn't actually lived, but past lives all the same. They had needed his help. He had obliged. Then he'd died. He hadn't wanted to. But it was for the best.

Now, through choice, he exists in a kind of limbo, in an orb, with those four past lives; waiting for their next chance to help others; the living.

Is that a carol I hear being sung?

Chapter 1

'Tra-la-la-la-la-di-la-la-lah!'

'You don't know the words, do you?' laughed one of the four, a waitress called Laura. Richard's attempt at carol singing was causing much wincing amongst those in the orb.

Richard sighed. 'No,' he admitted, 'But it's the thought that counts.'

'That's gifts you idiot,' said Laura, playfully correcting Richard. 'Of which sadly, singing isn't one you possess.' Richard's lack of knowledge where lyrics were concerned was matched equally by his lack of singing ability.

'I'd like to hear you do better,' said Richard.

'You're on,' said Laura, rising to the challenge.

Oh no! thought nearly everyone else in the orb. They had heard Laura "sing" you see.

'Right!' said the Chaplain, who had died sometime in World War One. 'What say we all contemplate on the meaning of this time of year? Quietly contemplate.' He turned to Sammy. 'Don't you agree?'

Sammy, who had thrown off his mortal coil when in his down and out years, after spending years treading the boards as an entertainer at only the best theatres, ignored the Chaplain.

'Sammy?' said the Chaplain, eager for backup. Still nothing from Sammy. The Chaplain determined that this would just not do, so he shared a discreet elbow contact with the little tramp's ribs.

It should be pointed out at this juncture, that each in the orb were dressed as they had died. The Chaplain as a First World War Chaplain, Richard as a football referee, Laura in her waitress garb, Sammy still in pork pie hat and evening wear; shabby and worn, and Geoff as an elf; long story.

'Oi!' said Sammy, scowling at the Chaplain. The Chaplain had incredibly bony elbows.

'I said it's time for quiet reflection. Don't you agree?' said the Chaplain.

'Wait a mo,' said Sammy, reaching for his ears, 'can't hear a thing.' Sammy proceeded to remove a wad of cotton wool from each of them. Where he had got said cotton wool from was a mystery. 'There. Now, what was it you were saying?'

'Never mind,' said the Chaplain, rolling his eyes to heaven.

Shrugging, Sammy went to put the wads back; he was a professional singer after all, but was stopped by Geoff wondering out-loud.

'I wonder what our job will be this time?' said Geoff.

'Job?' said Sammy, mid wad. 'What are you on about? What job?' He wondered if he had missed something while under the influence of cotton wool.

It was only then that everyone noticed what Geoff already had; that the orb was slowly dimming. A sure sign they were about to be paid a visit. An almost sure sign they were about to be assigned.

Chapter 2

'Deck the halls with-ow.'

'You okay love?' asked a concerned Rosemary, wife to Horace, and the world's only plant psychic.

'Just a little prick,' said Horace, sucking on his thumb.

Rosemary knew all about little pricks, she had a conservatory full to the roof with plants of all kinds, some of which were cacti. You could get a nasty one off one of those if you weren't careful. 'Here, let me see,' she said.

Horace showed Rosemary his thumb. 'Can't we have plastic holly?' he whimpered, as Rosemary inspected the injury.

He was treated to a stare one didn't mess with. 'I suppose you'll be wanting one of those pesky artificial trees as well?' Rosemary gave Horace's thumb a squeeze which made him yelp. 'There, all better, bleeding's stopped.' Sometimes you had to be cruel to be kind.

'No, of course not,' said Horace, inspecting his thumb.

'Glad to hear it,' said Rosemary, smiling. 'Now, before we put up the tree, how about a nice cup of herbal tea and a homemade mince pie?'

Horace liked the idea. Rosemary's mince pies were legendary, or would be if any of them made it past Horace to the taste buds of the outside world. Rosemary never stinted on the alcohol. Food and drink in one neat little package. 'That would be lovely,' he enthused, thumb forgotten about for the moment.

'A dash of cream dear?'

'Wouldn't be the same without it,' said Horace, salivating at the thought.

Rosemary gave Horace a playful curtsey and headed for the kitchen, blowing him a kiss on the way. Rosemary and Horace were very much in love. Horace caught and returned it. It was a love so deep it had the power to bring a tear to a total stranger. It could also bring on a feeling of nausea. It just depended on how one saw it. But it was love nevertheless; true love.

With Rosemary busy in the kitchen, Horace set about removing the netting from the tree. It was a Norwegian Blue. A fine specimen, roots attached. Rosemary had a place for it in the garden come the twelfth day; a hole already dug. Horace hummed as he worked. He was a happy man. He was a contented man. Not a cloud in the sky. Except... There was something, a something causing a blot on his blue sky outlook. A small worry, concerning a very far removed young cousin. A troubled young man Horace feared.

Chapter 3

The entrance to the orb opened and a figure filled the opening, well part of it; Roberta wasn't that big. Roberta was short for Australopithecus Robustus; an early inhabitant of planet Earth, a paver of paths, but now a link between Upstairs and the orb's occupants. She had a job for them.

'Hi Rob,' said Geoff, always pleased to see the hirsute Roberta.

'Roberta,' said Roberta, with a wry smile.

'A job is it?' said the Chaplain, always ready to get straight to the point.

'Yes,' said Roberta, retaining her smile, 'and a surprise.'

'A surprise!' said Geoff, eyes widening.

'What kind of a surprise?' said the Chaplain, also always ready to look a gift horse in the mouth.

Roberta's big brown eyes studied the Chaplain. 'It wouldn't be much of a surprise if I told you now, would it?'

A frown formed on the Chaplain's brow. 'I suppose not,' he conceded.

'So what's the job?' said Richard.

Roberta's big brown eyes now alighted on Richard. 'We are to help out an old friend,' she said.

Frowning looked to be the new thing as Laura joined in. 'Is that allowed? Isn't that nepo-something or other?' she said.

'Nepotism is the word you're looking for I think,' said Roberta.

'That's it,' said Laura.

'No,' said Roberta, her smile just as broad. 'Family, friends, strangers are all the same when they need help.'

'Who?' said the Chaplain, once more to the point.

'All will soon be revealed,' said Roberta. 'Now, please follow me.' Roberta turned and stepped from the orb.

Chapter 4

Charles, Charlie to his friends, sat in the stockroom of one of the rarer breed of shops in existence, the independent bookshop, opening a newly arrived box of books. It wasn't what he wanted to do, but it was a job. What Charles wanted to do, was to write that next bestselling novel. Problem was, he didn't think himself good enough. So there he sat, happy to wallow, neck deep, in the success stories of others.

This suited the shop owner, one Marley, down to the ground. He had other ideas in mind for young Charles. Marley was desperate to open another shop, albeit against the current of the financial climate, with Charles at the helm. Marley thought Charles would make a darned fine shop manager one day. That is, if he ever managed to get his head down from out of those clouds he frequented. Marley knew of Charles's aspirations you see, and also knew that Charles was big on self-doubt where his writing was concerned; which suited him. But Marley also knew different. He had secretly entered one of Charles's short stories, under a non de plume, in a national writing competition. And it had won first prize. This had perplexed Marley greatly. If Charles ever found out how good his work really was, his head may never come down from the clouds. Perhaps it would even lead to that bestseller Charles was always going on about. Which would mean Charles would most certainly leave his employ. Which would mean years of wasted time, and having to train someone else, which would take even more time, and Marley was dead against that. No, better Charles didn't know how good he was; best for everyone concerned. Charles would never be able to cope with the pressure. Besides, the second bookshop, the continuation of his book-selling empire, was on the horizon and fast approaching.

And that was why Charles was tucked safely away, out of harm's and temptation's way, in the storeroom. And why Marley, at every opportunity, cast doubt into Charles's mind as to the standard of his writing ability. And why, at every opportunity, Marley would big up the job he had planned for Charles. Writing clearly wasn't his forte, but managing a bookshop... Better a captain at the helm of a ship, than a dreamer cast adrift on a raft going nowhere.

Marley left the shop floor and stuck his head round the storeroom door. Charles was sitting at the computer. 'Cuppa Charlie?' he asked.

'Please Dad,' said Charles.

Chapter 5

Rosemary peeped from the kitchen to see how Horace was getting on with the tree. He wasn't, which was very jolly hockey sticks as far as Rosemary was concerned. The longer he took, the more time she had to prepare the surprise she had been planning for him.

Rosemary knew about Charles, Horace's very far removed young cousin, and worry. Horace wasn't as good as he thought he was at keeping his worries to himself. She wanted to help. And she knew just the right someone who would be able to help with that help.

Popping back into the kitchen, before Horace noticed her looking at him, Rosemary went to the window and surveyed the back garden. They should be arriving any moment now. She then had a thought. *Better safe than sorry.* She popped her head back into the lounge.

'Horace?'

'Yes dear,' said Horace, who had the tree in a half nelson. Or was that the other way round?

'Could you be a dear and pop down the shops for me?'

'The shops?' said Horace, stopping what he was doing; the tree held under an arm. He frowned. 'Are they open today?'

'They're always open, dearest,' said Rosemary, smiling at the love of her life. 'Silly of me, but it would appear I've run out of my favourite herbal tea.'

Horace's frown deepened. Surely he had seen a nearly full pack not that very morning, when making breakfast. But he supposed he could be wrong. And a journey down the shops would make for a pleasant respite from the mauling the tree was bestowing on him. The frown disappeared. There it was then; he would take on the persona of the White Knight and come to his damsel's rescue. He dropped the tree. 'I'll get my hat,' he said. Rosemary saw him to the door.

On returning to the kitchen, you would have thought Rosemary was now all alone, and she was, if it wasn't for the robin, the Jack Russell, and the heavily disguised hirsute lady – she had removed her scarf – taking up room around and on the kitchen table. Also present, and in the centre of the table, was a rather splendid spider plant. It spoke to her.

'Nice to see you too Geoff,' said Rosemary, smiling coyly at the spider plant; they had history. 'I hope you're well?'

'Rosemary,' said the hirsute lady sitting at the table.

'Roberta,' said Rosemary, switching the kettle on. 'Tea?'

'That would be lovely.'

'And how are you Chaplain?' Rosemary asked, as she opened a cupboard. She could talk to the animals and they could talk to her; psychically that is. And to plants; she was a plant psychic after all. But they did have to house a spirit of the poor departed. Although...

'Fine, thank you,' said the Chaplain, who then woofed, more for effect than any useful purpose.

The robin cheeped.

'Yes,' said Rosemary, turning to look at him. She smiled. 'Yes, very festive Sammy.'

You see, the poor departed cannot come back, unless in the vessel of a recently departed animal, or a plant; never in human form; an Upstairs thing. And very wise too, flora and fauna being better suited as they were less likely to raise an eyebrow. Coming back, using a departed human being had its problems; someone catching a glimpse of their late lamented relative seemingly healthy again, one of them.

Placing two cups and saucers on the table, Rosemary aimed a question at Roberta, but not to her. 'And how are you two?'

Richard had journeyed and arrived in Roberta. Something the spirits were allowed to do, travel in the living, having passed across during unconsciousness or sleep; with permission of course. Not doing so could cause problems; exorcism for instance. Call it a short time, time share. But two sharing a body was a little unusual, a bit of a tight squeeze; frowned upon. But then again Roberta was unusual, being able to exist in two planes, the spiritual and physical, as she did.

'We're fine, thank you,' said Laura.

'You speak for yourself,' said Richard, still smarting over the travelling arrangements.

'Glad to hear it,' said Rosemary, ignoring Richard. She knew what a grumpy groggins he could be at times.

'And yourself, marriage suiting you?' said Laura.

Rosemary's eyes shone bright. 'Wouldn't have my life any other way,' she said, smiling broadly. Peppermint Roberta?'

'Yes please,' said Roberta, who loved her peppermint tea.

'I'll be mother then.' Rosemary put peppermint tea bags into the cups, and added boiling water. She then filled two bowls with cold water and placed them on the table, one for Sammy the robin, and the other for the Chaplain, in his Jack Russell guise. The Chaplain had clambered onto a chair, and was now perched on it, his front paws resting on the table. Rosemary saw them as people and should be treated as such. They both thanked her. Especially Sammy when he discovered there was a little something extra in his bowl. Not enough brandy to do any harm, but just enough to warm the cockles of one's heart. Rosemary sat beside the Chaplain.

'So,' said Richard, eager to get down to the nitty-gritty, now that they knew who Roberta's friend in need was. 'What's the to-do?'

'Yes,' said the Chaplain, 'the to-do?'

Rosemary told her story.

Chapter 6

'Well-well,' said Marley, as he put the phone down.

'Problem?' asked Charles, alerted by his father's puzzled look.

'No, not really,' said Marley, still looking at the phone, the puzzled look now more a bemused one, 'more a surprise.'

'Surprise?' Charles stopped what he was doing, this sounded intriguing.

'Rosemary's invited us over for Christmas dinner. We're to go over Christmas Eve.'

'Blimey,' said Charles, who was now as surprised as his father, especially as Christmas Eve was tomorrow. 'That's a bolt from the blue.' It then dawned on him, that this year he might be able to escape his dad's annual burnt offering. 'You did say yes?' He then bit his lip. He hoped he hadn't sounded too eager.

But Marley hadn't noticed, having mentally left the room for a moment as he wondered if he would have to shut up shop early. 'What?'

'Did you say yes?'

'Er, yes. That okay?'

'Fine by me,' said Charles, trying to curb his eagerness. 'What time are we going over?'

Marley looked blank for a moment; it was a good question. 'I forgot to ask.' He picked the phone up. Maybe he wouldn't have to shut early.

Chapter 7

'And you're sure it will work?' asked a dubious Richard.

'It did last time,' said Rosemary.

'That it did,' Richard conceded, but still with reservations. It had not been the most pleasant of experiences.

'He just needs encouragement, and where better to get it?'

'Nowhere,' agreed Roberta. 'I think it will be very interesting and very instructive.'

'That's all right for you to say, but you're not going with him,' said the Chaplain, who should have been showing at least the tiniest spark of excitement by now, considering what a fan he was. But as with Richard, the idea of what they were about to do outweighed the where's and who's.

'Sammy will be with you,' Roberta reminded him; an attempt at easing the Chaplain's fears.

'Yeah, it'll be fun,' said Sammy, who was always up for whatever was thrown his way. As far as he was concerned, you only die once, and he had already done that.

'Yes, it'll be fun,' said Richard, who didn't entirely believe what he had just said, but it had to be, compared to the plan Roberta had laid out for him and Laura. She had even admitted she wasn't sure if their part in all this was possible. What if it wasn't? What then?

Just then the front door opened.

'Rosemary! I'm back.'

'It's Horace,' said Rosemary, suddenly filled with the butterflies.

'You had better tell him,' said Roberta.

'You haven't told him yet?' said Richard.

'He'll be fine with it,' said Rosemary, any fears she might have well hidden. She got up and went to head Horace off at the lounge. It was perhaps for the best if she told him before he saw the others. At the kitchen door she turned to her guests and put a finger to her lips. She then stepped into the lounge.

There was a moment of silence, followed by the sound of a hushed voice, then…

'You what!' exclaimed Horace.

'So far so good then,' said Richard.

Chapter 8

'I don't think you needed to wear a suit and tie,' said Charles, as he and his dad wheeled through the garden gate, onto the garden path, that led to Horace and Rosemary's front door. He had been itching to say so since leaving home, but hadn't decided on a right moment, until now, when it was far too late.

'Too much you think?' said Marley, looking down at his tie.

'Looks like you've got a date with the bank manager.'

'That bad eh?' Marley decided Charles might be right, a tad more on the casual side might be in order. He started to remove his tie, just as the front door opened to reveal Rosemary all dressed up in her Sunday best. She was smiling her best jolly hockey sticks smile.

'On second thoughts,' whispered Charles, who suddenly felt very much underdressed.

Marley returned Rosemary's smile. 'You look smart,' he said. Charles winced.

'Thank you,' said Rosemary. 'And may I say how dapper you look Marley.'

At this point, Charles attempted to use his dad as a shield. Perhaps he could squeeze in unnoticed. He wasn't sure about Rosemary in truth. He wasn't sure how to take her. Horace, on the other hand, was a different kettle of fish. Since his dramatic reappearance, he had often visited the bookshop, purchasing this and that, mostly books about the Orinoco. Charles thought him a good old stick, always ready for the old banter. Thought of him as someone you could tell your woes to. And there was also just that touch of mystery about the man. Perhaps one day, if his writing ever took an upturn, he would base a character on Horace in a book, as a spy, or something equally exotic.

'Come in, come in,' said Rosemary, standing aside and ushering.

In the hall, Horace was waiting to take coats and overnight bags.

Charles immediately brightened as he saw him, his attire forgotten for the moment.

'Hi Charlie,' said Horace, pointing the way. 'Go straight through, Rosemary's made mulled wine.'

Charles, followed by his dad, wandered from the hall into the lounge.

'Sit-sit,' said Rosemary, flouncing in behind them in her best hostess flounce. 'I'll get that mulled wine.' But stopped suddenly in mid stride as she remembered there was alcohol in the wine. 'You are old enough for alcohol Charlie? If not, I've got some splendid pop.'

'I'm twenty-two.'

'Of course you are. Right, good-oh.' Happy that all was above board, Rosemary headed for the kitchen.

In the kitchen, her other guests, who had stayed overnight, were patiently waiting. Richard though was a little grumpy.

Staying overnight was all right for some. There were steak titbits for the Chaplain, cake crumbs and sunflower hearts for Sammy, even a specially formulated plant food for Geoff. And what did he get? No sleep, that's what. The secret was out, Roberta snored. And, as for food and drink, Richard only got what Roberta wanted; herbal tea, more herbal tea, and enough raisins and sultanas to put a man off the sickly little things for life. Oh, what he would have given for one of those delicious mince pies he had spied. Buttery pastry, rum, brandy... but no, he had to have what Roberta wanted. And when he had broached the subject, nothing, no reply; it was as if an iron curtain had fallen, cutting him off. Pity it hadn't been there when she'd dropped off. Hopefully his next host would be more accommodating. He would have to wait and see. Rosemary entered the kitchen.

'Sacrificial lambs arrived have they?' said Richard, who had been stewing all day.

'Richard!' scorned Laura, appalled.

'Well.'

'He's just grumpy,' said Roberta.

'But no reason to be so rude,' said Laura.

'Laura's right Richard,' said Roberta.

Richard pouted non-existent lips. 'Sorry,' he said, a tad unconvincingly.

'Richard!' said Laura.

'Sorry,' Richard repeated, with a little more conviction.

'Better,' said Laura.

'Good,' said Roberta, 'I wouldn't want to have to cancel his part of the surprise.'

'I...'

'Thank you Richard,' said Rosemary, who sympathised with Richard, so didn't take his remark to heart. 'And yes, the lambs have arrived.' She smiled as she said it.

With the heads up regarding the arrivals delivered, Rosemary went back to the lounge, carrying four mulled wines on a tray, and something secretly secreted about her person.

*

'Mmm,' murmured Marley as he sipped on his mulled wine. 'Delicious.'

'My grandmother's recipe,' said Rosemary, preening. 'Just a moment, I've forgotten the napkins.' Excuse made, she went back to the kitchen.

'How's that?' she said.

'Loud and clear,' said Roberta. The baby monitor Rosemary had secreted about her person was working. 'See you in a mo then.'

Rosemary handed out the napkins and indulged in some small talk.

The niceties continued, with a nervous Rosemary occasionally glancing Horace's way. Those niceties progressed to idle chit-chat, to deeper conversation; the nervousness abating slightly but not going away. Dinner was served in the dining room. All relaxed further. Time passed. Games were introduced back in the lounge. More drinks. More chat. The question of hypnotism tentatively introduced into it.

'I didn't know that,' said Marley, when Rosemary mentioned that Horace had dabbled.

'In the past,' said Horace.

'Tell us more,' said Charles, mind perhaps on that book.

'Not much to tell really,' said Horace, throwing Rosemary a look. She batted her eyelashes back at him. He took a deep breath. 'The usual nonsense, you know regression and whatnot.' The bait had been dangled. But would it be taken?

'What happened?' said Charles, moving to the edge of his seat.

The bait had been nibbled at. Horace let the breath out. Across the room Rosemary, who had been holding hers, did likewise.

'They said they went back, some sort of royalty no less,' said Horace, who wasn't at all comfortable with the lie. 'But can't say I believed them. The jury's out on that one.'

'And there we should leave it,' said Rosemary. 'It's getting late and we don't want to be tired for Christmas morning, do we?' It didn't do any harm to play the line a little.

'Oh,' said Charles, closing in on the bait, 'can't we just hear a little bit more?'

Hooked? Rosemary wasn't sure. 'Well Horace,' she said, putting him into bat. Horace had been in two minds about Rosemary's plan since she had told him. It was time for him to step up, or forget about the whole thing. The decision to continue lay in Horace's hands now. Rosemary stared at him. In the kitchen, those that could held their breath.

Horace had his reservations. Had voiced his reservations. But it was down to him now. He didn't want to meddle, but he wanted to help. What to do? He could feel Rosemary's stare. He looked at Charles. He looked like an author, if there was such a thing? He didn't look like a shop manager, again if there was such a thing? But he shouldn't meddle. But when he looked at Charles, he could see how eager he was to succeed; reminded him of someone. The light bulb went on. Charles reminded Horace of a younger version of himself. And where would he be if he hadn't been given chances? It didn't bear thinking about. Horace looked at Rosemary. 'A little longer then,' said Horace. There was no going back now.

Charles placed his glass on the coffee table, taking care to put it on the coaster provided. He cast a nervous glance at Rosemary then looked at Horace. 'Could you do me?' he said.

'Whatever do you mean?' said Rosemary, playing her role to perfection.

'Regress me,' said Charles, again with a nervous glance at Rosemary.

The bait was taken. The wheels were in motion. There was definitely no going back now.

Rosemary rose. 'How spiffing,' she gushed, 'anyone for a mince pie?'

Safely behind the closed kitchen door, Rosemary made quick preparations. She needed cotton wool; it wouldn't do if she was accidently put under as well. Cotton wool gathered, Rosemary turned her attention to Geoff. He could only communicate via the mind while in his current situation but one could never be too careful.

'It's just a precaution,' assured Rosemary, as she went to cover the spider plant with a tea cosy.

'Will it hurt?' said Geoff.

'Only if she drops it on you,' chirped Sammy.

'Don't you take any notice of him,' said Rosemary, lowering the cosy over Geoff. He too needed to be protected. In an emergency Rosemary and Geoff might be the only chance the others had for getting back.

'It's dark,' said Geoff.

'Can you hear me?' said Rosemary, communicating through the medium of normal speech; talking.

There was no immediate reply, but that meant nothing. Geoff was quite capable of retreating into his shell if the mood took him. So a second opinion was needed.

'Could you Laura, please?'

'Can you hear Rosemary?' said Laura, mind to mind with Geoff.

'What did she say?' said Geoff, not in a shell, just the tea cosy.

'She asked if you could hear her.'

'Did she?'

'He can't hear you.'

'Right,' said Rosemary, girding up. 'Time to gather round the monitor, you need to hear everything Horace says.

They gathered.

Rosemary filled a tray with mince pies. 'Here goes,' she said, heading for the door. She hesitated. 'I'll say a few words and then come back to check all's working okay.' She left the kitchen.

A couple of seconds later Rosemary's voice rang clear but quietly. 'Oops, silly me I've forgotten the cream.'

A further couple of seconds and Rosemary was back in the kitchen. 'Well?' she said.

'All systems go,' said Roberta, giving Rosemary the okay sign.

Rosemary collected the cream from the fridge. 'Good luck everyone.'

'You shouldn't have,' said Marley as he licked his lips at the sight of the cream. 'But seeing as you already have.'

Chapter 9

The tray was soon empty, the plates clean, the conversation back to hypnotic regression.

'I don't know,' said Horace, playing it coy.

'But you said,' said Charles.

'Did I?'

'Well, no but…'

'Go on Horace,' said Marley, 'let the boy visit his past.' Marley didn't think for a moment such things were possible, especially with his business-like brain. But as that brain was well on its way to being nicely pickled, why not?

Horace finished the last of the ruby port in his glass in one gulp. And quite a gulp it was too as, apart from a small sip earlier, it was still quite full. Call it Dutch courage. 'Okay,' he said.

With sleight of hand Rosemary immediately removed the cotton wool from her cardigan sleeve. She held it in her hand at the ready.

'What do I do?' said Charles, excitement building.

'Just sit where you are and relax,' said Horace.

'I thought I'd have to lie down or something.'

'That's a psychiatrist,' said Horace, wondering if he might need one himself after this.

'Okay,' said Charles, shaking his hands. He had seen someone do this on the television. It relaxed you, or did it warm you? Whatever, he was ready. He then reached for his glass of whisky Mac and downed it. Now he was ready.

Horace started to do what he did.

Across the room, Rosemary discreetly plugged her ears with the cotton wool and looked away; going again with the "can't be too careful" routine.

Less than a minute later, Charles was under Horace's influence. As was Marley and most of the guests in the kitchen; thanks to the baby monitor.

Horace motioned to Rosemary, and she removed the cotton wool. 'You better check the others,' he said.

Rosemary went to the kitchen and looked in. Roberta was face down on the kitchen table, as was the Chaplain, which didn't look at all comfortable. Rosemary gently moved his snout sideways so his head was resting on its side. Sammy was on his back on the table, his little legs in the air. Rosemary again obliged and set him on his side. She then removed the tea cosy from Geoff. She enquired as to his wellbeing.

'All okay,' said Geoff, attempting, but failing to give the thumbs up.

'So far so good then,' said Rosemary, picking Geoff and his pot up before going back to the lounge to give Horace the news.

Horace looked up expectantly as Rosemary entered. 'All fine,' she said.

'Right,' said Horace reaching for his glass. He needed another drink but the glass was empty from before.

'Another one dear?' said Rosemary, placing Geoff on the coffee table.

'Please.' Horace watched Rosemary pour him another glass of port. 'They'll be all right, won't they?' he said, a concerned look on his face.

'We shall soon find out.' Rosemary handed Horace his glass and went to pour herself one. Glass filled; she returned and sat beside Charles.

Chapter 10

Everything went dark. Not the dark dark that they drifted in, when joining with the living; the scary dark that had one fearing they may never see the light again. This was a different dark; a dark with hints of grey at its edges. But even so, Richard tensed as he always did, when in the dark; whatever the shade.

Laura, who was beside him, felt him do it. 'You okay?' she asked, as she had asked many times before.

Embarrassed that Laura had felt his fear yet again, Richard did what he usually did and lied, saying that he was. Would he ever get used to doing this? He doubted it.

The dark began to recede. And as it did, a figure began to form. It advanced from the dark's depth.

Laura sought out Richard's hand. Richard took it and gave it a squeeze. How would he react?

'What the flipping 'eck is going on?' demanded the figure. The figure sounded angry.

Now they knew.

Chapter 11

'Here we go again old chap,' said the Chaplain, as he and Sammy entered the dark.

Not the dark dark of course, but the same sort of dark as Richard and Laura had just entered. The sort of dark with grey at its edges, but this was a totally different one, one with a different owner.

'Hold onto your hat,' said Sammy, who was doing just that, as he always wore one.

After a while this dark also started to recede. The Chaplain and Sammy had arrived at their destination. They stood waiting. A figure approached.

Sammy gave the Chaplain a look and darted behind him. If their host wasn't happy, he wasn't going to be the one at the front.

Chapter 12

Horace paced back and forth from the sofa to the kitchen door, his hands behind his back. Rosemary sat, sipping at her port. Geoff twiddled his leaves.

'How do you think it's going?' said Horace for the umpteenth time, as he turned to pace back to the sofa. A hole in the carpet was imminent.

Feeling a little apprehensive as the idea had been her's, Rosemary took another sip from her glass. But she was nowhere as bad as Horace was. She tried to calm him. 'As well as it is,' she said, her words not bringing a great deal of comfort to Horace, who turned and headed for the kitchen door again.

'They'll be okay,' said Geoff.

'Geoff says they'll be all right,' said Rosemary, relaying Geoff's words. Horace couldn't communicate with Geoff as he wasn't psychic or unconscious.

'That's okay then, 'said Horace, his uneasiness promoting sarcasm.

'We're only trying to help,' said Rosemary, her eyes showing the stab of hurt Horace's remark had caused her.

Horace stopped mid step and looked at Rosemary. He suddenly felt very guilty; he hadn't meant to be so sharp. 'I'm sorry petal. I…'

But his apology was cut short, there had been a development, the unconscious Marley had started to shout.

Chapter 13

'Limbo!' shouted Marley. 'What the flipping 'eck do you mean, limbo?!'

'It's a place between life and death,' said Richard, trying to explain.

'You saying I died?' snapped Marley, a look of horror etched on his face.

'No,' said Laura quickly, 'you're just unconscious, sort of.'

'Unconscious? I had some sort of accident?'

'No,' said Richard, wincing as he spoke, 'you were hypnotised.'

'I was…' Dawning arrived on Marley's face, then bewilderment, which was quickly followed by a look of anger. 'Horace did this to me, didn't he?'

There was no point denying it. Richard wished he could. But he couldn't. 'Yes,' he said. And as he did, he couldn't help but think he and Laura had definitely got the short straw this time.

Marley placed hands on hips and glared at Laura and Richard. Someone had some explaining to do, and it might as well be these two bozos, whoever they were.

Chapter 14

'Charles?' said the Chaplain, feeling he should ask. Nothing was ever certain, as he had found to his cost. 'Is that you?'

'Yes,' came a nervous reply. Charles had the appearance of a worried yet curious man as he appeared from the dark. 'Where am I?'

'You're in a sort of limbo,' said Sammy, peeping from behind the Chaplain.

'Limbo?'

'Yes,' confirmed the Chaplain. 'Do you remember Horace hypnotising you?'

The worried look deepened as Charles gave this some thought, only for it to completely disappear a moment later, his face brightening. He stared at the two men standing before him, the one dressed like a soldier, and the other, smaller man peering around the soldier's arm. A little excitement began to surface. 'Are one of you me?' he asked.

The Chaplain and Sammy exchanged puzzled glances before twigging what Charles meant.

'Oh no,' said the Chaplain. 'Good grief no, we're your guides.'

'My guides?'

'I think we should explain,' said the Chaplain.

Chapter 15

Marley was stunned. 'You're ghosts?' he said, this revelation adding to the rest of the things he was trying to get his head around. Like the fact that everything that was happening, was supposed to be happening in his head. That these "ghosts" were there, in his head to supposedly help him. Take him on some journey.

'No,' said Laura, intent on not complicating things, as Richard had just done by saying what he had just said.

'Sort of,' said Richard, intent on doing just that, even though he wasn't strictly meaning to.

His comfort zone clearly a million miles away from where he now stood, or existed, or whatever it was he was doing, Marley courageously gathered what wits he could muster, ones that weren't frazzled by what was going on right there and then, and looked at Laura and Richard, studying them in turn. He appeared to be thinking. He appeared to come to some sort of decision. He spoke. 'Why?' he said.

'Why?' said Richard.

'Tell me why you're doing this?'

What more was there to say? They were there to help him. Show him a few things and bring him back. There was nothing else to say. All had already been said. Laura looked at Richard. Richard shrugged. There wasn't anymore.

'There isn't any more,' said Laura.

'There isn't any more what?' said Marley.

'Any more to tell you,' said Richard.

'Then I won't be going anywhere.'

'But...'

'No buts, I've made up my mind, while it's still in one piece. Ghosts and whatnot bah, I'm just having a dream or something. I want to wake up.'

And that looked like being that, but for the thing up Laura's sleeve, put there by Roberta for just a situation like this.

'Fair enough,' said Laura. 'If that's how you feel, but I don't believe you really think you're dreaming this. But it's your mind.'

'It is,' said Marley, adamant that it was.

'Shame,' said Laura, half turning away, and winking at Richard as she did. 'I'd have loved to have seen what the future held.'

Ah, thought Richard, *nice one*. But the thing that had worried him most about this enterprise, back when they had been discussing it in the kitchen, was about to rear its ugly head. Was it possible? Really possible? He would soon find out. 'Yeah, shame,' Richard agreed. He glanced at Marley and gave him the look of the glum. 'Would've been nice.'

Marley stood there, his eyes fixed on some distant point, his mind suddenly a whirr as he took in what had just been said. The future? Had she just mentioned the future? She had. But that wasn't possible, was it? Of course it wasn't, he was just having a dream; the port and whiskey. He pinched himself. It hurt. But what if it was true? All of it? He would be able to… No, what if things hadn't worked out as he planned. Better not. It would be too much to bear. But then again, if things hadn't gone as planned; his plans for a bookshop empire thwarted somehow, he would be able to discover what had gone wrong and take steps to make sure it didn't happen when he got back. Marley chanced a look at the ghosts, they were chatting; discussing the lost chance of going to the future no doubt. Did he? Should he? Why not? As far as he could see, it was win-win. And if it was just a dream, well, nothing lost. 'Sorry,' said Marley, 'did you say something about the future?'

It was time to contact Geoff.

Chapter 16

'Rosemary arranged this?' said Charles, after recovering from the initial shock of being told that his somewhere removed relative's wife, had been in contact with the spiritual world on his behalf. 'But how did she know how I feel about my writing?'

'It would appear she wheedled it out of Horace,' said the Chaplain.

'But how did he know?'

'I suppose he wheedled it out of you.'

'Wheedlers huh,' said Sammy knowingly, getting his penny's worth, without actually contributing anything positive to the situation.

Ignoring Sammy's utterance, the Chaplain continued, 'Horace is under the impression your work is worthy of the top drawer.'

It was a positive comment, but Charles just sighed. 'But he isn't the editor of a publishing house, is he?'

'I heard tell, that old Horace is a bit of an expert when it comes to tall tales, so he should know what he's talking about,' said Sammy, trying to help in his own inimitable way.

'Yes, thank you Sammy,' hissed the Chaplain, planting an elbow in Sammy's ribs. The Chaplain was all too aware of Horace's past demeanours, but this wasn't the time or place for discussions on the matter.

'Ow!' said Sammy, rubbing at his chest. One of the perks of entering a living person's mind was the ability to feel again; along with other senses. For the moment though, feeling was more than enough as far as Sammy was concerned.

'He means,' said the Chaplain, giving Sammy one heck of a disdainful look, 'that Horace knows a good story when he hears one. And isn't that what writing is all about, giving the reader enjoyment?'

'I suppose.'

'No suppose about it,' said the Chaplain. The Chaplain had a thought. 'You have sent your work to publishers, haven't you?'

A sheepish looking Charles admitted he hadn't. 'There's no point.'

The Chaplain shook his head, such negativity. 'There is if you want that big break,' he said, only just refraining from the old finger wag.

'I mean there's no point sending anyone my work, because it's not good enough.' And there it was, for the world and her husband to see, Charles's low self-esteem, when it came to his writing.

Unfazed by Charles's borderline outburst, the Chaplain took the bull by the horns. 'Then let us prove you wrong,' he said.

Charles was wary. 'How?'

'By letting us stay in your head when Horace regresses you for real. Hopefully we'll be able to show you something that will help you.'

'What?' Charles was still not convinced.

'That's for us to know, and you to find out,' said Sammy.

'Not helping again,' whispered the Chaplain, causing Sammy's hands to go up in defence of his chest.

But it did. For all Charles's misgivings regarding the situation, and his literary prowess, his writers' curiosity had been piqued by what Sammy had said. But he didn't want to sound too eager, he still had reservations. 'I'd really go back in time?' he asked. 'Live another life? See through someone else's eyes?' His mind started to work overtime; his writer's mind. He might not think of himself as much of an author, but that didn't stop his writer's mind from gathering ideas.

'More a visit,' said the Chaplain, 'a bystander looking on, so to speak.'

A little bit of doubt crept back in. Charles suddenly wasn't sure again.

But the Chaplain was on the ball and noticed. 'We have a time in mind,' he said quickly.

'You do?' said Charles.

'Oh yes,' said the Chaplain enthusiastically.

'Time bystander!' added Sammy, speaking as if providing the hype for the next big science fiction film to hit the silver screen.

Whether it was the Chaplain's enthusiasm or Sammy's hyped description, Charles was surprised to find he was suddenly sold on the idea. *What the heck?* he thought. 'Okay, I'll do it.'

It was time to contact Geoff.

Chapter 17

Eyes twitched beneath their lids. Gradually they opened. The pair belonging to Charles was immediately rubbed. The pair belonging to Marley, glared at Horace.

'Ah,' said Horace, trying his best to avoid eye contact. Turned to stone sprang to mind. 'Glad to have you back.'

'Outrage is what it is,' spluttered an indignant Marley, 'a flipping liberty.'

'But you've agreed,' said Rosemary, quickly.

'It's not set in stone yet,' said Marley, bringing a wince from Horace. He moved his glare from Horace to Rosemary. Marley was having second and third thoughts now that he was awake again; regression, stuff and nonsense. People in your brain, talking to you, preposterous, that's what it is, a cheap parlour trick. He didn't like being made the fool of. 'Charles, get your coat.'

But as an indignant and increasingly angry Marley, went to rise from his seat, a voice whispered quietly in his ear. 'And what about us?' said Laura.

'What's this?' said Marley, shaking his head.

'We're still in here,' said Laura.

'With bells on,' said Richard.

'What?' said Marley, not sure what to make of what he was hearing. He glared again at Horace. It was time for the nonsense to stop.

'They won't be able to leave until you're under again,' said Rosemary, guessing the reason for Marley's "what's" and puzzled head shaking. 'The same for Charles.'

Sitting back in his seat, Marley's glare gave way to a look of realisation. *Surely not?* he thought. He looked at Rosemary. 'But that's not fair,' he mumbled.

'You've nothing to lose,' said Rosemary, confident they now had the upper hand, 'and from what I hear, perhaps something to learn.'

Marley slumped. It had all been real.

'Dad?' said a concerned Charles.

But resigned as he might be to what had just happened to him, it didn't mean he was happy about it. 'Let's get it over with then,' he said, with a total lack of conviction, 'if we must.'

'Good man,' said Richard.

'Bah,' said Marley.

'Good,' said Rosemary. 'Now if everyone is ready, Horace you may begin.' She swept Geoff from the coffee table and headed for the kitchen and the waiting Roberta.

'All fine?' asked Roberta, as Rosemary entered.

'All fine,' said a smiling Rosemary, as she placed Geoff on the table. She switched the baby monitors off.

'Leaves crossed,' said Geoff.

Chapter 18

The first thing to hit them, when they arrived, was the smell; the smell of the sea and seaweed, and all the smells that went with it.

The second thing to hit was the colours. Hit Charles that is. Why Charles had expected everything to be in black and white, he didn't know, but there you go. 'It's fantastic,' said Charles, taking in the scene before him.

'It smells,' said Sammy.

'That's the seaside for you,' said the Chaplain. 'Portsmouth eighteen-twelve to be precise.'

'Wow,' said Charles, eyes wide. Those eyes were then cast over the Chaplain and Sammy. They appeared as they had in his mind, but more so. They looked alive. 'You're a soldier,' he said, staring at the Chaplain.

'A chaplain,' said the Chaplain.

Charles turned his attention to Sammy. 'And you're a…'

'Disappointment,' said the Chaplain, proving that he did have a sense of humour contrary to popular belief.

''ere,' said Sammy, 'I'm an entertainer.'

'An entertainer?' said Charles.

'Right,' said the Chaplain, in his I'm taking control voice, 'pleasantries later. Time is upon us, and lots to see and do. Follow me please.' The Chaplain set off at a moderate trot, 'and stay close. We don't want anyone getting lost now, do we?'

Charles, eager not to do that, left the matter of Sammy's occupation hanging, and fell in behind. 'Where are we going?' he said.

'To see a master,' said the Chaplain, 'The Master.'

Charles turned to Sammy, who was a few steps adrift behind them, hoping he would be able to elaborate. But Sammy just smiled, shrugged and showed his willingness to go with the flow.

A few streets later, the Chaplain came to a halt. 'And there we have it,' he announced, gesturing towards a house.

'Have what?' said Charles, staring at the building the Chaplain was pointing to, whilst wondering if it perhaps held some significant position in the building world that merited it being known as The Master, whilst also wondering what on Earth a building had to do with why he was there.

'The birthplace of the great Charles Dickens,' said the Chaplain, with a flourish.

'Wow,' said Charles. He was even more agog than when he had arrived.

'Do you know much about Dickens?'

'Not a lot,' Charles admitted.

Sammy on the other hand, surveyed the building with suspicion. 'You sure?' he said.

'Of course I'm sure,' said the Chaplain indignantly. 'And to prove it, we are going in to watch the great moment in all its glory.'

'You're jesting me?' said Sammy.

'I joke not,' said the Chaplain, deadly serious. 'It's so Charles here can fully appreciate and understand what we are trying to do for him.'

'Fully lose his breakfast you mean,' said Sammy, who had heard all about the doings of childbirth. There was no way any woman was going to hold his hand so hard it would make him cry, then have every obscenity known to man wailed at him.

'Won't they see us?' said Charles, also erring on the wary at the Chaplain's plan, but for more rational reasons.

'Usually,' said the Chaplain, 'but for this trip we have been given special permission to act the ghost.'

'Do we?' said Sammy.

'Not listening again Samuel?' the Chaplain chastised.

'It's Sammy, as well you know,' said Sammy, who had been listening and had even done a little homework on their mission. But he would have to admit, yes, he had missed the ghost bit. *Oh well,* he thought, *might as well enjoy it while I can.* So Sammy stepped through the open gate and straight through the front door.

The Chaplain and Charles followed him, but with the Chaplain staying Charles with a hand on his shoulder, stopped just short of the door. 'Allow me,' said the Chaplain, reaching for the door handle. He turned it and the door opened. Ushering Charles inside, the Chaplain followed and closed the door behind them.

They were stood in a hallway, across from a flight of stairs. Sammy was standing at the bottom of them.

'That was pretty cool,' said Charles, referring to Sammy's entrance.

'Yes, in some quarters,' said the Chaplain, 'but also very rude. You can't just intrude on people's property like that you know.'

'And I suppose opening the door and just walking in isn't?' said Sammy, defending himself. 'And I bet the door was locked. Wasn't it?'

'We walk the Earth Sammy, not through it,' said the Chaplain, ignoring Sammy's rather valid question.

Sammy shoved his hands in his pockets and shrugged. He muttered something under his breath. Charles, who was wondering if he might get the chance to walk through something in the near future, grinned; he couldn't ever remember hearing anyone say piffle before. The Chaplain meanwhile, had started to ascend the flight of stairs.

'This way,' said the Chaplain. 'I believe we are about to witness a small miracle.'

'Miracle my…'

'I can hear you Sammy.'

Chapter 19

'Not what I expected,' said Marley, inspecting his new surroundings.

'What were you expecting?' asked Richard.

'I don't know, flying car perhaps. Clean pavements. The usual things associated with the future.'

'Well then,' said Laura, 'you shouldn't feel too disappointed, as this isn't the future.'

Marley turned on his two companions. Why were they dressed as a waitress and a football referee? But never mind that for the moment. 'But I thought you said we were going to travel to the future. You lied to me.' Marley did a bit of glaring; he was good at it. 'This looks more like the past.'

'I think you'll find the clue is in the word regression,' said Richard.

'But you said…'

'And we will, I promise,' said Laura, stepping in before Marley blew a gasket. 'But we have to go back first, to move forward.'

Looking at Laura through narrowed eyes, Marley digested her words. They gave him heartburn. Woman speaks with forked tongue, he didn't doubt. But as there wasn't much he could do about it. 'Why here?' he asked.

'We go where we are put,' said Laura.

'You mean you don't know.'

'That about sums it up,' said Richard.

Marley scowled at him.

'But I believe that house behind you has something to do with why we're here,' said Laura. 'Do you recognise it?'

Turning round, Marley realised he did.

Chapter 20

'Goodness,' said the Chaplain, who was considerably green about the gills.

'Blimey,' said Charles, who wasn't feeling so good himself.

'Only got yourselves to blame,' said a smirking Sammy, who'd had the good sense to stand well clear of the goings on in the room at the top of the stairs. Facing the wall had also helped.

They were now at the foot of those stairs, with Charles and the Chaplain sitting on the bottom step. Sammy was leaning against the hall wall.

'It was sort of wonderful though,' said Charles, starting to recover a little from his ordeal.

'If you like that sort of thing,' said Sammy. 'I suppose you have to be a parent.'

'Nature at its best,' said the Chaplain, recovering, but still a little stunned. Never in his wildest dreams had he thought childbirth could be so... so... He had always thought "pop" and there you have it, he, she, all wrapped up, powdered, and ready to be fed.

'And did you see the baby's eyes when he saw us?' said Charles. 'As big as saucers they were.'

'Poppycock,' said the Chaplain. 'Much too young, and besides, we're invisible to the world, remember.'

'I have to admit,' said Sammy, examining a fingernail, 'I have to agree with Charles, though more like dinner plates, I'd say.'

'As I said before, it's poppycock. And if I remember right, you were looking the other way.' said the Chaplain.

'Only during the, you know, the...'

'Birth?' said Charles.

'That's it.'

The Chaplain stood up and brushed imaginary dust from his trousers. He wasn't going to be drawn further on the matter. It was poppycock and poppycock it was going to stay. 'So Charles, I hope you have learnt something from this experience.'

'I...'

'Good, onto the next step of your journey then. Shall we?'

As one both Sammy and Charles shared a silly notion and looked at the step one up from where Charles was sitting.

Noticing this, the Chaplain glared at them. 'Really?' he asked, then tutted. 'From you Sammy, I can understand, but Charles I thought better of you.'

'I thought it might be one of those trick questions,' said Sammy.

'What are you talking about?'

'Sorry,' said Charles.

'I should think so too,' said the Chaplain. 'This is serious stuff we are about, your future no less. I hope you did learn something whilst here?'

'Well... I er...' muttered Charles, casting a hopeful glance in Sammy's direction.

But Sammy was as forthcoming as tea from a chocolate teapot.

The Chaplain couldn't believe it. Was he the only one to notice? 'The poverty,' he said.

'Don't look too impoverished to me,' said Sammy, giving the décor the once over.

'Behind the curtains,' said the Chaplain.

'What is?' said Charles, trying to understand.

'The poverty of course,' said the Chaplain, as if that explained anything.

'Is it?' said Sammy. He headed for the nearest curtain.

An exasperated Chaplain shook his head. 'Not the physical curtain you numbskull, the metaphorical one.'

'Ah,' said Sammy. 'I see.' He started to whistle under his breath.

The Chaplain rolled his eyes to heaven. 'I mean it's all a façade. Look, let's take that next step and you'll see what I mean.'

Sammy suppressed the urge to look at the second step again.

The Chaplain took Charles by the hand, and led him to the front door and that next step. A step that took them into the future, Charles Dickens's future that is.

'Coo, luvaduck and all that malarkey,' said Sammy. 'This place smells worse than the last.'

'Welcome gentlemen, to good old London Town, eighteen twenties,' said the Chaplain.

'What are we doing here?' said Charles, his eyes watering.

'Follow me old chap and all will be explained.'

'Which one is he?' asked Charles, as they crowded round a small, grimy, windowpane.

'That one,' said the Chaplain, pointing towards a small boy of about twelve, sitting on a bench at the far end of the room they were peering into.

'Looks like a girl, if you ask me,' said Sammy.

'No one is,' said the Chaplain.

'He's dressed like a girl,' said Charles.

'That's how they dress in these days,' the Chaplain explained.

'You sure?' said Sammy, having his doubts.

'Of course I'm sure, who's the expert here?' said the Chaplain.

Sammy decided it best if he didn't answer that question due to safety issues; his, and kept quiet.

'Exactly,' said the Chaplain, taking Sammy's silence as an acceptance of his authority on the matter. He turned to Charles. 'Now Charles, what do you notice?'

Charles concentrated on the scene facing him, but apart from the way the young Dickens was dressed, he was at a loss as to what the Chaplain expected. He had a stab anyway. 'He's got ringlets?' he said.

'Oh good grief,' said the Chaplain despairingly. 'Come with me.' And just like that, the Chaplain led Charles straight through the window and wall and into the room where the young Dickens sat. An intrigued Sammy tagged along.

'It's a workhouse,' said the Chaplain, 'where the poor come to work.'

'Warehouse,' said Sammy.

'Excuse me?' said the Chaplain.

'It says warehouse on the sign outside.'

'Tomato, tomahto,' said the Chaplain, annoyed by the interruption. He may have died before the immortal phrase was coined, but the Chaplain tried to keep abreast of things.

''ere,' said Sammy, 'that's my line.'

'I believe I first heard it from Laura's lips.'

'Potato, potahto,' said Sammy.

'He's fallen on hard times?' said Charles, no pun intended.

'His parents are in the debtors' prison,' said the Chaplain, fruit and vegetable talk over with for the moment.

'Poor lad,' said Charles.

'Precisely,' said the Chaplain. 'I'm glad you're starting to realise.'

A puzzled look. 'Realise what?' said Charles.

'What you are supposed to,' said the Chaplain. 'And now we move on. Come.'

And so they did. And did so, completely oblivious to the shout of dismay and clatter of things dropped, that followed as they left the way they had entered, through window and wall.

Chapter 21

'It's me,' said Marley.

'So it would appear,' said Laura.

'Can he see us?'

'No.'

'Happy little soul, aren't you,' said Richard.

'I was always happy as a child,' said Marley, watching his boy self, building a house from small bricks. A house that any crooked man, living down any crooked lane, would be proud of.

'The window's upside down,' noted Richard.

'I'm only four,' said Marley.

'But you're not happy now?' said Laura, sidestepping the whole building regulation issue.

'I didn't say that,' said Marley.

'I never said you did.'

'Not bad for a four year old I suppose,' said Richard.

'Tell my old man that,' said Marley, before he could stop himself.

Laura swopped a glance with Richard.

'Your old man?' said Laura.

'Forget I said anything.'

'Do you mean your dad?'

'Yeah, I mean my dad,' said Marley, not wishing to go there.

'Nothing was ever right for him, eh?' said Richard.

'I never said that either.'

'I don't believe that,' said Laura.

'I didn't,' said Marley, just short of snapping.

'I mean, nothing ever being right for him.'

'Think what you want.'

'But happy none the less?' said Richard.

'Yes,' said Marley.

The room began to blur around the edges.

'Looks like we're off again,' said Richard.

It was the same room. It was the same boy, but older. He was sat on the bed reading. The wallpaper had also changed.

'Nice wallpaper,' said Richard.

'Yeah,' said Marley, 'official Reading FC wallpaper. My old man put it up when they won the Champion's League.'

'A football fan were you?'

'I guess,' said Marley, not sounding at all convincing. 'Preferred my books to football to be truthful, but the old man was. Took me to all the home matches.'

'Doesn't sound as if you enjoyed it much,' said Laura.

'Oh I did, but not as much as my old man. I think he secretly harboured the hope that I might play for them one day.'

'You that good?' said Richard, eyebrows rising.

Marley actually smiled. 'Nah, two left feet. I remember when he took me down the local park for a kick about for the first time. I kept falling over, so that was that.'

'Did you feel you'd let him down?' said Laura.

'Not really,' said Marley. 'I don't think so, but maybe.'

'I don't see any books,' said Richard, who, out of curiosity, had scanned the room for a bookcase to see what the young Marley might read.

'They're under the bed.'

'Under the bed?' said Laura. 'Why?'

'After the football debacle, I had the silly notion that if the old man saw them, he'd be somehow disappointed.'

The young Marley on the bed flipped a page.

'What you reading?' said Laura.

Marley couldn't recall, so he went over to the bed to get a better look. Another smile appeared. 'Ah,' he said, 'I must be twelve.' He read the title out-loud. 'It's "Entrepreneurism for Young Dummies".'

'Phew,' said Richard. 'That's heavy stuff for a twelve year old.'

'Some people wanted to be astronauts, some a sportsman; I wanted to be a magnate.'

'Attractive thought,' said Richard, pleased with his little witticism.

Laura rolled her eyes. Marley just ignored the comment.

'But you're a happy twelve year old?' she said.

'Yeah,' said Marley, giving Laura a strange look, 'still happy.'

The room started to blur again.

Chapter 22

'At least he managed to go back to school,' said Charles, as they stepped into the latest future they were visiting of Dickens's life.

'And all the better he was for it,' said the Chaplain.

'Can I just say something?' said Sammy, as they strode along another London street.

'Of course Sammy, what is it?' said the Chaplain.

'He didn't have any ringlets, back there, in the school.'

'Who didn't?'

'Dickens.'

'There were curls, weren't there?' said the Chaplain.

'Not back there, there wasn't. And I'm sure he looked frightened when we came through the wall.'

'For the last time Sammy, no one can see us. And as for his curls or lack of, I dare say some school rule, short back and sides and such.'

'And I suppose the school rules had something to do with him looking totally different from when we saw him in the warehouse.'

The Chaplain stopped his striding. 'It was a workhouse Sammy, workhouse, and yes, he would look different. He was older in the school for one thing and, well, the workhouse wasn't one of the nicest places to be. He was bound to look a little different. They were dire places by all accounts. They left a mark.'

'But… '

But the Chaplain had heard enough and took up with his striding again, only stopping when he reached their destination. 'And here we have it Charles, the solicitors Dickens worked for before embarking on his career as a journalist.'

The three of them gathered round for more window peering.

'I can't see him,' said Charles, who could only see a couple of elderly gentlemen going about their business.

'Perhaps he's on holiday,' said Sammy.

'I hardly think so,' said the Chaplain, 'the very idea. No, I suspect he has had to run an errand.'

'So we're not going to see him?' said a disappointed Charles.

'It would seem not,' said the Chaplain, who was himself a tad disappointed. 'But suffice to say he was going up in the world. Work, work, work, was his ethic. Work, and work hard at it. You see Charles, keep on-'

'May I just interrupt you there?' said Sammy, swiftly doing just that.

Slightly more than mildly annoyed with Sammy's constant interruptions, the Chaplain turned from the window and looked at him. 'It would seem you didn't need my permission. What is it?'

Sammy stood on tiptoe and whispered something in the Chaplain's ear.

The Chaplain looked shocked. 'Did I?' he said, feeling fairly aghast that he may have just been about to divulge something he shouldn't have.'

'Nearly,' said Sammy.

'Well,' said the Chaplain, gathering his wits back about him, 'time to move on I think, nothing further to see here.' He mouthed a silent thank you to Sammy. Sometimes the little man had his uses. Not often, but…

They walked a few steps along the road and disappeared.

'Adversity,' said the Chaplain, as they stopped at another building of the grim persuasion. There seemed to be a lot of them about in London.

'Say again?' said Sammy.

'This is where Dickens started to really find himself,' said the Chaplain, turning a deaf ear to Sammy. 'How easy it would have been to give up along the way.'

'Ah-hem,' coughed Sammy.

A frown gave way to realisation. 'Ah yes,' said the Chaplain, looking a tad embarrassed, 'where was I?'

'Adversity,' said Charles, giving frowning a go.

'The newspaper where he worked,' said the Chaplain, pointing to the grim building.

'We going in?' said Sammy.

'Why not,' said the Chaplain.

They went in. They came straight back out again.

'Was that him?' said Charles.

'I think so,' said Sammy.

'It'll take him a little while to pick that lot up,' said Charles.

'I reckon I'd have dropped more than that if I'd just seen three ghosts walk in through the wall,' said Sammy.

'Charles is not a ghost,' said the Chaplain, correcting Sammy, 'and as I've said, on numerous occasions, we cannot be seen. It was just an unfortunate accident, and one we just happened to walk in on.'

'Must have been something else then, that made his hair stand up on end like it did,' said Sammy.

'Exactly,' said the Chaplain.

Charles said nothing.

They moved on.

Chapter 23

Marley and Charles had been under for almost ten minutes. Almost ten minutes of rapid eye movement and the odd jerk, but thankfully no thrashing about like something possessed, so far. This was a good thing, so all those sitting in Rosemary and Horace's lounge had decided.

'How much longer do you think?' said Horace, who had just looked at his watch for what seemed like the hundredth time. Rosemary was beginning to wonder if he had developed a nervous tic.

'They'll let us know when they're ready,' said Roberta, calmly sipping at her peppermint tea. She and Geoff had returned to the lounge as soon as Marley and Charles had been put under.

'I do hope they're all right,' said Rosemary, worrying that if anything did go wrong, it would be on her head. It had been her idea. She raised a glass of sherry to her lips. It was medicinal, to calm her nerves.

'They will,' said Roberta, sharing a knowing smile.

'I wish I had your optimism,' said Horace.

'Born with it,' said Roberta. 'But what can go wrong? The Chaplain knows his stuff.' Her smile broadened a little as she said that, 'and Sammy's there to watch out for him. Charles is in safe hands. And as for Richard and Laura, they have their ways, but I'm sure Marley will be safe too.'

Horace looked at Rosemary. Rosemary returned his look with a weak smile. She took another sip from her sherry.

Chapter 24

Rooms came, and rooms went. A young child's bedroom, full of innocence. A teenager's bedroom, full of hope and angst. A college classroom, filled with learning. These and many more appeared and then faded back to memory. In all, Marley was happy.

The surroundings changed again, another room appeared, filled with books. A bookshop; the bookshop Marley owned. A smiling Marley was serving a customer. The bought books were bagged. The customer left.

Alone, Marley looked at his watch and sighed. It was closing time; past closing time by a couple of seconds. Another day had passed, another dollar had found its way into the till. Marley went to the shop door and turned the welcome sign from open to closed, he then locked the door.

'Charles!' shouted Marley.

A muffled reply came from the stockroom. Marley headed for it, totally oblivious to the fact he was being watched.

'It's two months ago,' said the visiting Marley. The information gleaned from the calendar on the counter.

'It is,' said Laura. 'Come on.'

'Still happy by the looks of it,' said Richard, falling in beside Laura as she headed after the past Marley.

Marley scowled at him, this constant reference to his state of mind was beginning to wear thin. But he kept quiet, he had the feeling there was a point to it, a point he suspected he was getting closer to discovering.

Charles, the past Charles of two months ago, was stock taking, or at least that was what he was supposed to be doing.

'I hope you're at that computer for the right reasons,' said Marley, as he stuck his head round the stockroom door.

'No... I mean yes,' said Charles jumping up and so giving himself away. Why had he carried on? He had heard his dad coming. But he knew why, he was mesmerised by the written word, his written word. Just one more second, he had told himself, just one and he would finish what he was writing. And he had taken that one more second, and he had finished what he was writing; another short story. Even though he knew it wasn't any good, he'd had to finish it. He could dream couldn't he? He turned the computer off.

'I've shut up shop,' said Marley, shaking his head. 'You can finish the stock take tomorrow.'

Charles stood up, closed the computer and went to pick it up.

'And you can leave that,' said Marley. 'Enough daydreaming for one day, I think.'

Unhappy, but knowing it was a punishment he could have avoided by doing what he was supposed to have been doing, also because he was stupid enough to be caught, Charles reluctantly obeyed. 'I'll get my stuff.'

'Good lad,' said Marley. He hesitated a moment. 'Tell you what, how about a cup of coffee before we go?'

In no position to argue, but thinking the suggestion odd, Charles nodded and did as he was told. But he was back in a moment. 'We've no milk,' he said. Something Marley already knew.

Somewhere close, a silent invisible observer, cringed inwardly, he knew what was coming.

The corner shop's still open,' said Marley.

'But Dad... ' But it was no good. Charles sighed and went to get his coat.

Marley waited until he heard the door close behind Charles, then opened the computer, it didn't take him long to find what he was looking for.

'Shouldn't we be going or something?' said Marley, as he watched himself at the computer.

'What's your hurry?' said Richard.

'I just thought, you know, we've been here long enough.'

'We'll know when that is, when we're no longer here,' said Laura.

Marley bit on his lip. He wasn't so happy now.

Marley scrolled through Charles's latest offering, a short story which he must have finished as Marley had walked through the stockroom door, and read it. Sadly, it was very good. This might be a problem. But he wasn't an expert, so how good was it really? Then an idea came to him. While having his cuppa that morning, he had seen something in one of those magazines Charles always left lying about. Should he? He shouldn't. Why not? At least he would know for sure. Checking to make sure Charles was nowhere to be seen, he opened the computers Wi-Fi link to the shop printer and started to print the story.

By the time Charles returned, Marley had printed the story, turned the computer off and was waiting in his coat. His plan was in motion. He was going to enter Charles's story into a competition he had seen in that magazine he'd looked at earlier. If nothing happened and the story failed to hit any heights, the plan was to confront Charles with the news, tell him he had entered it as a surprise, but sorry, never mind. End of story; and in so many ways. It's time to move on. I just happen to know of an opening for a shop manager. But if the story was good, good enough to win even, well, what the heart doesn't know.

'Dad?' said a puzzled Charles, as he returned with the milk.

'Changed my mind,' said Marley.

Laura and Richard had watched all this happen in silence. Marley, for his part, had had the good grace to look increasingly embarrassed.

Chapter 25

'Well, that was impressive,' said Sammy, returning from another Dickens scenario.

'You can say that again,' said an equally impressed Charles.

'Yes indeed,' said the Chaplain, puffing out his chest. 'Our Mister Dickens has to be one of the youngest newspaper editors ever.

'I meant the way he somersaulted from the room like that,' said Sammy.

'And that,' said Charles.

'A very athletic young man indeed,' agreed the Chaplain, who hadn't been fazed one iota by Dickens's antics. Young men liked to show off. Why exactly like that though was a bit of a mystery, and just as they had arrived too, but boys will be boys.

'Very young,' said Sammy, who couldn't help thinking the cartwheeling Dickens looked younger than the last time they had seen him; more teen than twenties. And the curls were back. But, he had been holding a pen, so who else could it have been but an editor? So, faced with this compelling piece of evidence, Sammy decided to refrain from mentioning his doubts to the Chaplain and instead decided some nonchalant whistling was in order.

And while Sammy whistled, the world around them changed once more.

'Where are we now?' asked Charles, taking in his new surroundings.

'The publishers,' said the Chaplain. 'It's eighteen forty-three, and Charles Dickens is about to enter, with his first ever Christmas story.'

'Not… '

'Yes Charles. A Christmas Carol.'

'Wow,' said Charles.

'Blimey,' said Sammy.

The door to the establishment opened, a young man in his early thirties entered.

All held their breaths, some because they could again.

'Ah,' said a man's voice, 'Mister Dickens, please come in.'

'It is him,' said an astounded Charles.

'Yes,' said the Chaplain proudly.

'You sure?' said Sammy.

The Chaplain rounded on Sammy. 'Of course I am,' he said. 'Didn't you hear that man welcome him?'

Sammy had, but that didn't prove anything to his mind. There was something wrong with the picture he was seeing. 'But he hasn't got a beard,'

Sammy protested. Which was a fair point really, most people only knew Dickens as a bearded fellow.

The Chaplain let out one of his infamous sighs. 'He wasn't born with one you know.'

'Oh,' said Sammy, who although still doubtful, could see the Chaplain's point. Especially as now he came to think about it, none of the Dickens he had seen so far had sported one. 'Fair enough I suppose.'

'Good,' said the Chaplain.

They stood and watched as Mister Dickens was propelled towards an office door, and then disappear behind it.

'And that is that,' said the Chaplain, wistfully. He looked at Charles. 'We must what we must.'

Charles frowned.

Sammy shrugged.

'Time to go,' said the Chaplain, as the publisher's waiting room started to melt from existence around them.

But not before someone else entered the publishing house, a young man, spouting a mass of curls, and carrying a sheaf of paper. He headed for the reception desk, but suddenly stopped dead, staring in the direction of Charles, Sammy and the Chaplain.

'Here,' said Sammy, 'isn't that… '

But before Sammy had the chance to utter another word, the scene and the man, along with his curls, ceased to exist.

Chapter 26

'Post!' said Richard, as the bookshop's letterbox opened admitting a small avalanche of letters and circulars.

Six weeks had passed according to the calendar sat on the counter, as another past Marley rounded it to retrieve the mailman's offering.

'Anything interesting?' enquired Laura, who had an idea, the way things were going, that she might just know what to expect.

'How should I know?' said Marley, as he watched himself pick the mail up. He was still smarting from being observed stealing his son's story.

'Maybe because you're looking a little shifty over there as you're going through the post. Maybe because you're in work an hour earlier than you usually are. Maybe because you're expecting something you don't want anyone else knowing about.' Richard was on a roll. 'Maybe-'

'You finished?' said Marley.

'Maybe,' said Richard.

'How am I supposed to remember what came in the post two weeks ago?' But Marley did know, and he had the horrible feeling he wasn't alone in that.

Richard scratched his head. 'That's a lot of mail for this day and age isn't it? I thought snail mail had had its day?'

'Because I like it, it's more real somehow,' said Marley.

Richard nodded, it looked like they had at least one thing in common, not that he got much in the way of mail where he lived; none in fact.

The past Marley, having gathered the mail, strode back to the counter, sifting as he went. He stopped suddenly. A letter sifted from the others in his hand. He was staring at it. He then placed the rest of the mail on the counter and headed for the stockroom.

'It's the reply, isn't it?' said Laura.

Marley lost some colour. 'Like I said, how-'

'Oh come on,' said Richard, 'you know it is.'

'What reply?' Marley suddenly felt as if the walls were closing in on him. They knew.

'Let's go see, shall we?' said Laura. She headed for the stockroom.

In the stockroom, the past Marley had already opened the letter. His hands appeared to be shaking. The present Marley licked his lips nervously. The past Marley paled, just as the present Marley had.

'The story won, didn't it?' said Laura.

The present Marley's face now proceeded to do the opposite to what it had done earlier, and crimsoned nicely. 'You know it did,' he snapped, feeling he had been played somehow.

'Not really, not until you just said,' said Laura.

'But how did you know what I'd done? You can't read my mind. Can you?'

'Let's just say we had inside information,' said Richard.

'How happy are you now?' said Laura.

Marley wasn't happy at all.

Chapter 27

'It won't be long now,' said Roberta, placing her empty cup on the coffee table. 'That peppermint tea was lovely Rosemary. Thank you.'

'He doesn't look too good,' said Horace, looking at Marley. 'He's going a funny colour.'

'He looks angry,' said Rosemary.

'Perhaps some home truths are being learnt?' said Roberta. She spoke to Geoff. 'Anything?' she asked.

'Nothing yet,' said Geoff, fluttering his leaves.

'It's nearly quarter of an hour now,' said Horace, consulting his watch yet again.

'It will be done when it is done,' said Roberta. She smiled. 'I don't suppose I could have another cup of that delicious peppermint tea, could I Rosemary?'

Although Rosemary was as worried as Horace was, she managed a smile. 'Of course you can.' She collected Roberta's cup. 'Anybody else want anything while I'm up?'

Chapter 28

Charles peered into the fog-like surroundings; London smog? It had to be London smog they were in? But where and when in London were they? He broached the subject. 'Where are we this time?' he asked.

'In your head,' said the Chaplain.

'My head?' said Charles, not sure he liked the idea of the inside of his head being so pea soup like.

'It's where we started from,' said Sammy, when no further explanation looked to be coming from the direction of the Chaplain. The blankest of looks from Charles prompted more. 'You know, before we started our journey, the place between consciousness and unconsciousness. Except it's foggy because you're a little groggy.'

'Foggy groggy,' said the Chaplain.

'You okay old pal?' said Sammy.

'Just sad that it's all over,' said the Chaplain, wistfully. Charles Dickens was the Chaplain's hero.

'It's over?' said Charles, sounding disappointed.

The wistful look fell from the Chaplain's face. 'That is up to you my boy,' he said cryptically.

'Me?' said Charles. 'In that case I want to see more of Dickens.'

'That's not what I meant,' said the Chaplain.

'Not what he meant,' echoed Sammy.

'I don't understand,' said Charles. He looked confused.

'We took you on a journey so that you could learn,' said the Chaplain. 'The story with Dickens has finished. It now continues with you.'

'Continues with you,' echoed Sammy.

'Will you stop that,' said the Chaplain, glowering at Sammy.

'Sorry.'

'Learn what?' said Charles.

'We can't tell you that,' said the Chaplain, all serious. 'That's for you to work out. It was all there, laid out before you.'

Charles looked even more confused. 'I still don't understand.'

'Then think on what you've seen,' said the Chaplain, 'because our job here is done.'

'Yes,' said Sammy, 'think on it.' Something he himself was doing right that very minute, especially the bits with the screams, staring eyes and cartwheels. Something hadn't been quite right there, he was sure of it. Sammy decided he was going to have a quiet word with Roberta when he got back. 'Think hard,' he added, feeling the lad would have to.

Charles shook his head, the one he was wearing on his shoulders not the one he was in. He didn't get it. What did they mean? Had he learnt anything? He thought hard. And as he did, his eyes began to flicker. Not the ones he had in the head he was wearing on his shoulders, the ones in the one he was in. The fog began to lift. He was back in the darkness and it was giving way to light.

Chapter 29

They were now in Marley's head, a thick fog as surrounded Charles, surrounding him. Marley was quiet. He was a man deep in thought. Unlike Charles, he was all too aware of the purpose behind all he had just been through. As promised, and to Richard's surprise, Marley had been taken to the future. It had been a short, sharp and to the point journey. And that point had pricked Marley's conscience.

'He doesn't look too good, does he?' said Richard, watching Marley trying to come to terms with himself.

'Would you?' said Laura.

'I don't know,' said Richard, 'I don't know what it's like to be him.'

'You know what I mean.'

'He's had a shock, that's all,' said Richard.

'A big one though,' said Laura, 'but I suppose better now than later.'

'But would he have known later? You know, be able to see it, been conscience of what he had done, if we hadn't have taken him on the journey?'

It was Laura's turn not to know. 'It's lucky he has a friend like Rosemary,' she said.

'Relative so many times removed, you mean,' said Richard.

Laura smiled. 'Many times removed relative-in-law you mean,' she said.

'Hold up, he's coming over.'

Marley came over to them, his eyes slightly glazed. 'What now?' he asked.

'We go back.'

'I won't know what to say.'

'Can't help you with that one,' said Richard.

'Say what you have to,' said Laura, a tad more helpfully.

Marley looked Laura in the eye, the first time he had made eye contact since they had arrived back. 'I didn't like what I saw.'

'Neither did-oof,' said Richard.

'It can be changed,' said Laura, while smiling sweetly at Richard. 'You've been given the chance to change your future.'

'What if it's too late to change it?'

'I suspect that ball is in your court,' said Laura.

'You think?'

'I do.'

Marley straightened. 'Then I'm ready to go.'

'Good man,' said Richard, giving Marley a hearty slap on the back. Perhaps a little too exuberantly than was called for, but all through their adventure with Marley, he had had half an eye on what he thought of as the prize, the surprise Roberta had mentioned. A Christmas present perhaps? He rubbed his hands together. But what; the usual suspects, socks and aftershave weren't a lot of good when you were on the other side. Unless... He brightened. A new change of clothes, he was always going on about it; moaning about it. It was amazing how draughty the afterlife could be, especially for those wearing shorts. It would make the perfect present. It would be the perfect surprise.

The fog had lifted. The dark was giving way to the light.

Chapter 30

Rosemary had just entered the kitchen when Roberta called her back. Geoff had been contacted. It was time to wake Charles and Marley from their trance.

Horace clicked his fingers then clapped his hands. He wanted to be sure they snapped out of it. He then sat back and waited. Roberta made herself scarce.

Eyelids began to flicker. A bark was heard from the kitchen, followed closely by a chirp. Geoff wiggled his leaves with delight. Roberta's mind became host to others again.

Charles was the first to wake properly. Rosemary, glass of water at the ready just in case, offered it to him. Travel could be a thirsty business. He took it and sipped at it. 'Thank you,' he said, wiping a dribble from his chin.

'How are you feeling?' asked Rosemary.

'A little dizzy if I'm honest,' he said, 'but okay I think.' He then remembered his dad. He turned to look for him. 'Dad?'

'He's coming round,' said Rosemary, another glass of water at the ready.

Marley fluttered his eyelids. They opened. He looked a little disorientated.

'Marley?' said Rosemary, showing concern.

'Where am I?' Marley had never been a good traveller.

'In the lounge,' said Horace.

'Lounge?'

'At our house. Do you remember? You're here for Christmas dinner,' said Horace. And as an afterthought added: 'I hypnotised you.'

And then, as if a gate had been opened, it all came flooding back to him. Where he was, why he was there, where he had been and, weighing on him like a weight, the guilt. Marley looked at Charles. His mouth was dry. He took the glass Rosemary was offering, took a couple of sips, and handed it back. 'Could we have a couple of minutes alone?' he said.

After gathering Geoff up from the coffee table, Rosemary joined Horace and headed for the kitchen. They were greeted by a tail wagging Jack Russell, a feather fluffing Robin, and Roberta.

'Everything okay?' whispered Roberta.

'They want a moment to chat,' said Rosemary, placing Geoff on the table.

Roberta nodded, but she suspected they would need more than a moment to sort things out, going on what she had been told by the others. But she could wait. 'How about another cup of that delicious peppermint tea while we wait?' she said.

'Of course,' said Rosemary, more than happy to have something to take her mind off of the goings on taking place behind closed doors. 'Anyone else for anything else?' she said.

All needs in the kitchen catered for, they settled down to wait.

Chapter 31

The future Marley had been shown was a bleak unhappy time. Charles would gradually over time retreat into himself, any purpose he had for his own life draining from him. Marley, his guilt festering, would watch his boy change, become an empty shell until he was no more than an unthinking robot, helping steer a sinking ship onto the rocks. A robot of Marley's making. Marley's dream would also flounder on the rocks, his guilt, bringing about its demise as he self-destructed. He had been shown an empty shop, an empty son, a ruined dream and ruined lives. All brought about because of his selfish single-mindedness.

It was explained to Marley that what he had seen was just one of many futures that may be waiting for him. Things changed from day to day, hour to hour, minute to minute, but did he want to take the chance that this wasn't the future he and Charles were heading for? Marley decided he didn't.

It had been hard for Marley, telling Charles what he had done and why. But he had and it was now in the past. Charles had been disappointed, but not to the point of anger. He had understood, in part, why his father had done what he had done. Everyone, at some time, had a dream and some people would do anything in their power to see that that dream happened. There was nothing wrong with that, but not at the expense of others. His father had had a dream, but he had wanted that dream for Charles as well, whether he wanted to be a part of it or not. He had been wrong, but now he was trying to put it right. It would be wrong of Charles to stand in his way.

'I've got it here,' said Marley, taking an envelope from his inside jacket pocket. He had thought it the safest place to keep it as he never wore his suit; unless he was visiting the bank manager. Fate had obviously been at work. He handed the envelope to Charles.

Charles took it and removed the letter. He read it, his eyes widening with astonishment as he did. 'It really won,' he said, when he finished.

'The best they've ever seen,' said Marley, feeling a little strange. It then dawned on him why he was feeling the way he was. It was pride. He started to smile.

Charles reread the line again. 'It does, doesn't it?' he said, also breaking into a smile.

But Marley's smile faded at the sight of Charles's. 'I'm sorry,' he said. 'I've been utterly selfish. I shouldn't have done it.'

Charles's smile widened. 'But if you hadn't I wouldn't have won. And besides, it's only a small competition, hardly the Nobel Prize for literature. The shop is much more important.'

Marley laughed. 'Yeah,' he said, 'if you like having a millstone round your neck.'

'But you love your shop,' said a surprised Charles. 'You want more.'

'True,' said Marley, 'but it was taking me over. I can see that now. I couldn't before, couldn't see any further than my own nose. My dream had always been to own a shop. I somehow forgot that. An empire indeed, what was I thinking? And at my age. Running one shop is more than enough.' Marley shook his head. 'If only your dear mother was alive. She would have put me right.'

But sadly, she wasn't. Charles nodded and reflected a little. 'So what now?' he said, after a moment.

Marley placed his jacket on the back of a chair. 'I think I should stop trying to bite off more than I can chew.'

'What about me?' said Charles.

'I'll still need an assistant manager.'

'I thought that's what I was.'

'Where did you get that idea?' said Marley, smiling. 'Your contract says general dogsbody. I'm promoting you.'

'Does that mean I get more cash?'

'Don't push it. But there is something you'll get more of from now on.'

Charles frowned. 'What's that?'

'Time.'

'Time?'

'To write. It's what you're good at isn't it? Besides, if you do write that bestseller, who knows, I might get that second shop after all.'

'Don't push it.'

Chapter 32

The knock on the kitchen door drew a "what should I do" glance from Rosemary that fell on Roberta.

'I think they are up to meeting your other visitors,' said Roberta.

'Are you sure?'

Roberta nodded, but pulled her shawl closer about her.

'Rosemary?' said Marley.

Rosemary opened the door. Marley stood there, wringing his hands.

'Rosemary, I… that is Charles and I would like to… ' His voice trailed off as he noticed Rosemary and Horace had other guests. 'Sorry, I didn't know you had other… is that a robin on the table?'

'Take a bow Sammy,' said Roberta.

Sammy did a sort of curtsey. It was a wing thing.

'Tell you what,' said Rosemary, 'how about we move back into the lounge and make introductions? Mince pies anyone?'

The lounge was fairly crowded once all had piled in. Charles and Marley were sat on the sofa, sort of staring. Rosemary was in her favourite chair. Horace was in his. Roberta on a good stiff backed chair, something she preferred, from the kitchen. Geoff on the coffee table, with Sammy perched on the edge of Geoff's pot. And last, but not least, the Chaplain was sat on the carpet, in front of Charles and Marley, staring back at them. Richard and Laura were of course, still in Roberta's head.

'Why is your dog staring at us like that?' said a slightly unnerved Charles, aiming the question at Roberta. The Chaplain hadn't blinked since everyone had sat down.

'He's eager to know if you've learned any valuable lessons lately,' said Roberta, removing her shawl and placing it on the back of her chair. Charles and Marley's jaws dropped. They had never seen so much hair on a woman, and all over too.

'Ah,' said Rosemary, 'this is Roberta, she's an old friend.'

'Yes,' said Roberta, 'a *very old* friend.' She smiled. And as she did, something on a level way above their understanding passed between her, Marley and Charles. Their jaws closed and all was well with the world again.

'Pleased to meet you,' said Marley, standing and offering his hand.

'Please,' said Roberta, waving a hand, 'no formalities here.'

Marley smiled, nodded and sat back down again.

The Chaplain ceased his non-blinking and woofed.

'And this is the Chaplain,' said Rosemary.

'The Chaplain?' said Charles, goggle-eyed. 'But he's a dog.'

'Give the man a coconut,' said Richard, from somewhere in the confines of Roberta's mind.

'You're so mean,' said Laura, somewhere near him.

The introductions continued as Sammy chirped. 'And this is Sammy,' said Rosemary.

At this point Horace interrupted the introductions. He thought it wise, before Charles's eyes fell from their sockets. 'I think, before we go any further, my sweet, explanations might be a good idea?'

Rosemary, who was always the consummate host, blushed. 'Of course,' she said, 'what was I thinking?'

And so the explanations began. Which wasn't to say it was easy, because it wasn't, unworldly things never were. Thankfully though Horace had a head start, or rather Marley and Charles had. So the concept of having voices in their heads, along with their owner's, saved a little time. The rest took a little longer to explain.

The fact that Richard, Laura, Sammy, Geoff, and the Chaplain, "lived" in limbo, ready to help the living when called upon was fairly straight forward, if you can describe such goings on as straight forward. The fact that they could come back in the bodies of recently passed on animals wasn't so straight forward. Charles for one couldn't quite get his head around the patting of a Jack Russell that was in reality a First World War Chaplain. And a late lamented one at that. Or the fact that the spider plant was possessed by an elf called Geoff. Yes, not a real elf, but… and as for Roberta, the hairy lady, their guardian; how old? But as was said, Marley and Charles had had a head start where the strange was concerned, and so managed, with just the odd stumble, to take it all in their stride.

So the evening gradually wore on, the explanations ended, all became a little more comfortable with things, more so when the drink began to flow, and then, just before the witching hour was upon them, Roberta brought the proceedings to a halt. To Roberta's mind, all had been successful. All that had needed to be learnt had been. Charles, even though he didn't fully appreciate just yet what it was he had learned, that hard work, belief in one's self and persistence was needed when all was against you, was already showing a new found confidence in himself. And Marley, contrite but better for it after his lesson was already proving to be a better man. So her work and that of the others was done here.

'Time for us to leave,' said Roberta, standing and reclaiming her shawl. 'I believe our work is done here.' She winked at Rosemary.

'So soon?' said Rosemary, returning the wink.

'Yeah,' said Richard, who still hadn't tasted one of those delicious looking mince pies yet, 'so soon?'

'The Eve is nearly at its end,' said Roberta, 'and tomorrow is a glorious day waiting to happen.'

'Er... what?' said Richard.

'Sssch,' said Laura.

'But I only want to taste one measly pie,' groaned Richard, who could only be heard by Laura and Roberta, who was busy ignoring him. 'And there's the surprise. What about that?'

Everyone else now stood. 'If you must,' said Rosemary.

'We must,' said Roberta, holding out a gloved hand to Horace, who had offered his. She shook it, and then Charles's and Marley's who had also offered theirs.

Dogs were patted; much to the annoyance of the Chaplain. A robin hopped from one hand to another curtsying, indignity to Sammy, just a word to be ignored. Leaves were trembled. Goodbyes were said.

And then they were back in the orb. All that belonged there that is. Those that weren't were now safely tucked up in their beds, dreaming their dreams, snoring their snores. Those that were, were not.

'But it's not fair,' moaned Richard, all but stamping his feet, as soon as Roberta had left.

'What isn't?' said Laura.

'We didn't get the surprise she promised us.' He really had been looking forward to those long trousers he'd imagined he was going to have.

'She didn't actually say when exactly we were to have it,' said the Chaplain, who if he had to admit it, now he thought about it, was a tad disappointed himself. 'Though traditionally, tomorrow is the day for surprises.'

'That's true,' said Sammy.

'But you can never tell with Roberta,' said Geoff, sagely.

'That's also true,' said Sammy, more than happy to go with the flow as usual.

Richard's shoulders sagged. 'I couldn't even have a mince pie.'

'We can't always have what we want,' said the Chaplain.

'True,' said Sammy. Who then ducked for cover behind the Chaplain when Richard scowled at him.

'Tomorrow's another day,' said Geoff, absently.

And you know what, he was right.

Chapter 33

It was tomorrow, although, to be correct, it was technically today. Anyway, it was another day. But not just any old another day, it was Christmas Day.

The orb began to dim.

'Oh come on!' said Richard. 'It's Christmas.' He had been the epitome of humbug since arriving back yesterday.

'Charity,' said the Chaplain. 'Someone must need our help Richard. Our work doesn't stop just because it's Christmas Day.'

'It's Christmas!!' shouted Geoff.'

'Humbug,' said Richard, really going for it now.

'Cheer up,' smiled Laura. 'Perhaps it's Roberta bearing gifts? Or that surprise?'

'Humbug,' repeated Richard.

'Do you think?' said Geoff, referring to Laura's reference to gift bearing.

'Think what?' said Roberta, who had entered the orb unnoticed.

Geoff blushed. 'I... er... Laura... '

'That you might have our surprise,' said Laura, coming to Geoff's rescue.

Roberta's expression was stony. 'Do you think you deserve a surprise after the way some of you have been acting?'

All eyes turned to Richard.

'What?' said Richard, clearly hurt by the silent accusation, even though it was true.

'Well,' said Roberta, 'I for one... ' She left her words hanging in the air for a moment before continuing. '... think you do.'

'You do?' said Geoff, colour returning to normal.

'Yes,' said Roberta, 'even though it appears some of you haven't the faith you were born with.'

'Don't you mean sense?' said Richard, before he could stop himself.

'That too,' said Roberta, looking pointedly at Richard.

'Oh,' said Richard.

'Now,' said Roberta, 'if you've quite finished trying to sabotage your own good fortune Richard, perhaps you would all like to come with me?'

'It's a bit crowded in here,' said Sammy.

'I didn't think it was possible for anybody to hold so many at the same time?' said Laura.

'But I'm not just anybody,' said Roberta, reminding them that she could hear everything they were saying.

'Where are we going?' said Geoff, who now and again couldn't contain himself.

'He's wiggling again,' moaned Richard, who hadn't quite thrown off the shackles of humbug.

'Won't be long now,' said Roberta.

And it wasn't long. Only seconds to be precise. The very next second to be perfectly correct. They had arrived and Roberta was now stood in front of a familiar looking door. And in her head excitement began to build.

'Isn't that… '

'It is it's… '

'You're right you know.'

A moment later the door opened and a very Christmassy looking Rosemary, decked in tinsel, paper crown and Christmas tree earrings appeared, and smiling the already been at the sherry smile, greeted them. 'Merry Christmas!' said Rosemary, with enthusiasm. 'Come in, come in.'

It was the surprise Roberta had promised them. And what a surprise it was. Unbeknown to all in the orb, Roberta had had a secret word with Rosemary about arranging dinner; Christmas dinner! But even better than that, because Marley and Charles had agreed to be hypnotised one more time, it meant there were more people to go round, which meant they wouldn't have to eat in shifts, and so could now enjoy the festivities all at the same time. Like a proper family.

The Chaplain joined Marley. Sammy linked with Charles. Laura went to Rosemary. Geoff with Horace; Rosemary had to be trusted with that piece of hypnotism. And lastly, Richard stayed with Roberta.

'Have fun,' whispered Laura to Richard as she prepared to leave.

'I will,' said Richard, who had this horrible feeling deep down inside his stomach that perhaps he shouldn't have been such a grouch and that he wouldn't be tasting anything remotely as nice as a mince pie, anytime soon.

'He will,' said Roberta.

'Oops,' said Laura, as she left.

But, season of goodwill or no, Roberta always had it in abundance. So when Rosemary appeared in the dining room, carrying the turkey a certain Dickens character would have been proud to give to his long suffering employee, Roberta let out her belt and bellowed: 'A bit of everything for me please!'

And all were merry.

And all were joyful.

And as Richard observed: 'Bless us, everyone!' Or he would have done, if he hadn't been concentrating on that next mince pie so hard.

And now, in case you were wondering, an aside regarding the Chaplain's Dickens odyssey.

Sammy had something on his mind. Something put there during his Dickens odyssey with Charles and the Chaplain. So when the festivities subsided he took the opportunity, through Charles, who he had confided in and had found shared his concerns, to broach the subject with Roberta. If anyone knew anything, she would.

'Roberta?' said Charles, 'might I and Sammy have a private word with you?'

Roberta, who was always on the ball, and who had more than likely made the thing, suspected she knew what it was on their minds. 'Of course,' she said, and led them to the kitchen.

Inside, Sammy and Charles went to air their suspicions.

'Wait,' said Roberta.

'Oi,' said Richard, who had suddenly gone deaf.

'Okay,' said Roberta. 'But before you continue, is this about your trip with the Chaplain?'

'Yes,' said Sammy and Charles as one.

'Then the answer is no,' said Roberta.

'No?' said Sammy and Charles.

'No,' said Roberta. 'The Chaplain was, I'm afraid, misguided, and on more than a couple of occasions, as to the identity of Dickens in his venture. Apart from right at the end that is. That was Dickens in the publishers.'

Sammy and Charles shared a smile.

'But we won't tell him,' said Roberta. 'It will be our little secret. Goodwill to all mankind and all that.'

It was agreed, but Sammy and Charles had one other question they wanted answering.

'The man you caught a glimpse of at the publishers?' said Roberta. 'Yes, he was one of the Chaplain's cases of mistaken identity. But no, he didn't get his novel published I'm afraid. Two ghost stories in one day, was one too many for the publisher, even if he did claim it to be a true story, seen with his own eyes from the very day he was born.'

And so the story ends.

Bless us, everyone!

(As Richard, might well have said.)

Introducing
(with some trepidation)
characters from the forthcoming book

DANRITE WILLOCKY
(But not Danrite himself)
in

PRINCE BOTTOM OF
DOES
CHRISTMAS

Chapter 1

The embers from the dying fire still had enough strength to cast shadows across the room. Not deep dark creepy shadows you understand, the ones you see in movies where something waits in the shadow's depths waiting for its victim to turn away so that it can pounce, but warm shadows, the sort that greet you with a welcoming homeliness as you step into the room. A shadowy hug if you like. Ah, lovely.

But let's not get complacent here. For all that warmth and homeliness, there was something wrong, something amiss with the scene. Something that for some people would cause the skin on their scalp to tighten, the hairs on the nape of their neck to stand on end, their goose pimples to have goose pimples of their own.

Above the fire, where the embers that cast the friendly shadows lay, on the mantelpiece, two Christmas stockings hung, each with a name embroidered on their side. The one on the left had Millie on it in big red letters. The one on the right had Millie on it, also in big red letters. Weird. But perhaps the owner of the socks had wanted a bigger one, but couldn't find one? Whatever.

You see, it isn't what is written on the outside that should concern us, as strange as that might be, rather our concern is with what is inside the socks. Inside the socks lay the reason why scalps have tightened, hairs have stood on end, goose pimples multiplied. Each sock was bulging. Each sock had in its depths the same things, presents; if you could call them that. And not only these socks. Every sock that had been left out for Santa to fill had the same bulges, the same presents. No difference, no deviations, whether girl or boy, the same had been left, for each, right across the world.

No books. No dolls. No building bricks. No weapons of mass destruction (you'd be amazed what kids asked for these days). No bicycles. No i-this, i-that, or i-other. No electronic wizardry of any kind. Nothing but… are you ready for this? Is your hat pulled tight over your head? Have you pulled your scarf tight around your neck? Have you done whatever it is you do with goose pimples? Calamine lotion? Nothing but… small fishing rods! Small gardening implements! And small wheelbarrows! Yea gads! ("Yea gads" is just an expression, not a gift.)

No Christmas wish had been granted. Every child who owned a sock was going to be disappointed (unless they actually wanted what had been left). Then whoopee-do, get those wellies on!

It was the early hours of Christmas morning.

'Yea gads,' whispered a female voice, quiet so as not to wake the Millie or Millies, or whatever.

''as the mince pie gone?' enquired another whispering voice, a voice with all the characteristics of a cartoon Mexican.

'No.'

'Phew,' said the comical Mexican voice. 'That is good.'

'Nor is the sherry,' said a third whispering voice, with just a touch of the Transylvanian about it.

'Do you think the mince pie will be missed?' asked the Mexican voice.

'No you don't.' There followed the muffled sound of fingers softly slapping a snout.

'Ay caramba! It is only a little food I am asking for,' whined the Mexican voice. Its owner then fell quiet and wandered away.

'What do we do?' said the third voice.

'Nothing we can do, not for the moment anyway,' said the female voice. The female voice lowered into an even quieter whisper. 'Not if what I think has happened, has.'

'Not… '

'Yes.'

'No.'

'Ay caramba.'

'Afraid so Jose,' said the female voice, putting a name to the comical Mexican one.

But it was not out of anguish for what might or might not have happened that had caused Jose to utter. It was because of the pine needle that was sticking in his paw, the one he had used to steady himself, when leaning against the Christmas tree.

Chapter 2

It was world news. The media was in uproar. What had happened to Santa? What could it all mean? Was it some sort of message? From above? From below? In between? The Government? The bankers? The little boy who lives down the lane? No one knew. No one had any idea.

Well, not exactly. Someone had an idea. Only they didn't exist in the all-consuming, consumer world that the media, the governments, the bankers, or the little boy down the lane, lived in. Tell a lie, the little boy who lived down the lane didn't exist there either, or rather he did, but not as the media etcetera did. Anyway, suffice to say, he also knew nothing! So he said.

There is a world you see that runs parallel with the real world, as mankind likes to call it, where this someone with an idea lives. A world that has always been there, where myth, magic and make-believe eke out a living; a world given life and brought into being by the minds of man and woman. Where the little boy down the lane lives; in the minds of man and woman, and also in the world of make-believe. He makes a jolly good living too, selling sweaters and such, from the wool he keeps being given. But I digress. Someone had an idea.

'And the mince pie wasn't touched?' said an elderly man wearing a pointy hat, with stars and moons and other things astrological on it. He was your typical wizard sort. He was also the typical sort that lived in the world of myth, magic, and make-believe. Most called him Salor. To others he was known by different names, all of which were not said to his face. And it wasn't because his make-up was so bad. It was because he might just turn you into a toad or something equally damp. But he was slowly losing his magic.

'Nor the sherry,' said a voice with a Transylvanian twang. A voice you would have recognised, had you been at Millie's house earlier that morning. His name was Vlad. He was a vampire. A friendly one; if such a one exists? Which it did, because he was. He also had a problem; he could only be seen in mirrors.

'The mind boggles,' declared Salor.

'And Jose peed on the Christmas tree,' said a female voice, also from early this morning at Millie's. Her name was Twinkle, a fairy; a huge fairy. She was the size of a sumo wrestler; a huge sumo wrestler. She also had fairy dust, and if you were lucky, she would sprinkle some on you. But if you were lucky enough to have fairy dust sprinkled on you, it also meant, usually, that you were also unlucky, as Twinkle's fairy dust mainly fell when she was sorting someone out. The rage of a fairy should not be taken lightly; avoid. The rage of a fairy the size of a sumo wrestler, a huge sumo wrestler, should not be taken lightly; avoid with knobs on.

'Jose!' said an appalled Salor. 'Bad boy.' Salor wagged a finger at him.

Jose's tail fell between his back legs. He was a Chihuahua, a talking were-Chihuahua, who changed into a man, every full moon. It hadn't always been like that. But he was cute, in a Chihuahua sort of way, those big brown eyes, fluffy ears, funny little tail, razor sharp teeth. 'But I only do it in emergency,' he said in his defence, in his cartoon Mexican voice. 'The mince pie, it is still there.'

Salor's brow furrowed, but he decided to say no more on the matter. There were bigger dogs to fry. Not that he fried dogs. He loved dogs. He had always wanted a dog. He was going to call it Fido if he'd had one, but what with the rashes... 'So,' said Salor, turning his furrow and brow away from Jose, 'what do we know? Other than Santa's victuals weren't touched and Jose's misdemeanour.'

Vlad and Twinkle exchanged a nervous look. Neither of them wanted to give voice to what they were thinking, it was too horrible to contemplate, but one of them had to.

'Twinkle thinks she knows what happened,' said Vlad, getting in quick. He knew what happened to messengers.

Fairy dust fell from Twinkle's immense shoulders.

'Twinkle!' said Salor sternly, heading the approaching butt kicking off at the pass.

Twinkle collected herself. 'Sorry.'

'So what is it you think you know?' said Salor.

Narrowing her eyes at Vlad, Twinkle said what was on her mind, 'I believe people have stopped believing in Santa and he has stopped existing because of it.'

Salor raised his rather shrubby eyebrows. 'And, without the magic of Santa, how did all the presents, that are causing such a furore, get delivered pray tell?'

Truth be told, neither Twinkle or Vlad had thought of that. As for Jose, well, he was too deep for such thoughts. Now, any question regarding bones...

'I er... don't know,' said Twinkle.

'Knew that didn't sound right,' said Vlad, again with the quickly, this time to put space between him and Twinkle. He knew what happened to those that upset Twinkle.

'And you Vlad, what is it you think?' said Salor.

Feeling his face flush, a near miracle considering he was a vampire, Vlad struggled to find an answer.

'Thought so, hopeless,' said Salor, bringing a smile to Twinkle's lips. 'As hopeless as she is.' The smile passed into history.

'I know,' said a voice, belonging to a certain little Chihuahua.

Three heads turned to look at Jose. Each with a changing mixture of shock, bemusement and intrigue etched on their faces.

'You do?' said Salor, doubting he did.

'Sí,' said Jose. 'The jolly fat man was kidnapped I am thinking.' It was quite a statement coming from someone with supposedly so little brain.

'Kidnapped?' guffawed Vlad.

'Sí,' said Jose. 'And I am thinking it was before they, the presents, were delivered.'

'Before?' guffawed Twinkle.

'Go on,' said Salor, intrigued to see where the little brain addled Chihuahua was going with his theory.

And go on he did. 'And also I am thinking that the peoples that did this heinous crime is teetotal and health conscious regarding hydrogenated oils and fats. It is what I think,' said Jose.

'Hydro what?' said Vlad.

'I think Jose here might be right,' said Salor.

'You do?' said Twinkle.

'About Santa,' said Salor.

'What about the other stuff?' said Vlad.

'To be taken under consult I think,' said Salor. 'In the meantime, I suggest you follow Jose's lead and see what you can find; clues and whatnot, starting with that house you were at this morning.'

'Millie's,' said Twinkle.

'Right away,' said Vlad.

'And take Jose with you,' said Salor, 'but keep him away from the tree.' Salor called to Jose, 'Jose. Jose?'

But Jose wasn't listening. Instead he was standing, staring at the door, his tail wagging furiously.

'What's he doing?' said Twinkle.

'Beats me,' said Vlad.

'What is it Jose?' said Salor.

Tongue lolling, an exited look on his face, Jose responded by bouncing up and down on the spot, until he was facing Salor. 'I wait,' he said.

'Wait for what?' said Salor.

Jose cocked his head quizzically. 'For my lead,' he said.

'Your lead?'

'Sí, you say take Jose's lead, so Jose waiting to go for walk.'

'Take him out of here,' said Salor.

'But my walk,' wailed Jose as he was led away. 'Jose wants his walk?'

Chapter 3

It was Boxing Day, Saint Stephen's day, the day after Christmas Day, the why did I eat so much yesterday day, and all was quiet at Millie's, or the Millies's; whichever.

'What is it we look for?' said Jose, sniffing in the direction of the Christmas tree, the scent was still there.

'You're the detective,' said Vlad.

'Clues,' said Twinkle.

'The mince pie, it is gone,' said Jose, deducing.

'And the sherry,' said Vlad, open mouthed and perturbed. 'What can it mean?'

'They tidied up?' said Twinkle.

'Ah,' said Vlad, feeling just a little bit foolish.

Jose said nothing as he ambled closer to the tree.

Twinkle spotted the movement. 'Make sure he doesn't make another nuisance of himself over there,' she said.

'Nuisance?' said Vlad.

'Unwanted leg business,' said Twinkle.

'Oh,' said Vlad. 'Why do I have to watch him?'

'Because I have the magnifying glass,' said Twinkle, removing it from her tutu. She proceeded to study the mantelpiece where the socks had been hanging.

Jose meanwhile had made it to the tree and was giving it the wary eye.

'What're you doing?' said Vlad. Jose had moved on to warily sniffing.

'It smells,' said Jose, 'this stabbing tree of small creatures.'

'That's hardly surprising,' said Vlad, thinking about Jose's little episode of the day before.

'It smells of outside.'

'Give the dog a coconut,' said Vlad under his breath.

Another sniff and Jose was brought to another conclusion. 'It smells of gardens,' he said.

To Vlad's mind, this was one and the same, garden/outside, outside/garden. He had heard that people sometimes potted their Christmas tree in the New Year and brought it back in again for Christmas. 'Isn't that the same?' he asked.

'No,' said Jose, who was considered, in some quarters, to be quite the tree connoisseur; mostly the quarter filled with canines and were-botanists.

'All righty then,' said Vlad, glancing across to Twinkle in an attempt to catch her eye; it was pure comedy gold over where he was and he wanted to share the moment; at Jose's expense. But she was engrossed with her investigating and had her nose, and almost all of her head, stuck up the chimney. But it soon appeared again, when the sound of the front door opening reached her ears.

Twinkle, Vlad and Jose froze on the spot. Now there were voices. Voices coming from just behind the door that led to the room they were in. Tension started to rise. The door handle started to turn. The door started to open. A young lady with red hair entered. Someone called to her. It was Millie or one of the Millies. She said something back then entered the room. She stopped. Her eyes grew wide.

But no worry, Twinkle, Vlad and Jose weren't visible to people, unless they wanted to be, and Vlad was doubly safe; he being invisible to everyone. (In case you're wondering how the others know where he is, he wears a hooded robe, which was visible.) But they could be walked into. So it was time to move, especially as Millie had entered the room and looked to be on some kind of mission.

A sprinkle of emergency fairy dust later, and Millie was all alone in the room. She glared at the small table beside the Christmas tree. She filled her lungs with air and yelled to all that could hear her. 'Who's tidied the mince pie away?'

Chapter 4

'So,' said Salor, looking up from his desk, as his trio of intrepid detectives arrived back from their sojourn in the "real world". 'What have you found out?'

'The pie it is gone,' said Jose.

'And the sherry,' said Vlad.

'Oh, for goodness sake,' said Twinkle, 'they tidied.'

'Ah,' said Salor, not entirely sure what to think. 'Anything else?'

'Nothing,' said Twinkle.

'Something,' said Jose.

'Explain,' said Salor.

'The tree, it smell of gardens,' said Jose.

'Gardens?' said Twinkle, hearing about it for the first time.

Vlad let out a small titter, the laugh was going to be on Jose. 'I've already explained to him that trees are brought in from outside,' he said. Let the laughter begin.

'And of outside,' said Jose, looking very serious.

'Ha-ha,' said Vlad.

'Hush,' said Salor, not only taking the wind from Vlad's sails, but also putting him into dry dock. 'Tell me more Jose.'

'But… '

'Quiet Vlad, let Jose speak.'

'It smell of outside and garden,' said Jose.

'The tree, yes, you said,' said Salor. 'What about it?'

'It is the smell of the small fellows,' said Jose. 'The tree, it smell of the small fellows.'

A hush fell on the room. It lasted for a moment or two as what Jose had said sunk in.

'Good grief,' said Salor, breaking the hush with hushed tones, 'the small fellows.'

'Sí, it is what I say,' said Jose.

'We have to do something, and now,' said Salor.

'We do,' said Twinkle.

'Do we?' said Vlad, feeling he was missing something important. Perhaps someone would explain what was going on in a moment.

'Sí,' said Jose, 'the small fellows.'

'To the bat cave!' said Salor.

'Bat cave?' said Twinkle.

'Sorry, always wanted to say it,' said Salor, 'to the study!' It just didn't have the same ring.

'We're in it,' said Vlad.

'So we are.'

Chapter 5

In a rather cold place, as far removed from the South Pole as was possible, the sound of much hammering and drilling and cursing as thumb came between hammer and target, and painting and sanding, could be heard over the banging and crashing and howling of the snow storm outside.

'Tell me again why we are doing this?' said a small fellow, rueing his misplaced strike with his hammer and sucking on a sore thumb.

'Because it's what we do now,' said an equally small fellow, as he swung his mallet to knock home a dowel on the small wheelbarrow he was making.

'But why?' said the small fellow with the sore thumb.

'Because,' said the small fellow with the mallet, who had finished his wheelbarrow and was now stood admiring it.

'But it's not fair,' moaned the small fellow with the sore thumb. 'I could be fishing.'

'Then get a hat.'

'I have a hat,' said the small fellow, wondering how a hat was going to help him.

'Not one of the human's special hats I bet.'

'A special human hat?' said the small fellow with the sore thumb.

'Yes,' said the small fellow with the mallet.

With his interest piqued, could the human hat be magical in some way, able to whisk him off to his favourite fishing hole with a click of the fingers, the small fellow with the hammer wanted to know more. 'This hat,' he said, all conspiratorial like, his voice low, his eyes darting here and there, 'is it magical?'

'I don't think so,' said the small fellow with the mallet, bursting his co-worker's balloon of hope, 'but from what I gather, they have special words put on them.'

Runes! thought the small fellow with the sore thumb; *must be secret magical runes.* 'And what do these "words",' he winked at his co-worker, 'do?'

'Do? Nothing, they're just words,' said the small fellow with the mallet, gathering together the parts he needed for the next wheelbarrow he was going to build.

The new balloon the small fellow with the sore thumb had been inflating suddenly deflated. 'I don't understand,' he said.

Stopping what he was doing, the small fellow with the mallet, pointed to the front of the hat he was wearing. 'They print it here, or sew it, whichever takes the human's fancy I guess.'

'Print what?'

The small fellow with the mallet let out a small sigh of growing impatience. 'The words, the words that say what they would rather be doing of course.' He walked over to where his co-worker was sat and tapped the front of his hat. 'In your case your hat would have "I'd rather be fishing" on it, just there.'

'And that's it?' said the small fellow with the sore thumb, a sore thumb that wasn't throbbing as much as it was.

'As far as I know,' said the small fellow with the mallet, who then shrugged and returned to his pile of wheelbarrow parts.

'What's the point?

'I don't know,' said the small fellow with the mallet, picking up a wheel. 'Guess that's humans for you.'

The small fellow with the slowly healing sore thumb thought for a moment. He decided it didn't make any sense. 'Bah,' he said, returning to his hammering. 'Silly humans,' he muttered as he swung his hammer. 'AARGH!' screamed the small fellow. Silly, small fellow.

The door to the room where the two small fellows were working suddenly opened. The two small fellows fell silent, apart from a sucking sound and the occasional groan. Another small fellow then entered. Though to be fair, as small fellows went, he was a fair bit taller; perhaps an inch or two. He was imperial you see.

The imperial, slightly taller small fellow, stood and observed all that there was to be observed in the room and waited. And when the noise of industry subsided, as the other small fellows in the room, that weren't the small fellow with the doubly throbbing thumb, or the one with the mallet, realised they were being observed by another small fellow, who was a couple of inches taller and imperial, the slightly tall fellow who was imperial did a twirl.

'Well?' said the imperial, slightly taller small fellow. 'What do you think?'

Chapter 6

Their whereabouts confirmed; the study, Salor, Twinkle, Vlad and Jose got down to the business of what was afoot and what to do about it.

'We will need warm clothes,' said Twinkle, assuming the small fellows were where they thought they were. All in all, a weird place to start, considering.

'Sí,' said Jose, who was apt to feel the cold. 'A nice warm coat I am thinking.'

'Something warm to drink,' said Vlad, stopping the discussion dead and drawing stares from the other three. 'What?' said Vlad. 'Oh, come on, I meant hot chocolate or something like.'

'Glad to hear it,' said Salor, who had subconsciously pulled his collar tighter around his neck.

'You know I don't do that anymore,' said Vlad.

'I didn't know you liked hot chocolate,' said Twinkle.

'It has to be thick,' said Vlad. He averted his eyes and added quietly, 'with just a few of drops of cochineal mixed in.'

On the floor someone wasn't looking too well. 'I think I gonna be sick,' said Jose.

'There, there,' said Salor, patting Jose on the head. 'He wasn't talking about blood.'

'Sí, not blood,' said Jose. 'But he say hot chocolate. Argh! There, now I say it. It make me pukey.'

'Hot ch-'

'No, don't say it.' Jose had started to go a funny colour.

'Right,' said Salor, giving the were-Chihuahua a funny look to go along with his funny colour, 'what say we get this discussion back on track?'

And just like that the thought of hot chocolate was forgotten. Jose's little face brightened. 'We go on train?' Jose started to chase his tail. 'Jose like train.'

'No,' said Salor, hands in head, 'I meant, let's return to business. I said nothing about a train.'

Jose stopped his tail chasing and looked up at Salor with those big sad brown eyes of his. 'No train?' he said. Tears started to build. 'No train.' His tail suddenly became as lead and fell between his back legs. 'But Jose like train.' Now his ears began to droop. 'First I am to have no lead. Then I am to have no train. No walkies. No choo-choo. Jose's friends tease him. I am sad.' A tear rolled and dropped onto the floor. Jose sniffed.

'Right, order,' said Salor, trying to ignore what was going on at his feet, but it was no good, Jose was now lying on his back with his legs in the air, his eyes closed and whimpering. There was only one thing for it if they wanted to get on. 'Vlad.'

'Yes?'

'Get the, you know what.'

'The, you know what?' said Vlad, not knowing what the, you know what, was.

'Do I have to spell it out for you?' said Salor, nodding sideways at the door.

'Please,' said Vlad.

'Really?' said Salor, and then realised it might be for the best otherwise there was a chance they were going to still be there when the cows came home. 'The L-E-A-D.'

Vlad played the words through his head.

On the floor Jose had stopped whimpering and had opened one eye.

'Ah,' said Vlad, when he came to the inevitable conclusion. 'You mean the lead.'

Jose was so excited he was up on his feet and sitting staring at the door before anyone could say, well, anything really. His tail was wagging as if there was no tomorrow and on the floor was a little pitter-patter trail of droplets leading from where he had been lying to where he was now; and we're not talking tears here.

'And clear that up before you go,' said Salor, giving Vlad the evil eye.

'Me? But...'

'No buts, cleanies then walkies.'

'Oh fangs,' said Vlad.

'Sí,' said Jose. 'Cleanies, then walkies.'

Chapter 7

'I'm waiting,' said the imperial, slightly taller small fellow, growing impatient. He had been standing there for over a minute and as yet no one had ventured a comment.

At last, someone chanced their arm, and most likely their head as well if they weren't careful, they were talking to an imperial when all said and done, and everyone knew what they were like; impatient for one; choppy for another. 'Is that real fur?'

The imperial, slightly taller small fellow, who was better known as Prince Bottom Of, craned his neck to see who had asked the question, but a sea of heads suddenly looking at their shoes, preserved the enquirer's anonymity. He wanted compliments, not questions, impertinent little so and so. Only he need know it was faux. He tried a different tact to find the culprit. 'Who said that?' he said. But the only answer he got was the sound of foreheads hitting benches as small fellows tried to take an even closer look at their shoes.

'Right,' said Prince Bottom Of, 'let's try that again. WHAT DO YOU THINK?' That got the shoe studiers' attention. The room snapped to attention.

'Very regal,' said someone small, very quickly.

'Very original,' said Prince Bottom Of. It was true, but so passé.

'Royal,' said another.

'And why wouldn't it be?'

'Smart,' said someone else.

'Colourful,' said another, before Prince Bottom Of had a chance to reply to smart.

The flood gates were suddenly opening wide.

'Elegant.'

'Artistic.'

'Beautiful.'

'Chic.'

'Courtly.'

And suddenly everyone was reading off the same thesaurus page.

'Smart.'

And then they weren't.

'Someone's already said that.'

'Oh. Clever then.'

'Eh?'

'Very red.'

'Yuley.'
'Yuley?' said Prince Bottom Of.
'Loggy.'
'?'
'Scrumdiddlyumptious!'
And then...
'Alluring.'
'Saucy.'
'Raunchy cowboy!'
'Yeehaw!'

'Whoa there,' said Prince Bottom Of, not liking the sound of where things were going one little bit.

And then...

'Just like Santa,' said someone.

And that is just what Prince Bottom Of had been waiting to hear. For that is who he now was; Santa. And it was right, and it was legal; he had the proof you see. Prince Bottom Of beamed, preened and then with a wave of a royal hand and a further twirl of his gorgeous red and white faux fur-lined robe, he left.

The workshop stayed silent for a moment or two and then, when it looked likely his imperialist wasn't coming back, the sound of much hammering and drilling and painting and sanding and cursing gradually returned.

'Who was that then?' said the small fellow with the hammer, sore thumb and lump on his forehead, who was *so not* in touch with the latest who's who edition of important small fellows.

'Bottom Of,' said the small fellow's co-worker, the small fellow with a mallet and lump on his forehead.

'I was only asking!'

Chapter 8

By the time Vlad and Jose returned, the business that had started with a suspicion as to the small fellows whereabouts being somewhere cold, had run its course and had been concluded. And the conclusion of the concluded business, going on Jose's nose assumptions, regarding the involvement of the small fellows meant, should Jose be right, that they were where they shouldn't be and had almost certainly and possibly kidnapped Santa. Why? They didn't know. What had the small fellows done to Santa? That too they didn't know. So, after further discussion it had been decided that something had to be done about it. This would mean going and sorting the small fellows out and removing them, which meant more planning of the nature they had been planning before Vlad and Jose had left.

But there was a problem; to visit Santa's last known address meant having to travel to the human world, as Santa, for whatever reason, insisted on living there. True, Santa existed in a bubble of myth, magic and make-believe, but in the human world all the same; a world much harsher and much colder than their world. Colder being the operative word here.

So, as Vlad and Jose entered the study they were just in time to be back to where they were before they had left; both regarding the study and the planning. Had they missed anything? A little. Did it matter? Not really.

'Gloves?'
'Check.'
'Hats?'
'Check.'
'Coats?'
'Check.'
'Thermals?'
'Check.'
'Drinking chocolate?'
'Ergh!'
'Check.'
'Biscuits?'
'Check.'
'Doggie chews?'
'Sí, good.'
'Check.'
'Looks like we got everything,' said Salor.
'Looks like,' said Twinkle.
'Looks like, we're ready to go,' said Salor.

'Looks like,' said Twinkle. 'Just one thing though?'

'Yes?' said Salor, wondering what it was they might have missed.

'How are we going to get there?'

Now, hailing from a world with magic in its name as they did, you'd think magic, wouldn't you?

A sprinkling of fairy dust and whoosh!

A shake of the wizards' staff and poof!

A magic spell and shazzam!

A broomstick and away!

A magical portal and hello Santa!

Anything magical would do.

But the sad truth of the matter was they didn't have that much magic left; not for long haul. Not like they used to. Salor had been known to turn a stagecoach into a melon. Puzzled the socks off the passengers, and usually leaving them with the pip. But not now, magic was fast becoming a rare commodity. The world of myth, magic and make-believe was in a bad way, which meant it was in a worse way in the human world. A hero was needed. But that is a story for another day. Today they would have to make their journey the old fashioned way, using Shank's pony.

But Shank was having none of it, he was funny like that, and so they would have to make the journey on foot instead.

'Walk!' said Vlad. 'To the flipping North Pole, are you mad?'

'Did someone say something about a walk?' said Jose.

'Don't push it,' said Twinkle.

'What choice do we have?' said Salor, responding to Vlad's outburst. 'It's troubling times.'

'You are telling me,' mumbled Jose, who had just realised that one more walkies, added up to bath time. He would rather drink hot chocolate. Ergh! Better be quiet. He sloped off to find a shadowy corner to hide in.

'Isn't there another way?' said Vlad.

'Couldn't we just use a little magic?' said Twinkle.

'You got some to spare have you?' said Salor, suspiciously.

'No,' said Twinkle, 'I meant pool it.'

'Yes,' said Vlad, eager to agree with anything that didn't mean the wearing out of shoe leather. 'Pool it.'

In a shadowy corner of the room a certain someone, just as he was preparing to make himself comfortable, pricked his ears at the mention of pool.

Pool to Jose meant only one thing, water. And together with the mention of "it" after it caused alarm bells to ring. Had he been wrong about the number of walks he had had? Had his reckless questioning regarding walks nudged someone's thinking towards it? He decided this was no time to be asking questions. First walk no walk, then train no train, then walk good, but only one, bad, now bath and in a pool. No way Jose.

'Er,' said Jose, backing towards the door, 'Jose have to go.'

'What's that?' said Salor.

'I go,' said Jose.

'Good fellow,' said Salor. 'Shall I get the door for you?'

But the door was already ajar and as Jose suspected it was just a ploy to grab him, he made a break for it.

'Well,' said Salor, watching Jose make his exit. 'Good for him, never thought he'd get the hang of it, doing it outside and what.'

'Here-here,' said Vlad, who had been volunteered the dubious honour somewhere along the line, of official cleaner upper after Jose.

'Now, where were we?' said Salor.

'Walking,' said Twinkle.

'Ah, yes.'

The study door led to a flight of stairs that led to the hallway on the ground floor. Jose now ran down this, heading for the garden. No way was anyone going to dunk him like a witch on trial. But he couldn't hide for ever. Perhaps he could trade something for a bath reprieve? He had lots of things tucked away in his hidey-hole in the garden.

Jose reached his hidey-hole, sat down and gave behind his ear a good scratch. Scratch over, he started to mooch through the treasures he had accumulated over time. Something magical might do the trick. Jose had a little giggle to himself over that. There was a stick, like the one Salor waved over his head when he couldn't think of anything clever to say, but slightly chewed. One glass slipper, size nine, complete with glass pompom; one previous owner, not magical, but interesting; broken not chewed. A book of spells, very chewable, but in reasonable condition if you didn't mind the saliva stains. Would that do? He decided not and continued to dig and then got quite excited; he had found his old rubber bone, not magical, but very, very chewable. He gave it a chew, but then remembered why he had discarded it; the squeak had given up the ghost. Jose took a moment. He sniffed. It was sad. But life goes on. He continued digging and suddenly he found the something that might just be what he was looking for. If he remembered right, he had found it before the magic had started to drain from the world. Perhaps it retained its magic. It most definitely hadn't been used in a while. Not that the thought hadn't crossed his mind, but it appeared dogs didn't have what it took.

Jose stuck his nose into his pile of treasures, took grip and pulled. It held tight. He tugged harder. It finally gave, sending Jose tumbling backwards head over heels. Upright again, Jose inspected his prize, a bona fide magic lamp, except in this case it was a kettle. A bona fide magic kettle that he was sure was just crying out to be rubbed. Jose grabbed its handle in his jaw and triumphantly headed for the study. With a bit of luck it would save him from a ducking. And with a bit more luck, he thought cheerfully, if he played his cards right, perhaps a new rubber bone; one that came with a fully functioning squeak. A dog could dream.

Chapter 9

Smiling for all he was worth, Prince Bottom Of left Santa's workshop, heading for the big man's office. Not that it was the big man's anymore. It was a small fellow's office now. It would need a refit; Prince Bottom Of couldn't even reach Santa's chair, let alone sit on it without the aid of a stepladder, and then he needed a booster seat if he wanted to see over the desk. The refit would be sorted in due time, but more important things needed to be attended to first.

In the small fellow's office, Prince Bottom Of, or Santa as he now liked to be called, climbed the stepladder and deposited his bottom on the booster. There was business to be conducted and on the agenda was getting on top of things before next Christmas. He had coped admirably this time, considering the short notice he had been given, but if you don't take the chance when the opportunity arises – finding that scroll was a fantastic piece of luck – you've paid your lawyers a lot of dosh for nothing. And as for the small fellows under his command, limited as their abilities were, they had certainly risen to the occasion; the elves unexpectedly leaving him in the lurch like that. All in all things had worked out rather well. Not that he would ever tell the small fellows that, better they lived in ignorance than expect pay rises; not that they were paid.

Santa, formally known as Prince Bottom Of, leaned forward, and with the aid of his official stick, he pressed a large red button on the desk. The official stick was so called because that is what he had decided to call it. Otherwise it was just a stick. He now frowned, his smile fading for a moment. The first piece of business on the agenda was a conundrum, what did he do about the reindeer?

The door to Santa's office opened and a small fellow wearing spectacles, popped his head round it. He looked nervous. 'You buzzed your majesty?' said he.

'No,' said Santa, formally known as Prince Bottom Of, 'I buzzed you.' Santa gave the bespectacled small fellow a withering look. The small fellow wearing spectacles was sure he would laugh about it later. 'And where is your hat?'

The small fellow with spectacles put a hand on his head; he had forgotten to put it back on again. Nothing for it but to tell the truth, he supposed. He hoped it was enough. 'Sorry, your majesty, it's just that it's so hot in here I thought I might leave it off for a while.'

Santa, formally known as Prince Bottom Of, shifted uncomfortably; the small fellow was right, it was hot in here. More than likely why the old

Santa had such rosy cheeks. It would have to change, they were outdoors types, hardy, used to what the elements threw at them. Having said that there were hot days to endure, but not all the time. No, it would have to change.

'Okay,' said Santa, formally known as Prince Bottom Of, feeling charitable, 'but next time, ask permission before trying to think for yourself.'

'Yes, your majesty,' said the small bespectacled fellow, bowing for all he was worth. 'Thank you your majesty.'

'And call me Santa.'

'Yes your, er... Santa.'

'That's better. Now, what do you want?'

'Um... you buzzed for me,' said the small fellow wearing spectacles.

'I did?' Knitted brow. Thoughtful look. Finger on chin. 'I did! What was I thinking?'

'You weren't your majesty, I mean Santa,' said the small fellow, who's spectacles had slipped to the tip of his nose due to the sudden realise of perspiration, due to the sudden realisation of what he had just said.

Santa, formally known as Prince Bottom Of, was changing colour. From flushed pink, to outraged red, to furious purple. 'WHAT DID YOU JUST SAY?' he bellowed.

The bespectacled small fellow's spectacles raced backwards up his nose and settled on the bridge, such was the force of Santa's outburst. But the small fellow stayed resolute; it appeared it was his job to do so. 'Sorry, no offence meant,' he said, oh so humbly, 'but it's what happens.'

'Happens! What do you mean, happens?'

'It happened to Santa.' This brought a glower from the new Santa. 'I mean the last Santa.' The small fellow wearing spectacles ran a finger along his collar. Was it him, or was it hot in here? Both. He ploughed on regardless. 'It's a safety measure built into the job.' His glasses had steamed up.

Santa, the new one, leaned forward. 'Explain,' he said, his blood pressure slowly returning to normal.

The small fellow beset by spectacle problems took a tentative step into the room, making sure the door behind him stayed open. It never hurt to have an escape route planned.

'Well,' said the small fellow, 'it-'

'Stop,' said Santa, formally known as someone else, 'first tell me your name. I can't keep thinking of you as the small bespectacled fellow, can I?'

'No Santa,' said the small bespectacled fellow, who was at last getting used to not calling Prince Bottom Of, your majesty.

'Well?'

'It's Alf,' said Alf, formally known as the small bespectacled fellow.

'Elf?' said Santa, raising his eyebrows.

'No Santa, it's Alf, but some people call me Alfie.'

'Alf it is then,' said Santa, who didn't want to be seen as being too pally with the commoners. 'Now, continue with your explanation.'

'Yes Santa. It's the job you see. It's very high pressure.'

'Uh-huh,' said Santa.

'So, as a precaution against you, Santa, cracking up on the job, so to speak, as the job is so highly pressured, a safety measure was introduced to make sure that didn't happen.'

'A safety measure you say.'

'Something to help you become,' Alf had to choose his words carefully, 'relaxed, shall we say.'

'Relaxed?' said Santa. Relaxed? When he came to think about it, he did feel kind of relaxed, even though he had nearly blown a gasket just then. And when he thought about that, even that had been sort of relaxed; he hadn't ordered an execution or the like, had he?

'And jolly,' said Alf.

'And jolly?' And now he came to think about that as well, he had started to feel a little jollier since sitting down. Even the near gasket blowing had been jolly, the fact that he hadn't burst a blood vessel in one of his eyes was proof of that.

'And... ' Did he say it? Alf wasn't so sure he should. But if he didn't he might be held responsible in some way later. He decided to err on getting it over with.

'And?'

'Doolally.' Alf held his breath.

'Doolally, you say?' said Santa, who was indeed feeling a little doolally that very moment. How odd? 'Is it dangerous, this doolally? Does it impair one's reasoning? How long does the feeling last? What do you mean, doolally?' Santa was starting to look a tad irate, and unhappy, but in a relaxed, jolly, doolally sort of way.

Alf took a step backwards, he had also heard what can happen to messengers, and as messengers went, he felt this particular one was starting to skate on thick water. 'It's nothing to worry about,' said Alf, hoping to placate. 'It's just a condition of the job.'

Santa was now standing on his booster seat, which was a doolally thing to do, considering how high he was from the floor. 'Why didn't anyone tell me this before?' He was now waving his arms about and wondering if he could sue his lawyers for malpractice.

'I didn't... ' started Alf, before realising he might be incriminating himself. 'No one knew until we took over. It's pretty hush-hush, the ins and outs of this job.'

Bottom lip protruding, Santa glared at Alf. Surely someone should have looked into it. Someone then should have told him; given him the chance to weigh up his options. Why hadn't anyone thought to ask the old Santa about the doings of the job, asked the elves before they skedaddled? The glare started to falter. His anger was starting to subside. Why? He suddenly sat down. He could feel his cheeks flushing. He could feel something in his chest. Had he given himself indigestion? He wouldn't be surprised. But it wasn't indigestion. It was something else that was building. It passed his chest and reached his mouth. It opened. 'Ho ho,' said Santa. Where had that come from? He saw that the small fellow called Alf was staring at him. What the heck? No point in getting stressed on his first day. 'Okay,' said Santa.

'Okay?' said Alf.

'Okay,' said Santa, 'I'm hearing what you're saying. Time to get with the program. Go with the flow.'

'Okay,' said Alf, who hadn't expected what he had read about the safety measures to work this fast. He had expected stages. It had to have something to do with the room. Whatever it was that was affecting the prince had to be stronger here, in Santa's office.

'Right then, down to business,' said Santa. Flipping crikey and blimey but he was feeling relaxed all of a sudden. 'But first, would you do something for me?'

Alf had taken a pad and pencil from his pocket, but now stopped and stared expectantly at Santa. He just knew the way things were going had been too good to be true. 'Of course, Santa,' he said, wishing he could add conditions. Especially to someone as far down the doolally route as Santa appeared to be travelling.

'Excellent,' said Santa. 'Can you get a hot chocolate for me? With some squirty cream on the top. And a few marshmallows wouldn't go amiss.'

'Er, right away,' said Alf, putting pad and pencil back in his pocket.

'And get one for yourself, can't have you dehydrating, can we?'

'Thank you, Santa.' Alf turned to go get.

'Oh and just one more thing, before you go.'

And here it comes. He knew it was too good to be true. Alf squeezed his eyes shut. 'Yes Santa?'

'Ho ho ho!' said Santa.

Blimey, thought Alf, as he left the office, *it must work quicker on small fellows.*

Chapter 10

When Jose returned, the debate he left in the middle of was still going on.

'What about skis?' suggested Vlad, as Jose nudged the door open with his nose.

'Can you ski?' said Salor.

'I haven't tried,' said Vlad.

'What about one of those thingy things?' said Twinkle. Blank looks greeted her suggestion. 'You know, a snow thingy, they're like skis, but with an engine.'

'Do you mean a snowmobile per chance?' said Salor.

'Yes, that's what it's called, a snowmobile thingy.' Twinkle had always fancied a go on one of those.

'Have you got one?'

'No.'

'Do you know where to get one?'

'No.'

'How about a dog sled?' said Vlad.

On hearing this, Jose dropped what he had in his mouth and let out a severe whine of disapproval.

'Ah,' said Salor, 'you're back.'

'What have you got there?' asked Twinkle.

'It is my chewing toy,' said Jose, narrowing his eyes, daring anyone to say anything derogatory about it. He had gone back for his knackered rubber bone, to save time trying to describe what it was he desired as a reward for finding the kettle.

'Lovely,' said Twinkle, looking at it with undisguised disgust.

'But is not all that I find,' said Jose, turning and disappearing through the door. There followed the sound of the pitter-patter of tiny paws on the stairs. Then the sound of the flap that led to the garden opening then closing. Several moments later the sound of the flap was heard again, this time accompanied by some mild cursing. A noise of rearranging followed. The flap negotiated, the pitter-patter of tiny paws was heard once more on the stairs, together with the odd clang. The door to the study opened. Jose walked in with something in his mouth. He dropped the something at Salor's feet.

'I say,' said Salor, somewhat surprised. 'Is that what I think it is?'

'A tatty old kettle by the looks of it,' said Vlad.

'Upon my soul, I think it is,' said Salor, bending to take a better look.

'Am I right or am I right?' said Vlad, still thinking it was nothing more than an old battered kettle; which it was to be fair. He held up his hand for a high five, but as no one could see his hand he was disappointed. Dare say he would have been disappointed anyway.

'It's a magic kettle,' said Salor, his voice filled with wonder.

'He's right you know,' said Twinkle.

'Sí,' said Jose, looking on with some pride.

'A magic what?' said Vlad. Was he seeing the same thing the others were seeing? 'It doesn't look very magical to me. Look it's filthy. It could do with a good clean. Here, I'll give it a rub.' Vlad went to pick it up.

'No!' said Salor, putting himself between the kettle and the advancing Vlad. 'It needs to be treated with the utmost respect. It can be a dangerous thing in the wrong hands.'

''ere, what are you saying?' said Vlad.

'That you've got the wrong hands would be my guess,' said Twinkle.

'I'll take it,' said Salor. 'It will be safe with me.'

But Jose had other ideas. 'It is mine,' he said, standing over it. Until he got what he wanted that was.

'But it needs to be treated with care,' said Salor, backing off, as Jose sort of smiled at him. At least that is what it looked like, all those small sharp teeth showing like that.

'Looks like it's been chewed,' said Twinkle.

'Sí,' said Jose, through bared teeth.

'I don't understand,' said Salor, 'why bring it to us if you don't want us to use it?' He was fairly champing at the bit to get his hands on it.

'I give it you,' said Jose, 'but first I think we bargain.'

'Bargain?' said Salor.

'Sí,' said Jose. 'It is mine, look I make mark in it.' Jose pointed with his nose to a set of tooth marks on the spout.

'Ye gads!' said Salor.

'But I lend it.' Salor held out a hand. Jose smiled again. 'But first you give me something. Then I borrow it to you.'

'Lend it,' said Twinkle.

'Sí,' said Jose, 'that as well.'

Salor wasn't sure about all this, but his mind was working overtime. 'What you're saying is that you want to trade?'

'Sí,' said Jose.

'And then I keep the kettle?' said Salor, innocently.

'Sí,' said Jose.

'Then give it here,' said Salor.

'And then you give it back,' said Jose, who wasn't as daft as Salor hoped.

'Oh,' said Salor.

'I think what our Jose here wants, is a little something for the use of his kettle,' said Twinkle. 'Am I right?'

'Sí,' said Jose, 'a little something.'

'A little something?' said Salor. 'Did you have something in mind?'

Jose's tail began to wag. 'Sí, I wish a squeak.'

'A what?' said Salor.

'A squeak,' said Vlad.

'That's what he said,' said Twinkle.

'A squeak?' said Salor.

'Sí,' said Jose, 'for my bone.'

'For his bone,' said Vlad.

'Seems reasonable to me,' said Twinkle.

'But I thought he wanted something for the kettle?' said Salor, who could be terribly dense sometimes.

'Sí,' said Jose.

'I think for this,' said Twinkle, stepping in as Salor was looking increasingly confused. She pointed at the mangled piece of rubber that had once been a squeaky bone. 'That's his bone,' she said.

'Is it?' said Salor.

'He wants a squeak for it,' said Vlad.

'But I don't want a bone,' said Salor.

Jose looked at Vlad, who moved his hood in the direction of Twinkle, who looked at Jose.

'Perhaps it would be easier just to get Jose a new bone,' said Twinkle.

Jose's tail wagged again. 'Sí,' he said, 'with a squeak.'

'Yes, with a squeaker,' said Twinkle.

Salor threw his hands into the air. 'But what does he want for the kettle?'

'Vlad,' said Twinkle, 'go get Jose a new bone.'

'Where from?'

'Use your imagination.'

'I come too,' said Jose, an image of just the squeaky bone he wanted forming in his mind.

'Good idea,' said Twinkle. 'Salor.'

'Yes?'

'Put the kettle on.'

Salor made a move.

'Not that one.'

'But the... '

'I'll deal with that,' said Twinkle, feeling she had the safest hands for the job.

'But I… '

'Tea,' said Twinkle, in her sternest tone.

Salor toddled off.

'And you two. Off you go.'

Vlad glided off. Jose bounced off behind him.

Twinkle picked up the magic kettle, treating it with all the reverence an object as dangerous as it was deserved. She looked at it, turned it in her hands. The urge to rub it was strong. But she could cope, she was strong, she was a fairy for goodness sake.

Chapter 11

'They are much too big,' said Santa, the small fellow formally known as Prince Bottom Of; the one with a chocolate moustache.

'But they are the only ones we have,' said Alf, pleased with himself, after Santa had told him he makes the most wonderful hot chocolate.

Santa looked distraught. A hard thing to do when you're so relaxed, you're in imminent danger of sliding off your booster seat. 'But there have to be smaller ones,' he said. 'It says so.'

'If there are we can't find them,' said Alf, wishing he could be somewhere else right now, beside a pond would be nice. He looked up at Santa; he appeared to be in a little world of his own for the moment. Anywhere would be nice. Even the workshop would be better than this; at least he would be with his mates. Rumour had it, that someone in the workshop had discovered a magic hat that could take you anywhere. If only he could get his hands on it. He wouldn't have to do this job anymore. He felt his top lip, it was sticky. He took out his hanky and wiped the offending chocolate away. And just how had he got the job anyway? There must have been a thousand or more applicants for the flipping job. But he had got it. Oh yes, and he hadn't even applied! He took his spectacles off and gave them a wipe, smearing chocolate on them. He used the other end of his hanky to clean it off. *It had to have been these,* he thought, staring at them. He could imagine it now, "Look, he wears glasses, he must be a clerk of some sort, give him the job". Discrimination is what it is. And they aren't even real spectacles; the lenses are just plain glass. He had just been making a fashion statement. He only wanted to look intelligent; for the ladies. Well, that's the last time he ever did that. Look intelligent. Look where it's got him.

'Then what do we do?' said Santa, suddenly snapping out of his stupor. 'The big ones had to do this time around, but I could hardly control them. And what about the sleigh, I don't suppose you've managed to find a small one of those either?'

'No,' said Alf, popping his spectacles back on. 'We could put in a smaller seat.' He refrained from saying booster. 'Do something with the console perhaps.'

'No,' said Santa, 'we look harder. It must be hidden. It's there somewhere, it's written.'

It's written, thought Alf, *it's flipping written. If he's so certain it exists then perhaps he should go look.* Alf felt like saying so, but relaxed as he was, Santa was still imperial; dangerous. He tried a different tact. 'But, if you have a smaller sleigh, what about the presents? They wouldn't fit,' he said.

Santa frowned. 'I thought the special whatnot took care of that?' Showing he did know something regarding the world of Santa.

'Does it?' said Alf. He hadn't heard of a special whatnot before; he would have to look it up in the Santa's little helper manual.

'Beside the point anyway,' said Santa. 'A small sleigh existed, does exist, ergo so did the presents that fitted in it.'

He had him there. Alf's shoulders slumped. 'Shall I continue the search then?'

'Yes.'

'I'll be off then.'

'But I have more items to discuss.' Santa let the scroll he was holding unfurl; its end reached the floor.

'Ooh, what's that behind you?' said Alf pointing at something behind Santa.

'Where?' said Santa, almost toppling from his booster seat as he tried to see over his shoulder. 'What? I don't see anything.' He turned back. 'Alf? ALF!'

But Alf was gone.

Chapter 12

'What is your com… O-M-G! For the love of a good chiropodist, would you look at the state of my kettle.'

The exclamation, from a far from happy genie, coincided with the sound of cups smashing on the stairs. There followed the sound of hurried footsteps and the door to the study swinging open.

'Twinkle!' exclaimed Salor, his mouth hanging open, tea all over his gown. 'What have you done?'

'It was so grubby,' said Twinkle, a faraway look in her eye. All she had wanted to do was clean it; that's how they got you; the genies'.

'You can say that again,' said the genie, wiping a finger over the magic kettle. 'Is that spittle?'

Salor's gaze moved from Twinkle to the genie. He looked like trouble. They all did. The trouble with genies was that they were so unpredictable; mischievous; and not in a good way. One minute it was all, "what is your command O Master?" and the next, "well you should have thought about the lack of oxygen before asking to go to the moon". They just couldn't be trusted. There was always an angle. He was sure they invented small print. Genies had to be treated like an unexploded bomb, a temperamental unexploded bomb; very carefully, and preferably from some distance away.

'Er… ' said Salor, 'I… '

The genie looked up. 'Did you do this?' he said, pointing to the teeth marks on the spout.

Salor paled. 'Me? No. It was the dog. Jose.' Sorry Jose, but women, children and wizards first.

'What dog. I see no dog.'

'He's gone to get a bone.' Salor started to wither under the genie's stare. Its terrible stare. A stare that… he suddenly realised he had seen before. But that was ridiculous. He had never met a genie before. He had always hoped he would, the wishes and all, but the stare, where… He stopped cowering. 'Don't I know you?' he said, throwing caution to the wind. He could always take some antacids later, if he was still in one piece.

'I hardly think so,' said the genie, haughtily.

'You look awfully familiar.' And then it dawned. He looked harder at the genie, and then looked at Twinkle. He did a double take. 'Twinkle?'

Twinkle had been slowly coming down from her need to clean high. 'Salor?' said Twinkle, reacting as if he had only just appeared. She rubbed at her eyes and only then noticed that she and Salor were not alone. 'Tiny? Is that you?'

'Tiny?' said Salor.

'You got a problem with that?' said the genie.

'Problem? Me? No,' said Salor, nearly tripping over his gown as he stepped back. It was time for wizards to leave the sinking ship. 'Tea anyone?'

'Golden Needles for me,' said Tiny.

'Er, I'll see what we've got.'

'The usual,' said Twinkle.

Salor scurried off, picking up pieces of cup on the way.

'So,' said the genie, 'how do you know my name?'

Twinkle introduced herself. 'It's me, Twinkle.'

'No! Get away with you girl. You're soooo, different.' Tiny may be of mischievous ilk, but he still had manners. 'The last time I saw you girl, why you were only so high.' Tiny held up a finger. 'Excuse my French.'

Twinkle blushed. Tiny was her cousin. There had always been a family resemblance, a small one, but now, with magic the way it was, unstable, and her ballooning in size from elfin-like to sumo-like because of it, the resemblance was uncanny. Twin-like. Apart from the hair; she had some.

'It's because of the magic, its going.'

'I'd heard a rumour,' said Tiny. 'But that was,' he looked at the watch on his wrist, 'a hundred years or so ago. Got worse has it?'

'Much,' said Twinkle.

'Must say though, you're looking good.'

Tiny had always been Twinkle's favourite cousin, even when she knew he was lying. 'You get used to it,' she said, lying back to him.

'Now,' said Tiny, his expression hardening, 'what is your command?'

'Business, Tiny?' said Twinkle. She was enjoying the catch up.

'It's what I do cousin.'

'We need help.'

'Not what I asked.'

'Really?'

'You know what you have to do.'

'Three wishes?'

'Ah,' said Tiny, looking glum. 'It's two now I'm afraid. You know how it is.'

Twinkle did. 'Tell me about it.'

'Go on then, make a wish.'

'I wish- '

'Wait!' yelled Salor, arriving in what he thought was the nick of time. 'Twinkle, be careful what you wish for.' The tea swished in the cups he was holding. He was quick you're thinking; he's a wizard!

'I'm not a *total* idiot,' said Twinkle.

'I never said you were a total idiot,' said Salor, raising an eyebrow ever so slightly.

'And what is that supposed to mean?' said Twinkle, noticing the eyebrow twitch.

'What do you mean?' said Salor, playing the old looking innocent card again.

'The way you said total, and that face you pulled.'

A hole. Digging. Himself. They all came to mind, so Salor played the caring friend card. 'We have to be careful, that's all,' he said, 'you know.' He hoped she did, because he didn't want to have to explain what he meant with the genie in earshot, and so close at hand; and what big hands he had; all the better to throttle someone who upset him with.

'Do I?' said Twinkle.

'Tea, Tiny?' said Salor.

'Golden Needles?'

'As asked for.'

Tiny took the cup from Salor and held it up to his nose. He breathed deeply, savouring the aroma. 'It's been a while since I last had a cup of this.' He took a sip.

'Twinkle,' hissed Salor.

'Thank you,' said Twinkle, expecting her tea as well.

But Salor held it back and keeping an eye on Tiny, took a step back towards the door. 'Come here,' he said.

'Why?'

'I want a word.'

Twinkle tutted, but went over. 'What is it?' she said, taking the tea that Salor decided she could now have.

'We have to be careful,' whispered Salor.

'I know that,' said Twinkle. Of course she knew what genies were like, she was related to one.

'You also said that the kettle would be in safe hands,' said Salor.

'But it was filthy,' said Twinkle, which in all honesty, wasn't much of a defence.

'They always are,' said Salor, 'that's how they get you. Oh, look a dirty kettle, let's give it a rub and then, whammo!'

'Whammo?'

'They grant you wishes.'

'I thought that was the whole idea,' said Twinkle.

'Yes-yes,' said Salor, 'but they twist your words. You have to be careful. They can't be trusted.'

'I know that,' said Twinkle. 'You would have to be some kind of idiot not to. But he's my cousin.'

'And?'

'He's family.'

'He's dangerous.'

'I heard that,' said Tiny, taking a time out from his sipping. 'In fact I've heard everything you've said.'

'Everything?' gulped Salor.

'Everything,' said Tiny. 'And to be honest with you, and I'll hold my hands up to it, what you've said, it's all true.'

'Tiny!' said Twinkle.

Tiny laughed. 'Oh come on cuz, you know what I'm about. But I'll tell you what, if you see your way to getting a few of these dents out of the spout, I promise I'll listen very carefully to your second wish.'

'Hang about,' said Salor.

'Leave this to me,' said Twinkle, stopping Salor's protests with a hand in front of his face. She walked over to her cousin. 'I thought the deal was two wishes?'

'It is,' said Tiny, checking his nails, 'but I thought you could use the first one putting my abode right. You know what I mean, make the dents and all go away.'

'Let me see if I've got this right,' said Twinkle. 'You want me to use up a wish to help you save your magic on something you can do yourself?'

'Now you're on the same page cuz. Magic is in short demand, you said so yourself, so a little wish would be helpful, not much magic needed in mending a kettle, is there? And in return, like I said, I'll give you exactly what you wish for with your second. No strings.'

Careful, thought Salor.

'I'll tell you what,' said Twinkle, 'as you're my *cuz*, I'll help you to save your magic by asking for only one wish and *I'll* mend your lamp for you. How's that sound?'

'And is that your wish?' said Tiny, smiling slyly.

Slippery so and so, thought Salor.

'No,' said Twinkle, firmly. She didn't want to admit it, but Salor was right, she would have to be careful; very careful. 'What I wish, is that the wish I wish is not this wish but another, and that that wish that I wish, is a true and honest reflection of the wish I really wish, which is the next one.'

Tiny's jaw dropped. 'Say again?' he said, nearly spilling his Golden Needles.

'You heard,' said Twinkle, with a wink. 'Now, I wish for Salor, Vlad, Jose and myself, that is me Twinkle, to be safely transported to and deposited in, in a non-life threatening way, the stables of Santa's reindeer.'

Salor was standing, slack jawed. He hadn't understood a word Twinkle had said a moment ago and now she had taken the plunge and made a wish. *Oh dearie me,* he thought, *perhaps I should close my eyes.* He was feeling just a tad faint. Perhaps a lay down would be better.

'Santa's stables?' said Tiny.

'That's what I said,' said Twinkle.

'But surely your first wish was your wish,' said Tiny, not smiling.

'That was just a guarantee that my real wish would be followed to the letter,' said Twinkle, smiling for the both of them.

'But a wish is a wish, look, I have the small print.'

Ah-ha, thought Salor.

Tiny held up a yellowing parchment that was covered with small letters and words that were frantically trying to reform to cover the owner's butt, but couldn't. 'There, see. What the...?' Tiny's eyes were widening with shock, horror, surprise. 'I don't understand,' he said.

'I protected it with dust,' said Twinkle.

'Dust? I don't understand.'

'Fairy dust,' said Twinkle. 'It can't be corrupted.'

'I see,' said Tiny, his smile back. He liked his cousin. He would have hated to twist her. 'Go girlfriend.' Tiny was now laughing with admiration, she had twisted a twister. 'Then your wish is my command.' He went to clap his hands.

'Wait!'

'Wait?' said Tiny.

'I have to get the warm clothes and supplies.'

'Supplies?'

'Hot chocolate and dog chews.'

'Wow,' said Tiny, 'may I have some?'

'Dog chews?'

'Hot chocolate silly,' said Tiny. 'It's so hard to find where I come from. And I don't suppose you could throw in a pack of Golden Needles as well could you?'

'Salor?' said Twinkle. She hadn't heard of Golden Needles before today, so she figured Salor must have had something to do with it, appearing like it did.

'Can't see why not,' said Salor. He scurried off to conjure some up.

'A deal well done then,' said Tiny, 'but you will mend my lamp, you promised? And then keep it away from that dog of yours?'

'I will,' said Twinkle, her fingers crossed behind her back. She hadn't promised to keep the kettle away from Jose, but she wasn't taking any chances; Tiny had his small print.

'Then when the wizard gets back, to Santa's stables you will go.'

'All of us will go.'

'All of you will go.'

And they did.

Chapter 13

'Which one?'

'That one.'

'The blue one?'

'No.'

'The pink one?'

'Sí.'

'Really?'

'Sí.'

'Why?'

'It is more realistic.'

'Okay,' said Vlad, 'the pink one it is.' But how Jose thought the bone looked realistic was beyond him. Were bones pink? He thought they were white. Or was that when they were bleached by the sun in some inhospitable desert somewhere? He didn't know. And supposed it didn't matter, he wasn't the one that was going to be chewing on it. 'You know what to do?'

'Sí.'

'Off you go then.'

Jose made himself visible to humans, darted into the pet shop, and started to cause a commotion by running in a circle and yapping his favourite mariachi song as loud as he could. He didn't sing because one: he didn't want to alarm the humans any more than he already was, and two: he couldn't.

'What in tarnation is that?' yelled the American shopkeeper over the noise that was assaulting his ears, however hard he might try to press his hands against them.

The chap standing next to him, the shopkeeper's assistant, also with hands clamped firmly over his ears, yelled back, 'It's a mad Chihuahua and I think he's yapping the Mexican Hat Dance.'

Jose was, and was now standing on his hind legs and enjoying himself like only a Chihuahua can. 'Ye-yap-ye-ye-yap-ye-ye-yap-ye. Ye-yap-ye-ye-yap-ye-ye-yap-ye. Ye-yap-ye-ye-yap-ye-ye-yap-ye. Ye-yap-ye-ye-yap-ye-ye-ye. Ole!'

While this was going on Vlad, still invisible to everyone, slipped past the shopkeeper and his assistant and placed some money on the counter. He then went to the window display and removed a rubber bone. And just to be certain he had the right one, he squeezed it causing a small squeak. No point having a bone that didn't squeak.

'Done!' shouted Vlad, ready to hit the road.

'What did you say?' shouted the shopkeeper.

'I didn't say anything,' shouted the assistant.

'Ole!' yelled Jose, as an encore, before chasing after Vlad as fast as he could. He became invisible as soon as he was out of sight.

Safely away from the shop, Vlad and Jose stopped and took stock.

'Here you go,' said Vlad, handing Jose the bone.

'And what is this?' said Jose.

'It's the bone you wanted,' said Vlad, looking puzzled.

'But it is the pink one I was wanting.'

Vlad stared at his hand. 'Oh cripes,' he said. He was holding a blue one.

'Sí, oh cripes!' said Jose, but for completely different reasons.

Chapter 14

Santa, formally known as Prince Bottom Of, wasn't happy, even if he was smiling. Things weren't going as he had expected, but thankfully, thanks to feeling doolally, he wasn't unduly worried, even though his supposed right hand small fellow had added to his woes by performing a disappearing act.

Slumped, he stared at the big red button. He had pressed it several times since Alf's disappearance, but all to no avail. So what did he do next? He still had the reindeer to deal with, as well as finding the miniature sleigh, as well as numerous other things, like getting things ready for next Christmas. He slumped further then began to wonder if the old Santa had told him everything. He said he didn't know of any miniature sleigh or tiny reindeer, but had he been telling the truth? That was it! Santa suddenly sat bolt upright. There was only one thing for it, and it had been staring him in the face all the time, he would have to pay the old Santa a visit; find out what he really knew. Then Santa, the new one, would know too.

Santa clambered from his booster, climbed down the step ladder and wrapping his crimson cloak tightly around him, headed for the door. It would be cold where he was going. He stopped. Perhaps it would be wise to put on a hat and pair of gloves as well.

Chapter 15

'Ay caramba,' said Jose.

'You can say that again,' said Vlad, staring.

'Ay caramba,' said Jose.

'Hello boys,' said a familiar voice.

'Twinkle?' said Vlad.

'Ay caramba,' said Jose.

'Over here.' Twinkle waved at them from a stall. She beckoned for the confused duo to join her.

'Where are we?' said Vlad. He then heard a groan and noticed a sickly looking pile in the corner that looked suspiciously like Salor. 'What's wrong with him?'

'Travel sickness,' said Twinkle.

'I have the wrong bone,' said Jose, looking glum.

'Anyways,' said Twinkle, 'welcome to Santa's stable.'

'He had horses?' said Vlad.

'Reindeer stable, dolt.'

'Oh,' said Vlad. 'How did we get here then?'

'I have the wrong bone,' said Jose.

'My cousin,' said Twinkle.

'Your cousin?' said Vlad, a little surprised. For some reason he had never thought of Twinkle as having family. 'How?'

'She rubbed the lamp,' said Salor, his make-up smeared across his face to the four points of the compass, took a moment from his groaning to point the finger. 'Her cousin was the genie.'

'You didn't?' said Vlad. 'Did she have long brown hair by any chance?'

'No,' said Twinkle, 'he was a he, and he was bald. Why?'

'No reason.'

'You rub the kettle without me?' said Jose, dropping his bone. It bounced, but it did not squeak.

'It had to be done,' said Twinkle. 'How else were we going to get here?'

'She was weak,' said Salor. 'She couldn't *resist* it.'

'Sí, it is a dangerous thing,' said Jose, wisely.

'You having a go at me?' said Twinkle, squaring up to the prostrate wizard. 'I got us here, didn't I?'

'If you say so,' said Salor. 'We could be anywhere.'

Twinkle turned her back on him. 'Don't take any notice of him he's grumpy because he was sick in his hat.'

'It smell of reindeer,' said Jose, sniffing the air.

'His hat?' said Vlad.

'The stables,' said Jose.

'There,' said Twinkle.

Jose remembered his bone. 'I have wrong bone,' he said.

'What's wrong with him?' said Twinkle.

'I picked up the wrong colour bone,' said Vlad. 'It should have been pink.'

Call it her feminine side, but not to her face, Twinkle took pity on the poor little Chihuahua. 'But at least you have a new one,' she said. 'Have you given it a squeak yet?'

Jose looked up at Twinkle as if she was some god. He had forgotten all about the squeak. He picked the bone up, his face a picture of awe and chewed. It squeaked. 'It squeak! It squeak!' he squeaked, through a mouthful of rubber bone.

'Happy now?' said Twinkle.

'Sí,' said Jose, trying not to smile in case he dropped his bone. 'Jose, he one happy hombre.' He made the bone squeak to emphasise his joy.

'Good,' said Twinkle, 'I'm glad to hear it, but now we have work to... did you hear that?'

Vlad had. 'Someone's coming.'

'Quick, hide.'

Chapter 16

Alf wasn't happy, and neither was he smiling. He was still feeling hard done by. How dare they judge him by his spectacles. Clerkish indeed. He was a hardy kind of guy. Always ready to get down and dirty. Not shirty; white as in collar. A rough and ready kind of guy. A guy's guy. And as it turned out, an easily frightened guy.

'Yah!' screamed Alf, as three faces and a cloak he hadn't seen before appeared from one of the stalls.

'Yah,' to you too,' said the cloak, usually known as Vlad.

'Who-who are you?' said Alf, his underpants in turmoil. He backed away from the intruders. He didn't like the look of them, especially the large woman in the tutu. Or the one smelling of sick, smeared in multi-coloured camouflage paint and blinking like some maniac. Or the floating cloak. The small dog wasn't so bad, but as the small dog was nearly as big as he was, he still wasn't taking any chances.

'More to the point,' said Twinkle, 'who are *you,* and what are *you* doing *here*?'

'And what have you done with Santa?' said Vlad.

'Sí, Santa,' said Jose.

Salor didn't say anything, he still felt a tad dodgy, especially now he was standing.

Alf continued on his backward trajectory. He didn't like this. The cloak had spoken to him. He didn't like this one little bit.

'He's going to make a break for it,' said Vlad.

'Stop him!' said Twinkle.

Alf, already turning on his heels, turned them some more. He started to run, aiming for the stable doors. And he may well have made his escape – or not; very short legs were not good for creating distance between small fellows and any pursuer, unless they also had short legs, which in this case they didn't, except Jose, who was none the less quite swift on his pins when he wanted to be – if it wasn't for a well-placed hoof, unseen by anyone, appearing from one of the other stalls and tripping him up.

'Got him,' said Vlad, grabbing the still sprawling Alf.

'Hold him,' said Twinkle.

'What's happening?' said Salor, feeling a little better, but not being able to see because his smeared make-up had run into his eyes.

'Vlad, he has the small fellow,' said Jose.

'A small fellow you say?'

'Sí,' said Jose.

'Then you were right,' said Salor. 'Well done.'

'Sí,' said Jose, his little chest swelling.

'Right,' said Twinkle, looming large over the distraught Alf. And what a terrible sight it was too. 'You've got some talking to do, little fellow.'

'Small fellow,' said Alf, defiant to, he figured, his approaching end.

'I ask the questions,' said Twinkle.

'Sí,' said Jose agreeing, although not fully understanding why Twinkle had said what she said. He then realised, as his mouth was empty that he no longer had his bone. 'It is gone, my bone. I shall look.' Suspecting he must have dropped it somewhere in all the excitement, he wandered off to find it.

Chapter 17

Thankfully the storm had abated, but the snow was over three feet deep, a problem when you are less than two feet in height; well less than two feet in height. But that wasn't going to prove an obstacle to Santa, the one formally known as Prince Bottom Of, no sir. He was building a ramp. Usually he would have had them that did do it for him, but as he wanted it done properly, he had decided to do it himself.

'There,' said Santa, putting the last plank in place. He stood back to admire his handiwork. 'And that,' he said triumphantly, 'is why I am Prince... Santa, and you plebs in the workshop are... are... plebs!' They couldn't hear him, he was too far away, but it made him feel better and that's what counted, especially if you were a self-opinionated little prig. And talking of feeling better, Santa wasn't so doolally, now he was away from his office. Obviously the doolally factor was of stronger concentration there.

He stepped onto the bottom of the ramp, thought about naming it, decided as he didn't have a bottle of champers handy there was no point, and then made his way to the top. There he surveyed the vast whiteness that lay ahead. He hovered a foot over it but stopped short of placing it on the snow. A word perhaps? Why not? 'One small step for smallkind, one huge step for me! Aargh!'

Santa crawled from the snow to the base of his ramp. He got to his feet, brushed snow from his crimson attire, and shouted at the snow, 'You're supposed to be frozen solid, you stupid snow!' But it wasn't, so a plan B would be needed.

Ten minutes later, Santa arrived back at the bottom of the ramp. On his feet, a pair of snowshoes he had found. They were a bit on the big side, but if he was careful. He sidled up the ramp, like a crab with cramp. He reached the top. Again he surveyed the vast whiteness stretching before him. Again he wondered if he should say something. Yeah right. He once again hovered his foot over the snow. This time though, the snow was holding his weight. It wasn't perfect, he would have to sidle crablike, but he was on his way. He placed his second snowshoe on the snow. He waited. They were working. He took another step. A big one, the type you took when you were about to meet the world head on. 'Aargh!'

Santa, formally known as Prince Bottom Of, with his feet now firmly tied to the snowshoes, boldly stepped forward on to the snow for the third time. Third time lucky? One step. Two steps. Three steps. Four. They were working. He marched on, as only a crab with cramp could. Behind him, two stricken small fellows struggling to keep their beltless trousers up, ahead of him a white expanse and an ex Santa Claus with questions to answer.

Chapter 18

Jose found his bone and as he stooped to retrieve it, a voice whispered to him from one of the stalls.

'He is seeing Santa ja,' said the whispering voice, in a clipped stereotypically Scandinavian accent.

Narrowing his eyes, Jose gave a low growl; no one was getting his bone. But just in case the disembodied voice wasn't after his bone, he felt it might be a good idea to ask who the voice belonged to. 'Who says this?' he said, and then added as an afterthought, in case the owner of the voice was after his bone, 'The bone, it is mine.'

The stall where the voice emanated from was sheathed in shadow. After a second it emanated again from the shadows. 'I am not interested in your bone ja, I prefer my oats.'

Jose picked his bone up and clenched it tightly in his jaws. One just couldn't be too careful. 'Oo as?' he asked.

Silence fell on the stall sheathed in shadow as its mystery occupant digested what Jose had just said. A moment or two later, the mystery occupant decided that it was impossible. 'I am sorry, but I am not understanding what it is you are saying.'

This was understandable, as Jose hadn't either. He was loath to but dropped his bone to the floor anyway. 'I am saying, who is doing this thing of which you speak?'

'I am not understanding again I am thinking.'

Jose cocked his head to one side, was this some kind of windup? But he tried again, 'You say, "he is seeing Santa", sí?'

'Ja, that is correct. He is seeing Santa.'

Jose screwed his face up. He then spotted his bone. It needed chewing. He picked it up, deciding he had wasted enough time. He looked at the stall and then at his companions. Besides, he had enough idiots of his own to contend with without adding a stranger to the list. He bit down on his bone. It squeaked. Contented, he wondered off.

The other idiots as Jose called them were still gathered around Alf.

'But I don't know anything,' Alf protested.

'Oh yeah,' said Vlad, trying to play bad cop, but as he wasn't very visual it wasn't really working. 'Next you'll be telling us money doesn't grow on trees.' He gave Twinkle a wink, which went unnoticed.

'It doesn't,' said Alf. 'Does it?'

'"Does it?" he says,' said Vlad, shaking his head and throwing another look Twinkle's way.

'No,' said Twinkle.

'What?' said Vlad, the smug persona he had adopted draining from him.

'I don't believe you,' said Twinkle.

'It's true,' said Alf. 'One minute I was there, and then poof I was here.'

'I wasn't talking to you,' said Twinkle.

'*Poof?*' said Salor. He had managed to get most of the make-up out of his eyes and was feeling a little better now; the travel sickness starting to wear off.

'*Poof!*' said Alf.

'What do you mean, *poof?*' said Twinkle.

'What do you mean no money tree?' said Vlad.

'As in one minute I was there and the next I wasn't.'

'There?' said Twinkle.

'My garden,' said Alf.

'And then you were...?' said Salor.

'Here,' said Alf.

'The stable?' said Twinkle.

Alf frowned. 'No, in Santa's workshop, we all were.'

'All?' said Salor.

'The small fellows,' said Alf.

'Ah,' said Twinkle, 'we're getting somewhere.'

'Are we?' said Vlad, re-joining the loop after his money tree disappointment.

'And what did you do there?' said Twinkle.

'Yes,' said Vlad, now adopting the persona of the cocksure cop, 'did you frighten a mouse from under a chair?'

'What?' said Twinkle.

'Do what?' said Salor.

'No,' said Alf.

'Vlad.'

'Yes, Twinkle?'

'Why don't you go and look for some clues.'

'Good idea,' said Salor.

Vlad sloped off, shoulders slumped.

'Now,' said Twinkle, holding onto Alf and keen to get some sanity back into the situation, whilst also keeping an eye on Vlad to make sure he kept moving, 'you say you ended up in Santa's workshop. What then?'

*

'You go somewhere?' said Jose, as Vlad drew level with him going the other way. He had placed his bone on the floor when he saw Vlad approaching.

'I've been sent to find clues,' said Vlad, shoulders still slumped.

'Sí,' said Jose, full of understanding as to the suspected reasoning behind Vlad's quest. He had always thought of Vlad as being clueless. He decided to help him. 'The fourth stall on the right, try it.'

'You think there might be a clue there?' said Vlad, brightening a little.

'Sí,' said Jose, 'I think.'

'Thanks.' Vlad scurried off, a new vigour in his cloak.

Jose watched him go, then picked up his bone and trotted up to the others to see what was going on.

'Because the elves had done a runner?' said Twinkle, as Alf continued to be questioned.

'Yes,' said Alf, explaining why the small fellows had been drafted in as Santa helpers. 'It seems they decided enough was enough.'

'Just like that?' said Salor.

'Yes,' said Alf. 'They just skedaddled. Rumour has it they decided en masse to find pastures green. Some, it's said, headed for New Zealand looking for film work.'

'Piffle,' said Twinkle, 'film work, hardly seems likely.'

'Oh I don't know,' said Salor. 'I hear they're looking for wizards as well.'

'So,' said Twinkle, getting back on track, 'Santa set you small fellows to work?'

'Yes,' said Alf, who as it turned out was more a yes man than he-man. 'He said we had to pull our fingers out and stop standing there like Coneys caught in headlights. He said we had less than a year to get things ready, so move it sharpish.'

'How many of you?' said Salor.

'About a thousand, at a guess,' said Alf.

It made sense, thought Twinkle, all those toys. It also explained the nature of those toys.

But it didn't sound like Santa at all. He was a jolly character, not a slave driver. It sounded as if something was wrong with Santa. It also sounded like they were wrong about Santa being kidnapped. Twinkle was worried. So what was going on? Salor was also worried. How on earth was he going to get to New Zealand in time for an audition?

And so, even with inane interruptions, the interrogation continued.

'Just because you were the only one wearing glasses?' said Twinkle. 'That's so typical stereotypicalism.'

'What happened then?' said Salor.

Alf told them about being at Santa's beck and call, which brought him to the hunt for the small reindeer. He also told them about the hunt for the small sleigh. And then he told them that he couldn't take any more so had done a runner, which was why he ended up in the stable.

Jose sidled up at this point; it had taken him a while as he had stopped now and again for a quick squeak. He placed his bone on the ground. 'Sounds like he Santa, go loco,' he said. And it sounded, after all things so far said, that Jose might be right.

'So where is Santa now?' said Twinkle.

'I'm not sure,' said Alf.

'We have to find him,' said Twinkle.

'Is that a good idea?' said Salor. 'It sounds as if confrontation might not be a good idea, all things considered.'

'So what do you suggest?' said Twinkle. 'We have to find him. Find out what's wrong. I don't see any other way.'

'The organ grinder,' said Salor. 'That's how we'll find out what's going on.'

'No!' screamed Alf, trying to squirm from Twinkle's grip. 'Not that! I told you, I don't know anything!' He started to sob when he couldn't get free.

'I am thinking that it is not only Santa that is loco,' said Jose.

'What's wrong with you?' said Twinkle, gripping the small fellow even tighter.

Alf went limp.

'I think that perhaps you shouldn't be holding his neck so tight,' said Salor, noticing how bluish in the face Alf had gone.

'Whoops,' said Twinkle, releasing Alf, who immediately tried to make a dash for it, semi-conscious or not. Twinkle grabbed him by the arm. He started to sob again, but at least his face was returning to its normal colour.

'What's wrong with you?' said Salor, picking up from where Twinkle had left off.

Looking up at Salor through tear stained spectacles Alf, trying his hardest to keep the sobs that wanted to rack his little body at bay, replied and pleaded, 'Please, I don't want my organs grinded.'

'Organs grinded?' said Salor. Then: 'Oh.' when he realised what Alf was going on about. 'He must mean Missus Claus.'

'Ah-ha,' said Twinkle, shaking her head at Alf. 'You silly small fellow, Salor was talking about Santa's wife, not an actual, you know, grinder. He means no point in talking to the monkey if you can talk to the organ grinder, it's a saying. You're such a silly-billy.'

Alf looked puzzled; relieved, but puzzled, and also wary. 'But he doesn't have a wife,' he said. He wondered then if this wasn't all some test and that if he failed there would really be a grinder waiting for him. Alf now looked puzzled, relieved, wary, and worried.

'What are you talking about?' said Twinkle. 'Of course Santa's got a wife.'

'But he hasn't,' said Alf, 'I'm sure I would have heard about it if he had.' Unless Prince Bottom Of had secretly tied the knot. 'Has he?'

'He most certainly has,' said Salor. 'I've met her, wonderful woman. Santa calls her the boss among other things. The one in charge is another one. Then there's she who must be listened to. Even the puppeteer on occasion, but not to her face you understand. She makes the most wonderful hot chocolate.'

A groan emanated from the direction of the floor.

'But he said I make the most wonderful hot chocolate,' said Alf. And what did the one smelling of sick mean, he had met her?

Another groan from below.

'Tosh and fiddlesticks,' said Salor, 'only Missus Claus makes the hot chocolate.'

Ay Caramba, thought Jose, as a little bit of sick popped into his mouth. He quickly picked up his bone, a beacon of calm amidst a sea of madness, and bit on it. It squeaked. That was better.

'But… ' Alf was fit to sob all over again. It wasn't him talking tosh, he did make the chocolate. What was going on? Only Missus Claus makes the hot chocolate? They had to be playing with his mind. He whimpered. He had been poofed into *insaneville* and was now surrounded and being toyed with by its latest inmates. How he longed for his garden and its array of garden implements and pond.

'Jolly woman, Missus Claus,' said Salor.

Enough, thought Alf. 'But he hasn't!' he wailed. 'I'd have known about it if he had. Everyone would know about it. Gardens throughout the land would have known about it. It would have been heralded. There would have been bunting. There would have been path parties.' (Small fellows didn't have streets.) He stopped for a breath. 'A prince just doesn't get married without everyone knowing about it.' He took off his spectacles and wiped them. 'We get a holiday.'

'And rightly so,' said Salor. It took a moment. 'What did you say?'

Jose dropped his bone. He had a cousin called Prince, a Doberman. It couldn't be, could it?

'Say again?' said Twinkle, applying just a little more pressure on Alf's arm.

'We get a holiday,' said Alf, a glum expression building, as he now wondered if maybe he had missed it somehow.

'Not that bit,' said Twinkle, 'the bit about the prince. What do you mean?'

'He said prince,' said Salor. 'Yes, what do you mean, prince? We're not talking about a prince, we're talking about Santa.'

'Si, he did,' agreed Jose, eager to find out if they were talking about his cousin. And if they were, did that mean that his cousin was now Santa? And if they were, did that mean that he was now related to Santa?

'So am I,' said Alf.

'But you said prince,' said Twinkle.

Alf looked a little perplexed. 'Prince Bottom Of,' said Alf.

Not my Prince then, thought Jose. Hopes dashed, he returned to his bone.

'Who's Prince Bottom Of?' said Salor.

'Santa,' said Alf.

There was a squeak from the direction of the floor.

'I don't understand,' said Salor. 'How can this bottom chappie be Santa? Santa's... well... Santa.'

Twinkles eyes crossed in sympathy with the lines that had been doing it for some time. 'Are you telling us that you think this Prince Bottom Of, is Santa?'

'I don't think he is, I know he is. He has it in writing,' said Alf. 'He took over earlier this year.'

'Good grief,' said Twinkle, 'I think Santa's been usurped.'

'Yes,' said Alf. 'Didn't you know?'

'That doesn't sound right,' said Salor.

'No, it doesn't, and we've got to do something about it,' said Twinkle. 'So where is he?'

'Who?'

'Santa.'

'I told you I don't know.'

'Not yours, the real one.'

'But Prince Bottom Of is the real one,' said Alf. 'He has it in writing.'

'Okay,' said Twinkle, getting just a little frustrated, 'where then, is the *old Santa?*'

'I don't know,' said Alf.

'Don't know or won't tell us?' said Twinkle, looming menacingly.

'Don't know,' said Alf, shrinking in Twinkle's shadow.

'Don't know, don't know, or don't know whether you won't tell us don't know?' said Salor.

'Salor!' snapped Twinkle.

'What?' said Salor.

'Not helping.'

'I was only asking.'

Twinkle turned her attention back to Alf. 'You really don't know?' she asked.

'I really don't know,' said Alf.

'Well that's that then,' said Twinkle, wondering what the heck they were going to do next.

'Not quite,' said someone behind them.

Everyone turned to see a rather smug looking cloak hovering before them. And behind it, and not hovering, was a rather nervous looking reindeer.

Chapter 19

So far so good, the snowshoes were doing what they were meant to, thanks to the belts Prince Bottom Of had royally decreed as his, which kept his feet firmly in place, meaning the snow was where it was supposed to be, below him. All he needed to do now was find Santa.

Santa, the smaller one, continued his crablike snowshoe shuffle, one two three four – one two three four. He continually looked at a map. He had acquired it without the outgoing Santa knowing, just in case there was ever a problem. And there was, several of them.

One two three four – one two three four – pause. But what if the map was false? Why would it be? One two three four – one two three four – pause. Because the old Santa had obviously hidden the miniature sleigh and the tiny reindeers so that he couldn't find them. But why would he? He had been surprised when shown the scroll that exposed him as being a fraud, but he had taken it in good grace. Most jolly-like to be honest. But was that just a ploy? Why should it be? Well he would soon find out. He had questions and by jingo he was going to get some answers; if the map was real. One two three four – one two three four – teeter. Pause – one two three four – one two three four.

Chapter 20

As Vlad introduced his antlered friend, further reindeer started to appear from shadowy stalls. 'This is Hans, he's a reindeer,' said Vlad, stating the glaringly obvious. 'He says he has a clue to Santa's whereabouts.'

'I am pleased to meet you, ja,' said Hans, offering a hoof.

'Nice to meet you too,' said Twinkle, taking proffered hoof. She turned to Vlad as she did and raised questioning eyebrows.

'He's one of Santa's reindeers,' said Vlad, answering those eyebrows.

'Ja, I am,' said Hans, 'and this is Nees.' He nodded towards one of the other reindeer that had appeared. 'And to her left is Boompsa, and the shy one behind, is Daisy.'

'Hans, Nees, Boompsa-'

'Daisy,' said Hans butting in before Salor could finish, 'Ja.'

'And you say you are Santa's reindeers?' said Twinkle, getting it straight in her mind.

'Ja,' said Hans.

'But I thought Santa's reindeer were called-'

'We are reserves,' said Hans, jumping in again.

'Reserves?' said Twinkle.

'Ja, for when one of the first team have the injury.'

'It never happen though,' said Nees, moving closer to Hans. 'Perhaps that is why you are never hearing of us.' Nees had a much softer voice than Hans, being a doe.

'I see,' said Salor.

'So where are the others?' said Twinkle.

'They go,' said Hans, sadly, 'with the elves.'

'To New Zealand I suppose,' said Salor.

'No,' said Hans, 'I am thinking they went to greener pastures, ja.'

'Then why didn't you go with them?' said Salor.

'We weren't invited, ja,' said Nees, her expression reflecting Hans's sadness.

Twinkle suddenly felt sorry for them.

'But we also stay for Santa ja, just in case he need us,' said Daisy, surprising the other reindeer.

'Ja and that as well,' laughed Hans, Daisy's outburst bringing a little cheer to his and the faces of the other reindeer. 'Daisy is usually a doe of little words,' said Hans, explaining the reindeer's surprise.

'Good for you girl,' said Twinkle. 'Go girl power.' She was halfway to going for a high five before realising.

'Girl power,' said Daisy coyly.

A smiling Twinkle now turned her mind to business. 'So, Hans,' said Twinkle, 'you say you have a clue as to where Santa is.'

'Not a clue,' said Hans, 'we know where he is.'

'Great news,' said Salor, heartily slapping Vlad on the back. 'Well done.'

'But we are also knowing where the small fellow who says he is Santa is,' said Nees. 'He is already making the tracks ja, across the white wilderness to Santa's house.'

'He is, is he?' said Twinkle. 'Then we had better get moving, it sounds as if this Prince Buttons Off is up to no good.'

'Bottoms of,' said Alf.

'Off, of, all the same,' said Twinkle. 'Jose!'

Jose, who had been drifting in a world of his own that consisted of sausages, sausages and more sausages, and the occasional squeak, since discovering that he wasn't related to Santa, came to with a start. 'Ja, I mean sí?'

'Get that nose of yours into gear we've got some tracking to do.'

'But I am a Chihuahua, not a bloodyhound,' said Jose.

'Language Jose,' said Salor.

'I think he meant blood hound,' Twinkle interrupted.

'Ah,' said Salor. 'That's okay then.'

'Which way Hans?' said Twinkle.

Hans led the way to the stable's back entrance. Outside they could hear the small fellows, hammering and drilling and cursing as thumb came between hammer and target, and painting and sanding, in the workshop. There was a set of small of footprints in the snow leading to and from a side door. They ended at a wooden ramp that was leaning on a snow bank. 'The small one, he go that way, across the white expanse.'

Jose took one look at all that snow and decided it wasn't for him. 'Ay caramba! I cannot sniff that. I will drown.'

'I don't think you'll have to,' said Twinkle, who was tall enough to see the depressions Prince Bottom Of's snowshoes had left in the snow. 'Right Vlad, go gather up the supplies. We're going to visit Santa.'

'What supplies?' said Vlad.

'Sí,' said Jose, 'what supplies?'

'They're right you know,' said Salor. 'I don't remember seeing any supplies, or coats for that matter.'

'That flipping Tiny,' said Twinkle.

'I told you, you couldn't trust him,' said Salor.

'So what do we do now?' said Vlad. 'It's flipping cold out here.' He couldn't actually feel the cold as such, but he could freeze solid.

'My bone,' said Jose, suddenly remembering he didn't have it. He loped back into the stables to retrieve it. Boompsa followed him.

'Now what?' said Salor.

'We give chase the best we can,' said Twinkle. 'There are bound to be some blankets lying around in the stables somewhere.' She turned to Hans. 'How long ago did he leave?'

'About half of the hour, ja,' said Hans.

'And how far away is Santa's house?'

'About three quarters of the hour, ja,' said Hans. He looked glum. 'I am thinking the small fellow will be there before you.'

'We're not going to catch him, are we,' said Twinkle. How she wished she had one of those snow thingy's. 'Don't suppose you've got a snow thingy hanging about have you?' she asked.

'She means a snowmobile,' Salor explained.

'No,' said Hans shaking his head, 'I am sorry, we do not.'

'It's not good, is it?' said Salor, as he stared at the snowshoe prints, winding away into the distance.

'No,' said Twinkle.

Just then, Jose arrived back on the scene. He appeared to be a little on the excited side. 'Eth's as gonth,' he said.

'Try that again without the bone in your mouth,' said Twinkle.

Jose spat his bone on to the ground and gave it a try. 'He 'as gone,' said Jose, bouncing up and down on the spot.

'Who has?'

'The small fellow.'

'Drat, I'd forgotten all about him,' said Twinkle. 'But there's no need to get in such a lather about it Jose, I doubt he'll be much trouble.'

'It is not that that makes me excited,' said Jose, just as Boompsa appeared at the stable carrying something in his mouth. 'It is that.'

'Well I never,' said Hans, 'where in the world did you find that?'

Boompsa dropped what he was carrying onto the ground. 'It is the emergency supply, ja,' he said. 'I saw where Santa hid it. And I am thinking one day it might be important to know, ja.'

Hans nudged the small brown bag Boompsa had dropped towards Twinkle. 'I am thinking Boompsa has been finding something better than a snow thingy, ja.'

Curiosity abounding, Twinkle picked the bag up, and looked inside.

Chapter 21

The door flew open, snow swirling through the space it had vacated. It was very dramatic.

'Aaaah!' screamed a female voice. Crash! Went the crockery she had been carrying.

'Where are they?' demanded Santa, formally known as Prince Bottom Of. He stood in the open doorway, no way filling it, snow billowing past him.

A large man who, until a couple of seconds ago, had been enjoying a leisurely smoke on his electronic pipe; fake smoke and all, rose from his large comfy chair. 'You!' he shouted. 'What do you mean by bursting in here like this?' Very old school was old Santa.

Small Santa ignored the question, slammed the door behind him as he was in danger of disappearing in a drift, and removed a scroll of paper from his pocket. He untied the ribbon that held it. He unfurled it. He read from it, 'It is written, look.' He held the scroll up as high as he could, which wasn't really high enough, and pointed to a paragraph. 'So where are they?'

Old Santa sighed. They had been on this merry-go-round before. 'I've told you,' he said. 'I don't know where they are. I've never seen them.' His famous jolliness was being pushed to the limit.

The small fellow stamped his feet, a mixture of anger and frustration. 'But you must have seen them,' he said, 'when you forced your way into the job.'

'He never did,' said Missus Santa, as she cleared away the broken crockery.

'Missus Claus is right,' said old Santa, whose belly was beginning to shake like an agitated bowl of jelly, 'and I never forced my way in, I've always been Santa.' He pointed his pipe accusingly at small Santa. 'If anyone has it's you.' It was most unlike Santa.

Small Santa was furious. 'But it is written!' he shouted. He held the scroll out at arm's length and shook it. 'It is you that is the imposter sir as you well know, and I demand answers!'

'Aargh!' screamed Salor, holding on for dear life with one hand, his other hand clasping hat to head, as a sudden gust of wind attempted to dislodge him.

Jose wasn't far behind, gripping tightly with everything he had. 'I think I am being sick,' he suddenly wailed, releasing the grip he had with his teeth for a moment, but quickly grabbing hold again when he started to slip backwards.

'I should hold that thought if I was you!' shouted Twinkle, as she travelled in Jose's wake, the wind hitting her in the face. *For both our sakes,* she thought.

Jose decided to try and take his mind off things and thought of sausages. He immediately gagged. Think of something else. His bone, he thought about his bone, all alone back there in the stable. He hoped no one snaffled it. He growled, slipped, grabbed hold again. Rubber bone – rubber bone – rubber bone.

'Yahoo!' yelled Vlad, his cloak billowing out behind him. He had always wanted to fly and had been disappointed when he found out that not all vampires turned into bats. But that was forgotten for the moment as he soared high in the sky. 'Yahoo!'

'How far?' yelled Twinkle, attempting to be heard above the noise of the wind rushing past her.

'Not far,' said Hans. 'There in distance, is smoke, ja.'

Twinkle peered ahead, through the wind and snow that had started to fall. And yes, there was smoke rising just as Hans had said.

'Hold tight, preparing for landing ja,' said Hans. Twinkle wrapped her arms around his neck. A moment later he passed the other reindeer, banked to the left, straightened up and headed for the smoke. The other reindeer tacked in behind Hans, following his every move, making their descent.

Hans, Nees, Boompsa, and Daisy, all in a row, all grinning like the cat that had got the cream, all their passengers holding tight. Down they went. Down, down and down they went, heading for the vast whiteness below them, all concentrating on the smoke.

Old Santa's belly was in danger of wobbling out of control, so angry was he becoming. 'I told you, I know nothing of what is written on your piece of paper!'

'Oh yes you do,' said small Santa.

'Oh no I don't!' said old Santa, his belt at breaking point.

'Oh no he doesn't!' said Missus Claus, joining in and moving to stand by old Santa's side.

'Oh yes he does!' Small Santa snapped back.

Things were beginning to look ugly, the situation in danger of turning into a pantomime. And then…

'Behind you!' screamed Missus Claus.

The door had flown open and a tangle of fish, fur, feather and snow catapulted across the carpet.

'I thought you said you knew how to land?' said Twinkle, straightening her tiara.

'Ja, I do,' said Hans, lying upside down on the floor, wedged between a sideboard and a coffee table. 'But I am not seeing bird and fish until it is too late.'

The bird in question, a seagull, dazed but none the worst for its experience with the flying reindeer, was already up and about and looking for its dinner. It found the fish; just a little wool from the carpet stuck to it, but no apparent damage otherwise, picked it up in its beak, flapped its wings and disappeared outside to enjoy a late, but better than never, lunch.

Nees had managed to keep her feet, but Salor had lost his grip as she landed and had screamed like a little girl. He then lost his grip and somersaulted over her head. He was now sat on the floor, seeing stars and moons and other astrological entities. Posh hat he had; print on the inside and outside. But he would be okay, once someone had managed to remove his head from it. Nees went to help Hans.

'Yahoo!' whooped Vlad, 'That was fun.' Boompsa had taken evasive action by looping the loop and defying the carnage and was all for doing it again.

Jose and Daisy had been a little behind the others so had also missed the pile up. 'Ay caramba,' said Jose, sliding from Daisy's back. 'Sí, it is fun if you have one of the many screws that are loose.' Jose had never been so pleased to be on terra firma once more. If only there was a tree handy. Daisy shook herself and went to help Nees as she was having trouble getting Hans upright.

'No, that is not me,' said Hans, as his back appeared to shout for help for the second time.

'Who are you?' said a befuddled and shaken old Santa, struggling from behind his chair. It was where he had landed after the reindeer storm had struck.

'Who are you?' said Twinkle, offering the old man with the white beard a helping hand.

'Ay yi yi,' said Jose, 'are you loco? It is Papá Noel.'

'Who?'

'Santo Clós.'

'Who?'

'Ay caramba, it is the jolly fat man.'

'Do you mean Santa?'

'Olé!'

'Santa?' said Twinkle pulling him to his feet.

'Yes,' said old Santa. He then looked extremely alarmed. 'My wife, where is she?' Everyone turned to Hans. Oh no!

'I'm in the kitchen dear,' shouted Missus Claus. 'I'm making us all a nice mug of hot chocolate.'

'Ugh!'

'Jose!'

'Sí.'

'Make yourself useful and go help Salor with his hat.'

'Sí, I do that.'

'Santa?' said Vlad. 'Did you say Santa?' And then he saw him. 'It's Santa!' he yelled. Reindeer rides forgotten he hurtled towards Santa with arms outstretched. Santa started to shy away from the inevitable collision, but thankfully, in his excitement Vlad failed to see Salor's outstretched legs. He went a tumbling.

Steering Santa safely away from where Vlad had sprawled, Twinkle headed towards Hans. She had just acquired the feeling that she might know who it was that was trapped beneath the reindeer. 'Here, let me help.' Together with Nees and Daisy's help, they managed to get Hans back on his hooves.

'Hans?' said old Santa, looking confused, as the fog began to clear from his head. 'Is that you?'

'Ja,' said Hans. 'Hans and Nees and Boompsa, Daisy is also coming to help, ja.'

'To help?' Old Santa still wasn't quite up to speed, but he was getting there. 'I don't understand.'

'Ja, we bring help for to un-usurper you.'

'That's right,' said Twinkle. 'We've come to save you from the usurper and return you to your rightful place.' She looked at the small red mass struggling to find up between the sideboard and coffee table, where Hans had landed. 'And it looks like we were just in time.' She grabbed the struggling bundle, gave it a shake and revealed small Santa. He didn't look very happy.

'Unhand me!' demanded a squirming small Santa.

But Twinkle ignored him. 'What do you want us to do with the little small usurper?'

Old Santa, who was older than anyone could imagine, suddenly looked older than was possible; he staggered and leaned against a table. 'But he isn't,' he said, a weariness in his voice.

'But-'

'No, let me finish,' said old Santa. 'He has proof, written proof, that I cannot be the real Santa, I don't know how or where he got it, but it is written.' Old Santa took a second, fending off questions with an open palm, 'and as it is written, and has been verified as a bona fide document by the new Santa's lawyers, I bowed to his right of claim to the title of Santa. And all I ask now is that I may spend my retirement in peace.'

The room fell quiet with the exception of the part of it where Salor and Jose were still trying to remove Salor's hat. Everyone, again with the exception of Salor and Jose, were stunned, nay shocked, nay rocked to their very core.

'I have a scroll!' said small Santa waving it.

'Ay Caramba, that is sounding painful,' said Jose, who had only been half listening to what was going on, 'but that is what is happening if you are walking waist deep in the snow.' And as he had his back to everyone he didn't notice the funny looks.

'But I can't find the miniature sleigh,' wailed small Santa.

'Miniature sleigh?' said Twinkle.

'He claims one exists and that I am keeping its whereabouts secret from him,' said old Santa, 'but I really don't know anything about it.' He jumped a little after saying this and looked down at his leg. He was surprised to find the cloak that had charged at him clinging to it.

'You'll always be Santa to me,' said Vlad staring up at Santa.

'Ah-ha!' said Salor, as his hat was finally prised from his head. He could hear again, and because he could he immediately noticed the silence. 'What did I miss?'

'He has a scroll,' said Jose. 'I think it caused by the snow.' He tapped his nose with a paw.

'A scroll?' said Salor, and, as he gathered himself quite the aficionado where scrolls were concerned, his interest was instantly piqued.

Twinkle filled Salor in on what had passed while he had been side-lined.

'May I see it?'

'Ay ay,' said Jose, wrinkling his nose in disgust. 'I am thinking you bang your head.'

'Perhaps you should,' said Twinkle, remembering old Santa had said it had been authorised as the real thing by small Santa's lawyers. Only small

Santa's lawyers, did she smell a rat? She should ask. 'What about your lawyers?' she asked. 'What did they say?'

Old Santa blinked as if caught by a sudden light. 'My lawyers?' he said. 'Oh, I've never used lawyers, I exist on goodwill.'

It was enough to set the old alarm bells off as far as Twinkle was concerned, and if she had known about the existence of doolally, she may well have taken up extreme campanology.

'It is mine,' said small Santa, who was still swinging from Twinkle's wrist, 'and put me down; do you know who I am?'

'A small fellow usurper until proved otherwise,' said Twinkle. 'But I tell you what, I'll put you down if my learned colleague here can have a gander at your scroll.'

Small Santa duly surprised Twinkle by agreeing. When she placed him on the floor he handed the scroll over to Salor. 'Thank you, and when you realise your mistake I shall expect apologies and grovelling, and old Santa here to tell me exactly what he knows.' He watched Salor unfurl it.

The room fell silent again, except for the stirring sound of a spoon at work in the kitchen, as Salor read the scroll. Was Prince Bottom Of really the new Santa? Or had numerous sheep been shorn for the wool used for the pulling over of many eyes?

Salor read it once, he read it twice, he then checked to see if the document was on papyrus or rice. It wasn't, it was on ordinary paper. Frowning, he handed the scroll to Twinkle.

'Hey!' said small Santa, making a grab for it, 'that's mine.' But being so short he failed miserably.

Twinkle read it once, she read it twice, but didn't bother looking at what paper it was. She looked at small Santa. 'This is your proof?'

'As is written,' said small Santa, holding out his hand for the return of the scroll. He looked rather smug. 'Now, if I may ha—'

'You are kidding right?' said Twinkle. 'This is your proof? This?' She dangled the scroll in front of small Santa.

'It is,' said small Santa, 'now give it to me.'

'My size fourteens it is,' said Twinkle.

Small Santa made another grab at the scroll, again missing it by at least two feet, even though he had jumped as high as he could this time. 'Give it to me. I demand it! And do not scoff at me.' He stamped an indignant foot. 'I will not be scoffed at.'

Instead, Twinkle passed it to old Santa. 'Have you read this?' she asked.

'Not all,' old Santa admitted. 'His lawyers said I only needed to see what I needed to see, the highlighted parts, the parts about the sleigh, the reindeer and the part about me being too big to be Santa.'

'Lawyers,' said Vlad, tutting.

'Si, lawyers, I spit on them!' said Jose, making a spitting noise. 'What is this *lawyers*?'

'Then take a good look at it Santa,' said Twinkle. 'I think you'll find it isn't all it seems.'

Old Santa started to read the scroll from the beginning, and the more he read, the redder his rosy cheeks became.

'Give it to me,' demanded small Santa.

'Oh, I'm sure he will,' said Twinkle, with a twinkle in her eye.

Old Santa finished reading the scroll. And so thunderous was the look that he gave small Santa, it made the small fellow take a step back. 'Do you know what this is?!' he said, his voice matching his look.

'It is what is written,' said small Santa, defiant but uneasy, as if the ground beneath his feet was starting to shift.

'It is a *poem*!' snapped old Santa. 'I suspect the best poem ever written about me, but just a poem none the less.'

'But it… ' Small Santa's voice faltered. 'It… ' He had heard of poems, they were different from scrolls. But it was a scroll. Surely it was. His lawyers had said so when he had handed it to them. Small Santa was now certain of nothing. 'But it is written.' He looked from face to face. 'It is not a poem.' His voice was as small as he was.

'It is,' said Twinkle, speaking softer now. She had the feeling that maybe small Santa had been duped as much as old Santa. Believed what he was told as much as old Santa had.

'But it says the sleigh is miniature,' said small Santa, a last throw of the dice perhaps.

'Really depends on from what height it was seen from,' said Twinkle.

'But the reindeer?'

'Ditto for that as well I'm afraid.'

'But the driver was lively and quick,' said small Santa, gesturing at old Santa's bowl of jelly. And we're not talking desserts here.

'Si,' said Jose. 'He has the point.'

'Thank you Jose,' said Twinkle, giving him her sternest look, 'but it also says that the driver was old, jolly and fat.'

'Where?' said small, rapidly becoming more prince than Santa, Santa.

Old, rapidly becoming the only Santa again, Santa, handed the poem to small Santa. 'There,' he said.

Small Santa read it. He re-read it. His eyes widened.

'You haven't read it before, have you?' said Salor.

Small Santa looked up at Salor. 'Only the highlighted parts,' he said.

'Ah,' said Salor.

'I think you might want to talk to those lawyers of yours,' said Twinkle.

Prince Bottom Of, formally known as small Santa, appeared to shrink a little. 'I can't,' he said.

'Why not?' said Salor.

'They said they were retiring and going to live in a garden called Hawaii.'

'Ah,' said Santa, formally known as old Santa.

'It's not a garden is it?'

'No.'

'But they were the best lawyers money could hire.'

'Who said that?' asked Twinkle.

'The garden centre,' said Prince Bottom Of.

'Oh.'

There fell a hush on the room.

'So what's your real name?' said Vlad, still clinging to Santa's leg, too embarrassed to actually let go.

'Prince Bottom Of,' said Prince Bottom Of.

'Sí, really?' said Jose. 'Bottom of what is it you are bottom of?'

Prince Bottom Of screwed the scroll up. He had been duped, made a fool of, but at least he was a prince. He could still hold his head up high. 'The garden,' he said, holding head high.

Thankfully he said it just as Missus Claus appeared with mugs and bowls of steaming hot chocolate. 'Hot chocolate everyone!' she yelled merrily.

'Ugh,' said someone who shall not be named.

Chapter 22

And, as it does, time came to pass. It hadn't been a scroll at all, and just to put Prince Bottom Of's mind at rest, the greatest minds that knew, the Sandman, Jack Frost, the Easter Bunny and the Tooth Fairy, who was still fairy size, were called on to verify that what it was, was really nothing more than a poem.

Santa got his job back, and with brand spanking new letters after his name. He was to be known from now on as: Santa Claus KK SN PN etcetera etcetera. But he would never use them, not unless another scroll happened to turn up that is.

Prince Bottom Of, ruler of garden gnomes everywhere in the garden, eventually managed to get over what had happened to him and met a beautiful gnome princess, whom he got engaged to. A national gnome holiday was proclaimed. He also opened an international franchise selling children's garden implements, and was very successful.

The small fellow in Santa's workshop never did find a magic hat but enjoyed the national holiday and spent the whole day fishing. He also went on to become the Gnome Universe Bodybuilding Champion. Not bad for a gnome with only one thumb.

Alf ran away from the stable and kept on running until he was asked why by a Gnome National Newspaper. It was from the photo that went with the article that his successful modelling career took off. He kept his glasses though; he didn't want anyone thinking, because of the body beautiful, that he was some kind of a *gimbo*.

Twinkle, Salor, Vlad and Jose and his bone, went home. Another story had been written you see and they were needed toot sweet. I'm sure you'll bump into them again sometime.

*

And as for Hans, Nees, Boompsa and Daisy, if you listen carefully next Christmas Eve, you just might hear Santa saying something like this: 'On Donder, on Blitzen, on Comet and Cupid. Away Hans, Nees and Boompsa, Daisy, on and away!'

You will let me know if you do!

Happy Holidays everyone!

Other Titles
By
Stefan Jakubowski

Supernatural comedy starring Richard Ross
STRANGE RELATIONS
DEAD PECULIAR

Fantasy comedy nonsense
MISCREATION

Time travel comedy starring Tom Tyme
ONCE UPON A TYME
TYME AND TIME AGAIN

Comedy tales of the short kind
NOT JUST FOR CHRISTMAS

(Three Christmassy short stories to be enjoyed at any time)

COMING
~~**SOON**~~
(In a little while)

DANRITE WILLOCKY

Half GIANT – Half Dwarf
ALL HERO

**The World
of
Myth, Magic, and Make-believe
is in dire straits.
It needs help.
It needs a hero!
What it gets is a matter of opinion.**

Oh dear.